I0760760

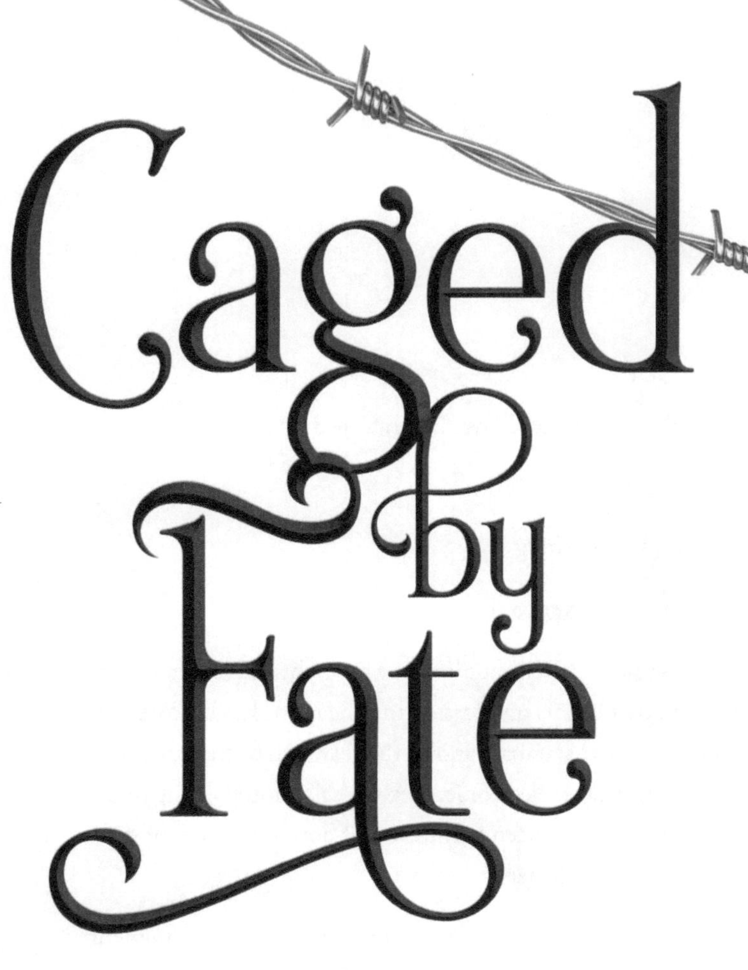

Caged by Fate

NEW YORK TIMES BESTSELLING AUTHOR

SHANNON MAYER

HiJinks Ink Publishing

www.shannonmayer.com

Mayer, Shannon

Caged By Fate, The Alpha Territories, Book 4

Thank you to Christine Bell who helped me immensely with building the characters for this one. You are a real lifesaver when it comes to pulling ideas out of your ass and making me write them. Couldn't have done it without you!

CHAPTER 1
Diana

SIXTY YEARS AGO...

The forest was blooming with color and scent, the sound of small animals scurrying ahead of me, the feel of a late spring breeze tangling through my hair. I breathed it in, letting the earth center me when all I wanted to do was rage.

I slowed my feet and closed my eyes, fighting the urges threatening to take over. Still, the blood in me ran hot, vampire and werewolf combined, and after all these years, I struggled with keeping myself in check.

My mind dipped back to the argument with my father earlier today, which only spiked my heart rate again.

"You need to find a mate. That is our way, Diana."

Lycan didn't move from his spot behind the big wooden table. His breakfast was spread in front of him, and he barely lifted his head as he spoke.

"No. I don't," I bit back. "There is none that so much as flicker my interest."

"Not even Lochlin?"

I snorted. "He's a brother to me. A cousin. Not a lover."

Lycan tipped his head to the side. "Our pack is not just you and me. I am king, Diana. And one day when I am gone, you will reign as queen, and you will need an heir."

I barked a laugh, though my ire rose with each of his words. "Perhaps I will make myself an heir, as you did."

His face closed off. "Do not mock—"

"I'm not. I am the last of your children, but I was not born here. Why can I not—"

His fist hit the table, making every plate on it jump, and the legs below groan. "Because of what you are. That will never be forgotten no matter how many years pass. Even now, there are whispers that I should not trust you."

My heart felt as though an icy fist reached through my chest and took hold. "And do you trust me?"

"Of course I do!" he bellowed. "Even if any of your siblings had survived, I still would have named you my heir. And I would not have named you heir had you not been the best choice! But there are some who will never trust you. Some who only see you for what you once were."

My wolf inside of me, she fought to break free, to unleash on those others.

In part because they were not entirely wrong. I was a werewolf, but I had not always been. Born as a half-human, half-vampire, biologically the daughter to the vampire king, my blood was stained in the eyes of my pack. Even though I'd undergone the most brutal of changes to become a werewolf in truth, burning the vampire blood out of my body...it was not enough, even now.

"I have defended the pack against our enemies, and that includes the vampires." My voice deepened, as I fought to keep my wolf in check. "I have been obedient to my king and done everything in my power to serve our people!"

Lycan grunted and went back to eating, but I knew him. Knew that this conversation was not done.

Soon enough, he spoke again. This time, with a note of finality in his voice that made my stomach turn.

"Find a mate, Diana. This is not your father speaking, but your king. It is a must. I don't care if you love him. I don't care if he means nothing to you and is just a trophy. But do it. Before the year is out."

I knew a dismissal when I heard one.

Spinning on my heel, I'd left at a good clip, heading for the deep forest bordering us on the north.

And so here I was, feeling sorry for myself.

"A mate I do not love."

I opened my eyes and kept walking, finding myself in the graveyard, beyond the black willows that wept with us when our dead were buried. Past the north creek, and deeper still until I stood on the border between us and the angels. Angelic in nature in only their own minds.

What had drawn me here?

My mate?

I laughed at myself. "You're a romantic fool."

The crack of a twig spun me around and I dropped to a crouch, my hand going to the knife at my belt. Shifting would take too long. But a blade would protect me just fine.

Movement across the border stilled me further, and I lowered myself until I was almost flat to the ground.

Stumbling, a man tripped over a log and fell, sprawled out on his belly. He should have sprung up, but he didn't move. A low groan slid out of him, a sound that cut into me. Whoever he was, he was clearly injured and in pain.

Did I dare try to help him? He was still technically on the other side of the border...

I pushed myself back into a low crouch and peered over the brilliant, orange poppies that hid him from view.

Face up, he'd rolled onto his back as he'd fallen.

I just stared at him, not sure why I couldn't look away. His hair was long, a deep brown, and in a few places around his face it was braided, beads set into the ends. His face was covered in a bit of scruff that hid the fact that he was a bit baby-faced still—as if anyone couldn't see that from the smooth skin of his cheeks.

His shirt was peeled open and large gashes ran in patterns over his chest.

Demon sign. He'd have had to cross at least two borders to get here.

"Fuck," I whispered. I crept forward. Demons did not mark their own like that. They marked captives. I was on the edge of the border when the sound of wings snapped my head up, the animals around us going silent.

Decision time, Diana. Help him, or leave him?

I had my hands under his arms and was dragging him across the border before I even had a chance to change my mind. Bending at the knees, I scooped him up over my shoulders and ran back the way I'd come.

A screech in the air behind us set the hair on the back of my neck on end.

Why was I risking my life for this human? Because human he was, I could smell it all over him.

A second screech ripped through the air, and I had no choice. I set down the human and wheeled around to face the incoming demon. Demons running through the territory held by their high and mighty cousins? What was going on?

"You cross our border, and you will start a war!" I yelled as the demon ducked in and out of the trees, weaving through darkness.

"Ah, but you took something of mine, little wolf! He did not make it to your lands."

I grinned, baring my teeth. "Finder's keepers."

"Then prepare to weep," the demon laughed and shot toward me, wings and body coming into view as the shadows around his—no, her—body gave way. She flung a five-pointed star at me, and I knocked it from the air with my blade. The clink of metal on metal rippled through the air.

She did not slow, and I met her head-on, weaving and ducking to one side so I could grab a hold of one, black wing. Digging my fingers in, I gripped the leathered skin and yanked hard, dragging her off course and away from the human.

"He's mine!" she shrieked.

The wolf in me howled, and I snarled back. "No. He's *mine.*"

We went down in a tangle of limbs and claws. I wasn't just fighting for my life; I was fighting for his—even if I didn't understand this need to protect him.

Her fingers raked across my neck, grappling for a hold on me. She slid through a shadow, her body turning into smoke, only to solidify behind me. Her one hand was around my neck, the other my head.

I knew I was about to have my neck snapped like a pencil. Father would have to select another heir. Maybe he'd choose one who could find a mate. Despite my maudlin thoughts, there was no regret. If I had to do it again, I'd have done the same. Something about saving this human felt like...my destiny.

Behind me the demon stiffened, and a gargled shriek slid out of her. Her hands loosened on my neck, and she fell to the ground twitching.

Behind her stood the human male, a glowing blade in his hands. His eyes slowly lifted to mine. One blue, one green.

"Are you...all right?" He swayed where he stood, asking if I was okay.

I looked down at the demon. "Y-you saved my life."

"You saved mine first." He shrugged. "It was nothing."

Only it was more than that, it was very much something. "Stay here."

He popped off a jaunty salute with the hand that still held the glowing knife, and then slumped to his knees.

"Don't mind if I do. I...don't feel particularly well."

His chest was still oozing blood, but it was the rivulets running down the side of his face from his hairline that had me worried.

Shit.

"I have to move the demon's body. I'll be right back. Don't move."

I wanted to ask him his name, ask him what he was doing here, ask him how he came in possession of a blade that could kill a demon with such ease...all the things. But I had to get rid of this corpse first. If it was found on our lands, war would break out, and it would be all my fault. That wouldn't do at all.

Scooping up the body, I took it to the river. The waters ran into the angel's lands and from there to their demon cousins. The current would carry her home as well as wash away some of mine and the human's scent. Perhaps the combination of distance and time in the water would be enough. The fact that she was killed by a blade that I had no knowledge of would help.

I hoped.

Once she'd floated well out of sight, I made my way back to where the human knelt. I found him motionless, his chin dropped to his chest.

For just a moment my heart seemed to stutter. Had he died while I'd been gone? I hurried to where he was and dropped to my own knees beside him.

"Hey! Wake up. Please wake up!"

He startled and the blade came up so fast, I didn't have time to move. For the second time in the space of only a few minutes, I was sure I was going to die.

He had the blade pressed to my throat, the steel of it glowing a bright bluish-white. But he didn't cut me as his wild eyes tried to focus. "Who are you?"

"Diana," I said, my throat moving against the blade. "And I just saved your life, remember?"

His jaw and throat worked and his eyes fluttered closed. I yanked the blade out of his hand and tucked it into my belt as he slumped forward, his head landing on my shoulder. "Maverick. My name is Maverick."

"Well, Maverick, seems like you've found yourself in a bit of trouble."

"Thought you said your name was Diana," he mumbled.

A laugh huffed out of me as I stood and helped him to his feet.

The moon was high in the sky by the time we made it to one of the old and rarely-used hunting lodges that dotted the Territory. I had brushed the cobwebs off the bed and tucked him in with a coarse blanket before heading over to the keep. It didn't take long for me to dig through the laundry sent down the chutes and recover a pair of pants and a shirt that smelled like Hamish, one of the guards. Hopefully, between the remote location and Hamish's clothes masking his scent, that would be enough to keep anyone from finding him.

A tiny part of me wondered why I was hiding him, but

I already knew. He was...different. And if only for a little while, I wanted to keep him to myself.

Crazy. This was sheer insanity. Or the influence of my father's discussion with me over breakfast about finding a mate. I surely had not found it in this scruffy, demon-slaying human.

Once I returned, I helped him wash and change into the new clothes, doing my best to be careful of the wounds on his chest. I asked him no questions until I had tossed his clothes in the fireplace, burning them into a pile of ash. There could be no evidence of the female demon's death.

"What happened to you?" I sat on the edge of the bed, tending his wounds. The ones on his chest and back were deep, but not so deep that he needed stitches. And, although the knock on his head had stopped bleeding, it had lumped up nicely. I'd need to watch him carefully. He probably had a concussion.

"I was a prisoner of the demons. I...I overheard them talking about a blade they had confiscated from another prisoner. One that could kill them. A week ago, while they were sleeping, I was able to escape my bonds and search our camp. That's when I found it. I snatched it and made a run for the hills, as they say. Almost made it, too..." He winced as I wiped alcohol across his chest. "Why are you helping me?"

I shrugged and shook my head. "I've been asking myself that same question, Maverick."

"Are you human?"

I lifted my eyes. "You think I could have taken on a full-grown Fallen female—a demon—as a human?" I wasn't offended so much as surprised. He had to be new to the Territories. There was no way he couldn't understand how incredibly dangerous it was to fight one of the Fallen. The fact that both of us had survived was still something that made me wonder just how we had pulled it off. His stolen magical weapon had definitely helped.

"Where's the blade?" He suddenly sat up and I pushed him gently back down.

"I've hidden it. If the demons come around asking questions, we need to make sure there is no evidence."

He frowned. "Why would they come here?"

"If they figure out that she died on Werewolf Territory, then they will come. They have been looking for a reason to start a fight with us for a very, very long time." I sat back and dropped the cloth into a bowl. "That is the best I can do for now. You need to rest, and heal."

"And then what?" His eyes searched mine, and despite the injuries done to him, I could see him working over the choices for his future. A quick and agile mind lay behind that pretty face.

"Then we see what you're made of." My smile was

stupid, and sudden...and stupid. Something about him drew me in. He was different. I was different. And in that, I felt a connection to him. For whatever reason, I got the sense that I could trust him. So I let my guard down. We spoke for hours in our little lodge in the forest, and I felt my heart slipping into his hands. Felt myself sharing more of who I was with him than I had with anyone else in my life ever.

Two weeks passed, and they were the most amazing two weeks of my life. My father, in a bid to give me more time to find a mate, had relieved me of some of my duties, and I used it all on Maverick. To my surprise, nothing ever came from the demons. If they hadn't come by now, I knew they would not, and my worries faded.

"You look happy, Diana," Lycan's voice called to me across the dining table the morning of the fifteenth day.

I smiled. "That's because I am happy."

He lifted an eyebrow. "And?"

"And what?"

"You're going to make me ask, are you? Fine then. Who is he, and when do I get to meet him?"

Panic settled in my chest.

"What do you mean?"

"Well, clearly, you've got your sights set on a mate now. You've hardly been home, and you're practically walking on air. When do I get to meet my new future son in law?"

My heartbeat slowed some and I managed a weak smile.

"I promise, if it gets to that point, you'll be the first to know."

It was going to have to happen, and sooner than later. But it would be a fight, I knew. And I wasn't ready to share yet. I just wanted to keep Maverick to myself, hidden away for a little while longer.

Back at the lodge a short while later, I flung the window open to let in some fresh air. "Are you feeling well enough to sightsee tomorrow, maybe? The merchant ships will be here, and we can walk the harbor. Maybe we can even take you to meet my father soon. We will just have to come up with a story of how we met. A story that doesn't involve border-crossing and murder..."

Maverick leaned against the headboard, his shirt flaring open to reveal his wounds mostly scabbed over, some even smooth already. "You think the wolves are ready for me?"

I laughed softly and shook my head. "Never. But my father is suspicious. He knows I am hiding something."

Or someone.

I made my way over to the chair beside the bed. We'd been careful not to touch too much. I could feel the tension in him, could smell the desire rolling off him. He wanted me. But he never so much as leaned too close.

Never tried to take advantage of me, though he watched me when he thought I wasn't looking.

"I brought you something," I said, grinning as I reached into my pocket. His eyes widened as I produced the four-leaf clover, I'd found on my walk back to the cabin. "I've heard they're supposed to be lucky in your world."

"I've never found one before," he said, eyes shining as he accepted it. "Though I've been so lucky lately that it almost seems like I had. And I've been meaning to give you a gift as well."

I cocked my head, wondering what it could be as he reached for the bedside table. He hadn't had much of anything when he'd arrived, and had spent all his time in the lodge, so what could he possibly have to give me?

"It's an anklet," he said, gesturing for my leg. The green thread was strung with shells of all kinds, with lots of deep purples and bony whites.

"It's beautiful," I said, eyeing it closely. "Where'd you get all these shells?"

"Here, try it on," he said, smiling softly at me, ignoring my question.

I raised my leg instinctively, and my ankle tingled as he gripped it lightly in his hands and tied the beautiful anklet in place. "Thank you," I said. "The colors are beautiful."

His hands lingered for a moment, caressing my leg before letting go to gesture to the room around us. "I tried to find lots of purple ones, since you seem to love it so much."

My heart stopped for a beat.

"Find? From here?"

He looked away. "I wanted to do something for you, some kind of gesture for taking care of me for all this time. I snuck out to the beach a few times earlier this week, while you were off at the keep."

I rolled my eyes, but the warmth inside me only grew, even as I chastised him. Hot, daring, and thoughtful. "That was reckless, Mav. You could've been killed."

"And it wasn't reckless when you ran headfirst into that demon to save me? We both have a bit of a reckless streak. Besides, if there's one thing I'm good at, it's being slick," he said, waving off my concern. "All that matters is that you like it."

"I love it," I said, warmth rolling through my body in waves. I paused for a long moment, just staring at the anklet and enjoying the moment. Just a few weeks earlier I'd been so certain that I didn't want a mate, and now I was here, giddy and starting to fall in love.

I ran my fingers over the back of his hand. "Mav. If... there was a way...would you stay here? With...me?"

He turned his hand over, lacing his fingers with mine. "A way? What do you mean?"

We'd talked at length already about him not wanting

to be a prisoner, and I felt him tense. I held onto him a little tighter.

"A way to become...like me. A werewolf. A way to stay here in truth, a part of this world."

His hand tightened on mine. "You told me there was a way your kind could hide their true nature when you went to the mainland. I thought maybe you could come back with me—"

My stomach flipped. Leave my pack? My family?

"No. The Crimson stones are kept in my father's chambers. There is no way he'd give us one. And even if he did, I need to stay here for my people." I shook my head. "But you could..." Gods of the forest, this was hard. To be vulnerable...tell him how much I wanted him to remain here with me. "If I could find a way to keep you safe, would you stay?"

His hand slid up to my cheek, his mouth finding mine. Tentative and careful. Sweet. Kind. He was so very kind. "It would be my honor."

It would be his honor...

But that, like so many of the things he'd told me, was a lie. Instead, he had betrayed me and left me heartbroken and alone.

Present Day

A knock at the door snapped me out of the memories that burned in my gut. I stood in front of my window holding two items in my hands.

"Enter."

"Your Majesty, the meeting is set to start in under five minutes. Are you prepared?"

"Yes, I'll be there in a few moments. Just gathering my thoughts."

The item in my left hand was the second of two crimson stones. The other had been stolen by Maverick that same night he'd kissed me and then escaped to the mainland, hidden in one of our ships.

In my right hand lay the hilt of the dagger that Maverick had used to save me. A blade that still glowed bluish-white.

I balanced them as I stared out the window of my room. The skies should have been brilliant with a noonday sun, but instead were black as night. The window flung open, clattering and slamming the panes against the wall, and the storm ripped into my room, flinging objects around, and scaring my attendant right out the door. The wind howled like a bitch on the hunt for blood. I bared my teeth as I gripped both the dagger and the stone, the storm matching my mood.

I'd managed to put him out of my head eventually, but it had taken decades. And now, here we were, full circle once again. If we had any hope of saving the world, I would first have to face the man who had broken my trust and then stomped on my heart. Only this time, I was a lot older and a hell of a lot smarter.

Maverick was going to wish that I'd let that demon have him by the time I was done with him.

CHAPTER 2

Give me the strength, father, one last time, to see this through despite my grief...

I sucked in a deep breath and let it out, pausing to study the faces around the table of my war room.

It had been a scant five weeks since he'd been killed, and the grief had not eased one bit. I'd felt it before, when I'd lost loved ones, siblings and friends, but it had never been like this. Wolves lived for many centuries, and I was very much in my prime, but since I'd lost my father, it was as if the life had been sucked out of me. My heart beat heavier, my steps slower, even my dark green eyes had been leached of color, leaving them ice-blue and cold. Just how I'd felt on the inside, until I read that note.

Now, I was flaming hot with purpose and rage, and grateful for it. At least I could still feel something...

Lochlin, seated in the chair beside me, where my father used to sit. My packmate, long-time confidant and friend. Now, my right hand and advisor. Usually quick to smile despite the scar that bisected his face from one brow to the corner of his mouth, the auburn-haired, bear of a man was stoic today. I had no doubt he wouldn't like my plans, but that was alright. We'd locked horns plenty over the decades, and while I appreciated his counsel, I was Queen.

We'd do it my way.

Beside him sat Will, the youngest of my three brothers. Now that we'd defeated and killed our oldest, Edmund the Vile, Will was King, and he deserved the title. A good man. A fair man...despite being a bloodsucker and all. His brand-new wife Bethany was seated to his right, holding his hand in a quiet show of support. That was good. He'd need it. Despite enjoying the backing of most in their Territory, there was still a fringe faction of his kind who would never accept his marriage to a natural-born human, even if she was a vampire now...

I turned my head and locked gazes with my other brother, Dominic. Dark, dangerous, and General of the Vampire Army. He'd been crucial to the success of our mission to take Edmund down. But just as crucial, his wife and beloved, Sienna. I still marveled at that one. A human

—or so we'd thought—with powers beyond anything I'd ever seen. Stories of her healing magic had spread across the Territories far and wide. And now that she could ride the bloody Hunters as if they were her own private ponies, she'd reached an almost god-like status. And still, she stayed humble and kind...and stubborn and foolhardy at times.

All part of why I liked her, honestly.

Next to them sat Nicholas of Southwind. A vampire aristocrat raised in a family of diplomats with an interesting skill set I'd yet to witness personally. And Raven, another vampire whose presence I still questioned. He was far too handsome, and charming in a way that raised my hackles. If it wouldn't please him so much to get under my skin, I'd have already demanded to know why he'd even come to this meeting.

Finally, I shifted my gaze to the woman directly across from me, Evangeline. My savior. The woman who had protected me from Edmund as a child, and spirited me away to Werewolf Territory. Defying the king himself and risking her life to save mine. A Duchess with a heart of gold and a spine of steel.

Although you wouldn't know it now. She looked like a husk of her former self. Those snapping silver eyes, always lit with determination and wit, were now downcast as she stared at the intricate pattern on the mahogany table. Losing Lycan had been tough on us all. It was as if a live grenade had been tossed in our midst, tearing through us all. The pack was still reeling, friends and clan members from far and wide had been in mourning for weeks now. And me? As much as I tried to play it off...show the strength and fortitude so necessary in a Queen, some days it was hard to even put one foot in front of the other and get through the day.

And still, Evangeline was suffering more. She'd barely left her quarters and seemed so deep in a fog, I was starting to wonder if she'd lost her grip on reality. Or maybe she'd just been lost in memories of the past.

I'd spent a fair amount of time doing the same lately, so I could hardly judge. Still, I hated having to leave her like this. Especially without knowing when—or if—I'd be coming back.

I spared one last glance out the window and pursed my lips. There was a fair chance it didn't matter what I or any other creature on this planet did now. The end was near. Ever since the Veil had fallen fifteen years before, we'd been on a downward slide.

It had been slow at first. So slow, we didn't even notice. But then the winters grew colder. Longer. The summers sweltering. The winds and tides unpredictable. And lately, especially these past few weeks, the weather was off the rails. Storms even while the sun shined. Snow and sleet mixed with hail and thunder. If we got caught at sea in something like that, we'd all be at the bottom of the ocean. Wolves were stronger and hardier than humans to be sure, but Mother Nature was the great equalizer.

Shoving aside the big-picture problems, I focused on the ones I had a shot of actually solving.

"I think that's everyone," I said, forcing a smile to my lips as I rose to stand. "Let's begin. I'm sure you've all seen how—"

The door flew open, banging off the stone wall with such a crash that I instinctively laid a hand on the hilt of my sword.

"Sorry I'm late!" rasped the tiny, misshapen woman who hobbled into the room. Her face wasn't visible due to the towering plate of food she held balanced in front of her, but I didn't need to see it.

"Myrr?" I demanded, immediately irritated. "What are you doing here?"

She plopped into a side chair closest to the door and shot me a mostly-toothless grin. "I'm the Oracle, ain't I? I need to be kept apprised of all the haps, don't I? I swear, I won't interrupt. I'm just going to sit here and eat my breakfast while you all do your plotting and scheming and such, hmm?"

I let out a sigh. I wanted to remind her that, as the Oracle, technically, shouldn't she already be apprised of "the haps"? But I wasn't about to call her on it. Dominic, a non-believer who was only just starting to come around to the idea of someone truly seeing the future—barely—had no such reservations.

"Aren't you supposed to be all-knowing?" he demanded. "All-seeing?"

"Not all, no." Myrr hefted what looked like an entire haunch of venison in her gnarled hands and glared at him through one, milky eye. "But I knew you lot were meeting here without me so I guess I know *some* things, eh, big boy?"

Sienna laid a hand on Dom's arm as he seemed ready to fire back, and he settled against his chair with a sigh.

"Fine, do as you please. You will anyway," he muttered.

It wasn't that Myrr wasn't helpful...exactly. It was just that it took some time—a lot of it, in some cases—to see how she was helping. Since I'd found the note my father had left for me in the event of his death, I'd met with her to talk over breakfast—at her request—a half dozen times to get some guidance. All I wound up with was a headache from grinding my teeth in irritation after listening to her chew for an hour straight. Now, with my journey imminent, she was just as likely to harm as she was to help. Many of her visions were cryptic and erratic, muddying the waters more than they offered clarity. Others were so ominous and full of impending doom that it made it hard to stay the course and keep morale high. If the weight of the world was on my shoulders, I needed morale at its highest, and the water to be crystal clear.

The time for prophecies and the doubts they could bring had passed. Now was the time for action.

I turned to her and lifted a brow in stern warning. "Just observing, yes? If you have something to add, we can meet afterward."

Or not.

The Oracle set down her venison to mimic the locking of lips before throwing away the key.

I dipped my head and then turned to face the others at the table.

“The reason I’ve asked you here is because I...” I glanced at Raven and Nicholas of Southwind and let out a sigh, “Or my brothers trust you implicitly. As you all know, Sienna has an enemy out there working behind the scenes to wreak havoc on both her and on the Territories as a whole. This enemy, she has considerable power, and she is using that power to prevent the rebuilding of the Veil, a process that apparently involves Sienna and four other keys.” I turned to Sienna. “Care to step in and share your experiences with this entity?”

Sienna sucked in a breath, her expression darkening as she spoke. “She was feeding me false prophecies and dreams for some time. She was also the one responsible for the werewolf Elka’s possession, and subsequent attack on me. She has the ability to intrude on my dreams somehow, and even cause injury from within them. It's jarring because you don't know what she'll do next. She even spoke to me through Will's bloodworm at one point. Her powers are chillingly strong, and largely unknowable at this point."

I nodded. "So be wary of strange dreams or other such intrusions. Beware of voices giving false directives, no matter how alluring they may seem. We theorize that Elka was targeted because of her dark emotional state at the loss of her brother, Jordan. We believe that the entity is most likely to make her move at times of strong emotion, or weakness."

"In hindsight, I'm fairly certain that my second in command, Scarlett, was possessed by her too," Dom cut in, and Sienna nodded at his side. "Perhaps for quite a long time. Unlike Elka, Scarlett didn't seem like a woman possessed. It was almost as if this entity prayed on her jealousies and insecurities, and wore her down over a long period. It's also very likely that she has a way of keeping track of us, given the nature of her powers. She clearly doesn't need to be directly present to invade someone's mind."

I turned to Myrr as I continued, "But it's not all bad news. There does seem to be another force out there that is trying to aid us. Elhimna, the enemy called him. He has spoken through Myrr on several occasions, and seems familiar with our enemy and her tricks. He has counseled us to gather the remaining keys and keep them safe at all costs."

Myrr nodded, setting down her venison for a moment to add, "There's something about his words that rings true. I'd stake my name as Oracle on his words being reliable."

"We have scholars studying the history books for any record of his name or of a dark force with powers like the entity we're facing, but have found nothing. For now, keep your guard up at all times. This will be most important when it comes to this next bit." I reached for the stack of papers before me and handed them to Loch. "Can you take one and pass the rest down?"

I didn't need to keep one for myself.

"I found this note shortly after my father's death. I've spent over a week trying to decide how to handle this, and now that my path is clear, I wanted to share it with you all."

I cleared my throat and began to recite from memory.

"'If you've found this, Diana, that means I am gone. Likely too old and too slow to keep up with the pups in battle. Such is life. What you need to know most of all is that you were my greatest joy. I cannot imagine how empty my life would've been without you in it, and if that was all my Evangeline ever gave to me, it would've been enough. I am so proud of you, and all you've accomplished. You are already a better leader than I ever was.

Enough of that, though. Now, for the hard bit. I hate to burden you further, my daughter, but I'm afraid it can't be helped. I've been in search of something that might help us fix what has been broken. Something the Oracle told me in secret could save you all. Decades ago, when I was still king and you were more trusting, a man came to our keep. Charming, silver-tongued, and handsome. That man left our territory with a jewel he had no right to take. I believe he is still in possession of that jewel, and we need to get it back, daughter. Only then can we find the other keys...Only then can we restore the Veil.'"

The rest of the room was silent, except for the Duchess's now-labored breathing.

She met my gaze through the thin, black lace of her widow's veil as she pushed back her chair and stood.

"I'm sorry, Diana, but I can't be here. I hope you'll forgive me."

I swallowed past the lump in my throat to reply. "Of course."

She swept from the room, closing the door behind her. I knew it had been a gamble to request her presence, but I didn't want her to feel excluded.

It was probably for the best that she wasn't here. Emotions were sure to run high and we needed to think with our minds, not with our hearts, now more than ever.

I glanced around the table as I continued. "I know who this man is. I know the gem my father spoke of. In fact, I am the reason it was so easily taken. But that's a story for another day. What's important is that I own its mate, so I know exactly what we're looking for. And, thanks to our amazing tech team, I know that it's located in the human realm. What I need now is a few volunteers to come and help me find it."

Sienna's arm instantly shot high. "I'm in."

Dom grabbed her hand and yanked it down. "*I'm* in."

Bethany shot Sienna a glance. "If she's in, I'm in too."

Will nodded. "In."

"Me too," Loch said.

I pinched my eyes closed and let out a sigh. *Gods give me strength.*

"As much as I appreciate your loyalty and passion here guys, none of that's going to happen. Loch, I need you here in my stead. And William and Bethany are the brand new King and Queen of the Vampire Territory. They need to be here for their people to waylay any concerns and ensure that the last of Edmund loyalists have all been rooted out. Dominic cannot be separated from Will. It's his literal job to ensure his safety. And obviously, Sienna, being the one key we *do* have, needs to be protected at all costs."

I crossed my arms over my chest.

"I brought you all here because I need some recommendations. Dominic," I said, turning his way. "I need one of your men to come with me and offer some cover.

Someone strong who can handle himself if things go sideways, but also smart and well-connected, with deep knowledge of the human world, whose presence won't be questioned. Someone who can call in some favors if our quarry proves to be hard to find."

Raven cleared his throat and hunkered down in his chair, silent as he eyed Dominic through heavy lids.

"That's Raven," Dom said with a clipped nod. "He's been my right hand since...since Scarlett's passing and spent more time in the human realm than any other warrior I know."

I instantly balked.

"Raven? What's he going to do, seduce Maverick into giving him the stone?"

The man in question met my gaze, a grin stealing over his firm mouth. "Your Majesty, make no mistake. While there's no doubt I could do it that way, I'd be much more inclined to fight the man than fuck him. I like my lovers...softer, if you will."

Heat stole over my cheeks for no good reason, which pissed me off. What was I, some blushing maiden? Hell no. I was a werewolf queen, damn it.

"Be that as it may," I said with a tight smile, "I was thinking Nicholas of Southwinds."

Anyone but Raven.

"Nicholas should go as well," Dom agreed. "His talent for...reading people could be useful. But you have your pack and this whole Territory relying on you, Diana. You need protection as much as anyone else in this room. If I could convince you not to go, I would."

I opened my mouth to speak but he held up a hand.

"*But* since I know I can't change your mind, it has to be Raven. There's no man I would want beside me on the field of battle more than him. If I have to put your life in someone's hands, it will be his."

"I'm honored to go," Nicholas said, his tone solemn.

Dominic turned to look at Raven, who slumped back in his seat and let out a groan, his eyes rolling hard enough that I wondered how they stayed in his head.

"I mean, yeah. Alright, then. I did swear fealty to King William, and now report to Dominic. If he says I go, then I go."

"Your enthusiasm for the task gives me the utmost confidence," I said through my teeth.

His smile never faltered. "I'd be a lot more willing about the whole thing if you didn't act like such a high-handed bitch all the time."

Something inside me snapped, and an instant later I was across the table, my short blade pressed against his neck.

"You dare call a queen such a slur in her own home?" I whispered, adrenaline pounding through my veins, making me feel more alive than I'd felt since before Lycan's death. I held Raven's mocking gaze, getting angrier by the moment as I called over my shoulder. "Brother...you say this is the strongest fighter you know? He couldn't even stop me from getting the drop on him."

Raven had the balls to wink at me. "Alas my Queen, if I chose violence today, you'd already be dead."

"Raven!" Will snapped. "Enough!"

Raven's voice dropped to a whisper, low enough for only me to hear.

"I get it. It's not your fault. Most women have a hard time letting me go."

As much as I wanted to take all the pent-up anger and grief of the past weeks out on this bastard, I couldn't. With all eyes on the two of us, it was best to let this little pissing contest die a quick death or risk creating a rift. Our pack had a strong ally in the vampires for the first time ever. I needed to keep it that way. No matter how satisfying it would've been to wipe the smirk off his face.

I lowered my knife and stepped back, smoothing the braid down my back as I forced a smile.

"You see I'm right, though. He's difficult, Dominic. There is zero chance he'll obey me. The last thing I need is to be dealing with a wild card bloodsucker who can't do as he's told. And while I understand that you and Will trust him, I do not. For all I know, he'll try to eat me while I sleep."

His mouth quirked. "If I decide to eat you, Your Majesty, you wouldn't be asleep for long."

"Godsdamnit, Raven!" Dominic growled, thumping the table with his fist. "You're not making this any easier."

"Just pick someone else. Anyone," I managed, suddenly flustered and trying not to think of this irritating man bent before me, mouth pressed to my–

"Wordplay aside, our brother is right, Diana," Will said, clearly not thrilled by the thought, but resigned. "I know he can be vexing, but in this time of political upheaval, there is no one else I would trust with your life, either."

Will pursed his lips and shot a glance at Dominic, who leveled his friend with a cold stare.

"Raven. Apologize. Now."

With a sigh, the bastard rose from his chair to stare down at me just long enough to let me clock his sheer size and presence that far overwhelmed my own before dropping to one knee.

"Forgive me, Your Majesty. It was never my intention to offend. I apologize for my insolence and offer my fealty." He bent his head low to the ground until it touched the tip of my boots and I was staring down at his gleaming, dark hair. Then he looked up. "From this day forward, I am yours to command."

He looked so solemn, his voice suddenly ringing with such sincerity that I actually believed him. Raven mocking me and acting a fool was one thing. This Raven was far more unsettling. I could hear the pulse in my neck pounding and, judging by the way he was staring at it with barely repressed hunger, so could he.

He had just ceded control to me, but somehow I felt more out of control than ever...

Nope. Not happening.

I was about to put this nonsense to bed once and for all when Myrr dropped the iced bun she'd been holding and spoke, her tone the low drone of prophecy.

"Yes. Our Queen Diana, Nicholas of Southwind, and Raven of the mainland. This is the trio that will save the Empire."

Oh, sure. *Now* her visions were clear as glass?

I knew I should've kicked her out when I had the chance.

CHAPTER 3
Raven

The waves on the rocks outside my window mimicked the waves in my dreams, the ones that crashed against the shoreline and threatened someone I couldn't protect. Panic and fear raced through me as I struggled to get through the surf, my hands outstretched as I screamed for her. Fought to get to her.

Too late, I was too late.

Sweat soaked through my sheets even though I'd gone to bed naked.

Jerking to a sitting position, I swung my legs to the side and bent at the waist, sheets pooling around my middle.

"Fuck." I growled the word, hating that I could still be denied a good sleep from something that had happened too damn long ago. Then again, I wondered if the dreams were even real now, because no one else remembered the things I did.

My skin was tight and hot, and my guts ached.

Curling my tongue over my fangs, I was reminded I had to feed today. Before we left on this so-called quest. Or Diana was right, she might just wake up with me eating her.

A flash of her on her knees in front of me instead of how it had actually happened was a pleasant enough thought that I considered relieving myself right then to the image but…no. I was not about to let her get to me.

Something about the woman dug at me in a way that made my skin itch, made me want to poke at her. Made me want to force her to deal with me. Which was only another reason for me to not go with them back to the mainland.

Yet I could not deny my King, or my friend.

"She's not even my type," I muttered under my breath as if saying it out loud would help me.

To be fair, the women who found their way to my bed were typically soft, with generous curves, and hair like silk that I could bury my face in while I fucked them ragged, making them beg for more before I brought them screaming to completion. Mind you, they rarely lasted more than a night or two—didn't want them getting attached, after all. But there was always another waiting in the wings. A maid who'd heard someone's panting through the walls.

My lips turned upward and then immediately slid into a frown.

Diana...she was everything that I would expect from a wolf queen, right down to her leather pants and the weapons she was never without. Her body was lean and strong, her muscles tight, and the way she held herself, with more confidence than I'd seen in any other leader.

I wanted pliable. Sweet. Not a sharp-tongued, battle-hardened she-wolf.

Grumbling to myself, the last remnants of my nightmare banished at the thought of the queen staring down at me when I'd apologized. I'd known exactly what I was doing, looking up at her, the same way I would have had I been feasting on her pussy.

Sure, she hated me, but I could see the blood rise to her cheeks as that knowledge had hit her, and the darker thoughts rippled through those frosted blue eyes. Her wolf had stared out at me with curiosity even while the woman was pissed as fuck to even consider the thought.

And now I had to spend goddess knew how many weeks with her.

"Stake me now and be done with it," I muttered as I slid into a dark shirt and pants. I ran my hands through my hair, not caring if it was tousled. It would give the impression I'd just fallen out of a lady's arms after pleasuring her all night. An image I had to uphold if I was to continue as the rogue.

I grimaced, anger snapping through me. There had been no woman to take my attention away from this stupid political game—the only two that had caught my eye were married to my two closest friends.

Strike one and two. And worse, I now considered them family, and would fight to protect them.

I made my way to the side table and opened the refrigerator hidden behind the panel in the wall. I stared at the stock of cold blood with mild distaste. Nothing like taking it straight from a warm, willing woman, but Dominic had reminded me that I had to drink and drink deeply before I got on the damn boat...A deadline that was rapidly approaching.

Familiar footsteps sounded outside my door.

"Bossy bastard." I smiled as I reached for the first of four bottles.

"Talking about me again?" Dominic opened the door as I spun the lid off the bottle and tipped it back.

Even cold, the flavor wasn't unpleasant. This vintage was from a human, female, early thirties and she tasted of chocolate and fruit. Not bad.

I put the empty bottle down and reached for a second. "No, of course not. How many bossy bastards are in my life? Wait...I suppose that it's just you."

Dominic raised a brow and leaned on the edge of the door frame. "Still mad?"

"You're sending me on a quest of some sort, with a woman who despises me, and a whelp who has barely been tested in battle, on a boat that likely was made when the Territories came into existence." I looked over my shoulder. "Sounds like the start to a bad joke, don't you think? Why would I be mad?"

I spun off the cap on the second bottle and snapped it back. Female, human again, and tasted strongly of whiskey and...peanut butter? It was an odd combination, but smooth and it slipped down my throat with an ease that had me sighing. I set the second bottle down and picked up a third, but didn't open it just yet. Instead, I turned to my friend.

"Choose another to go. Your sister doesn't want me there, and conveniently, I don't want to be there either. I came back to the Territories for a reason and this surely was not it." I pointed the bottle at him. "You have many, many men and even some women—who would be more than capable of doing this job, and you fucking well know it. So why me?"

"Diana is strong enough to take care of herself," Dom said. "But you know the mainland better than anyone else. You have the connections she might need to find this thief. And despite how you behave, you're skilled in areas outside the bedroom. Your swords are deadly, Raven."

I smiled at him over the third bottle and gave him a wink. "You would know it. You still bear the scars of our first fight, do you not?"

Dominic's nostrils flared. "You cheated."

"I won. Have you not yet learned? All's fair in a fight to the death." I tipped the bottle at him and then poured it into my mouth. This one caught me off guard. Werewolf, female, tasting of a wild spring storm and driving itself into my veins in a way I hadn't felt in so very, very long, making me want to run and howl at the moon, to find a partner and fuck her until I couldn't breathe any longer, then lay in her arms as the stars burned above. Eyes closed, I put the bottle down and leaned on the wall. "Gods, I forgot how hard other Territory blood hits. That was a doozy."

Dominic grunted. "I do not forget."

I lifted my eyes to him, my veins still humming with the unknown female's blood. "Sienna?"

He gave me a sharp nod. "When it tastes of magic, I believe you might have found your mate."

I grabbed the fourth bottle, almost hating that I had to drink it down and wash away the previous one. "There is no magic in blood that comes from another Territory. Power and strength, yes. But mates are for those who believe in fairy tales and happily ever afters." I paused and put the drink back. "I lost faith in those many, many years ago."

Dom motioned for me to follow him. “So did I. Then I met Sienna. Things change, Raven. Let them. And... drink your last bottle before you leave.”

I saluted him. “Yes, you bossy bastard. Where are we going now?”

“You need a tune-up. I want to make sure you can protect my sister.”

I laughed, blowing a kiss to a maid as she scurried past. Her eyes widened and her mouth dropped into a perfect O that would fit right over my—

“I want to see if you can still spar. I’ve no doubt you’ll be in a few fights before you find the thief.”

I stared after the maid who had slowed and was looking over her shoulder at me. Yes, that one would be lovely to hold and yet...I winked at her and turned back to Dominic.

“Sparring, sure. I do keep up, you know.” I tapped a hand on my chest. “Ladies don’t like a man who lets himself get soft.”

Dominic looked over at me, his eyes thoughtful as I kept my smile pinned in place. Let the fool I was thought to be stay on the surface.

“I see you, Raven,” he said finally. “I know who you are. You will protect her with your life if you need to, as would I. Which is why I am sending you. Because I trust you to do what you must to make sure you get the job done and both come back alive.”

His words cut into me, his faith in me still shaking me from time to time. I was just the palace maid's boy, before we were cast to the mainland. I did not come from blood, or fancy titles.

Dominic had never cared.

"You have my word," I said, all the light teasing tones gone. "I will protect her as if she is family."

He nodded and that was that—an understanding from one to the other.

We made our way to the covered courtyard, set up for the vampires who'd stayed behind in the Werewolf Territory. Will would need to leave soon, he'd gone back and forth for the last five weeks, dealing with both his own court and supporting Diana. Now he would finish his official takeover of the Vampire Territory as our new king.

The courtyard was empty. The day was only just beginning. We'd leave for the mainland this afternoon—just the three of us, if you didn't count a bare bones crew to help man the boat.

Diana, Nicholas, and myself. That was enough to draw irritation through me again, and I scooped up not one, but two swords.

Dominic lifted his eyebrows. "In a mood then, are we?"

"You said to spar. So let us spar." I lifted both swords and settled into a waiting stance.

Dominic scooped up a sword and a shield. A more

traditional set of tools for this fight. "Come at me then. Bird boy."

An old insult and one that only made me roll my eyes. "You can do better than that, you bastard."

He grinned. "Bird brain?"

"Perhaps that's what I will call you from now on."

Diana's voice made my hands flex of their own accord around the hilts of both swords. Though she wasn't my type, even I couldn't deny that she was striking as she came into view. Stalked into view was more like it.

Her long dark hair and frosty blue eyes like a winter morning could make you feel like kneeling at her feet.

Again.

I bowed at the waist. "Ah, the queen of all arrives. Come to watch the peasants fight for your honor?"

Dominic sighed so heavily, it fairly rattled the air. "Must you, Raven?"

"Oh, I must." I smiled and dipped my head. "I cannot feed on this trip. I cannot bed any women, and I must be subject to the ice queen's whims. Fairly played, but let me have a little fun."

Diana's eyes narrowed on me. "I barely saw you on the battlefield against Edmund, and have yet to ascertain with my own eyes if you have any skill, or if all you do is talk your way out of having to fight."

I shrugged. "A win, is a win, is a win. I don't care how

I survive, *Your Majesty*, only that I do." And, now, that she did too.

Diana moved into the sparring square that had been marked out, her eyes locked on me as she circled around. Hunter and prey, I could see it in the way her body shifted ever so slightly.

Another woman I might have laughed at, seeing her set herself up to attack me. With her, I was going to have to be careful. She'd just as soon tear my throat out.

"How are you going to track this thief?" Dominic asked, cutting through the growing tension. "He's been gone for years, correct?"

I was not so stupid as to take my eyes off the stalking wolf. She paused and turned to her brother, and I realized that had been his goal. To draw her ire away from me. I stabbed the tip of one sword into the ground and leaned on the handle.

"Yes, I'd been curious about that as well. Unless you're hoping I'll do all the work for you?"

Dominic shot me a look and I just grinned at him. I couldn't help it. She was fun to irritate, and I liked the way her eyes flashed at me a little too much.

"My tech team has been studying the crimson stone here, and have found a way to mimic the resonance within. They then sent out a similar sound and got back four pings."

My eyebrows shot up. That was...actually pretty clever. "Four pings, better than the whole world at least."

Diana tucked her hands behind her back. "Of the four locations, there is only one that Maverick would willingly go."

"Indulge me," I drawled. "I'm curious as to the other places we might end up."

"Antarctica, Madagascar, Moscow," she said and I winced as she went on. "But from what I know of him, he'll be in the fourth place. Isla Naranja..."

"How can you be sure?" I asked. "Being wrong will truly fuck us over."

I thought the question would piss her off, but she laughed and the sound caught me off guard, wrapping itself around me.

"Because that's where the party is. Casinos, brothels, pubs. And he is, at heart, a scoundrel and a gambler. And he sure as shit isn't gambling with penguins." Her eyes sparked and she turned to her brother.

"Hand me your weapons. I want to see if he's any good."

"He survived the battle unscathed," Dominic said. "And I've seen him fight. He's that good."

Good enough to beat the General himself more than once. But while I might brag about my skills in the bedroom, my skills on the battlefield...I chose to keep that to myself as much as possible. The more someone thought you were good at fighting, the more challenges came your way.

"You want to spar with me, Frostbite, far be it for me to stop you. Although I can't help but wonder if this is just a ploy to get close to me." I flashed her a wide smile as I tugged the blade from the ground and swung my two swords up into a ready stance.

"I'll get close enough to run you through the heart, just for giving me that stupid nickname." She smiled so very sweetly up at me, that I knew I was in trouble.

We circled one another, and Dominic watched from the sidelines. "He's weak to the right."

"Fucker," I growled at my supposed friend. "You'd help her cheat?"

"Giving her advice, it's a rather brotherly thing to do." Dominic laughed as Diana came at me, fast and low, springing up with her sword and shoving me backward.

I could have beaten her right then, her belly exposed to my right-handed blade, but I fell back, letting her push me around the ring.

Always keeping just out of reach.

Letting her direct the flow of this dance. Watching her body work, and admiring it none too little.

Keeping pace with her and noting when I could strike. Because I didn't want to hurt her—despite how she was getting under my skin.

On two legs, I outmatched her in speed, and reflexes,

so I kept myself reined in. If she got seriously pissed, and shifted to four legs...well, that would be a whole other ball of wax. Werewolves were far more deadly when they had claws and teeth that could tear your head from your shoulders.

Not that I'd ever admit that.

The fight rolled into ten minutes of parrying and thrusting, and her softly golden skin had a sheen of sweat coating it, beads sliding across her collarbone and down her neck. Her lips were parted as her breath came in harder and faster with each passing minute, the sound drawing me closer, wanting stupidly to feel her breath against my ear.

The top of her shirt slid just a fraction of an inch, exposing the very top swell of her breast and my eyes locked onto a bead of sweat as it ran down her skin there as I wondered how she'd feel under me, sweating and writhing, panting for air.

A bit of material that was not her shirt caught my eye. Binding? She bound her breasts to keep them out of the way?

The shield snapped into my face and sent me backward, flat onto my back, the world spinning. The tip of her sword followed, settling into the hollow of my throat. "If you can't keep your eyes on the prize, then you will die, Raven."

I laughed and smiled up at her, letting her see my fangs

as I ran my tongue over them. "Who said I didn't have my eye on the prize, Frostbite?"

The flush of her cheeks could have been from the exertion of the fight, but I didn't think so. With a snarl she tossed her shield and sword away and strode from the covered courtyard.

I pushed to my feet and dusted myself off as Dominic picked up the weapons and set them in the racks. "You just can't help yourself, can you?"

I shrugged. "I find I enjoy getting under her skin. If I must go, at least give me this."

Dominic sighed and shook his head. "Just try not to get yourself killed."

CHAPTER 4
Diana

The skies above the keep cleared, and the cold storm that had come up over dinner was gone as fast as it had arrived. Thick layers of ice from hail the size of fists made walking to the beach awkward, but everyone managed.

Raven strode along like the balls of ice were nothing, scooping them up and juggling them as we headed toward the ship.

Nicholas walked on my left; his young face marred with worry. "We are going to have to be below deck during the day. How are we to protect you if a battle comes? It's not like at home, where the sun is kept at bay."

I gave him a quick smile. "Trust me. My people are brilliant, and the tech team has sent us with some aces up our sleeves. I have something that will help."

The young vampire glanced at me. "You are confident?"

I nodded. "They've tried them out earlier, with Dominic offering to be the guinea pig. They worked without question." I didn't like thinking about the moment that Dominic had willingly walked out into the sun. Even though he'd been close to shade, and he could have jumped back quickly, despite trying to keep it from happening, somewhere along the line, my brother had become someone I cared about deeply. Hard times either brought people together or tore them apart. Through our battle with Edmund, and in the weeks since Lycan's death, Dominic had become more than just my brother in blood. He'd become my brother at heart. And the idea of him being hurt bothered me more than I wanted to admit.

I never thought my first family, the one I'd been born to, would be anything but enemies to me and my werewolves. Yet in Dominic and Will, too, I'd found that the ties that bound us together were stronger than I ever could have imagined.

Gratitude slipped through me, calming any fears, stealing away the last of my worry for the moment. A trick I'd learned years ago, and one that I could share if I was so inclined. I reached over and put a hand on Nicholas' shoulder.

He took a deep breath, and I could sense it as his worries eased, just a little.

"How did you do that?"

"A little bit of magic." I smiled.

"Vampire magic," he said, his tone sure.

I snatched my hand back from his shoulder as if it were hot. It had never occurred to me that my little trick was anything but a gift I'd received once I was a werewolf. "I doubt it."

Nicholas frowned. "Your inner circle knows what you went through to become a werewolf. I don't think any of them would doubt your loyalty, I just find it interesting that you still retained some magic that traditionally is a vampiric trait. A strong one, mind you, one that—"

"Nicholas," Raven drawled. "You are giving me a headache and we aren't even on the boat yet. Stop yammering."

Nicholas did as he was told, snapping his mouth shut and staring straight ahead.

I did not want to be grateful to Raven, but I was happy for the distraction. There was not a day that went by that I was not reminded of what I had been. Of what I'd come from. And there were days that I still worried what could happen to me if the moon goddess ever revoked her blessing on me. When the sun kissed my skin, it didn't melt my flesh from my bones, but there were days that I...felt that it could.

I sighed and tried to put those thoughts behind me.

"Get on the boat; I want to take this window while the weather is clear for a change, and get out of the harbor."

Nicholas hurried ahead, putting distance between him and Raven.

"Do not be cruel to him," I said.

"I wasn't. He was stressing you out," Raven said so nonchalantly that I couldn't believe there wasn't something else coming.

"So?"

"My job is to protect you, Frostbite. From all sides." He dropped each of the balls of ice he'd been juggling at the edge of the water and jogged up the boat plank.

I struggled to swallow. Was it so obvious that what Nicholas had been saying bothered me? I prided myself on my poker face. It was a must in diplomacy. I didn't think I'd given away my hand, and yet Raven had seen something in me react to Nicholas' casual observation. It wasn't like Nicholas had been spilling secrets.

Everyone in the Werewolf Territory knew I'd been born half vampire and made into a werewolf.

But not everyone knows how ashamed you are of that fact.

Hamish stood on deck. "Your Majesty—"

"Just Diana from here on out, Hamish," I said. "I don't need anyone finding out that I am royalty. The last thing we need is an attempted kidnapping or blackmail."

He dipped his head. "Diana. As soon as you are on board, we can go."

I turned to see Lochlin, Dominic and Sienna making their way through the ice field to see us off. Will and Bee had already headed back to the Vampire Territory. The new king and queen could not delay their trip home any longer. The Duchess had not joined them, choosing to stay at the keep. My guess was that she felt closest to Lycan here. But she had not come to send us off. I looked to the keep and the light at the top left-hand side. Her room was there and with my keen eyes, I could just make out her silhouette in the window. I lifted a hand, and she returned the gesture.

Thoughts of my father, and of her...my heart ached, and I struggled for a moment to breathe through the grief that threatened to overwhelm me.

No, I had to keep moving.

We had to find Maverick. I locked my wolf on the man who'd betrayed us and pushed the grief aside. I'd grieve my father more when I had time—this was not that time.

Dominic reached me first and he pulled me into his arms for a surprisingly tight hug. "Be safe, Diana. I do not want to gain a sister, only to lose her."

Damn it, so much for not feeling anything. My brother—*my brother*—held tight to me, as if it did not matter that we were in a hurry. There was no embarrassment from him to be hugging his sister.

I loved him all the more for that simple fact.

Sienna was next and she also held tight. "I echo his sentiment. Come back to us as quickly as you're able." She stepped back and her eyes went wide as she gazed past me. "The kraken will go with you as far as he can, to keep you safe. Until the second day at least."

I looked where she was looking to see the long tentacle of the kraken who'd once been a feared monster, and who was now an ally. What a strange time we were living in. "Thank him for me."

She smiled and stepped back. "He already knows."

Lochlin was last and he set aside the usual respectful distance he showed me since I'd become queen, and scooped me off the ground like the old days. "Lass, you need to be careful out there. Don't worry about nothing here, I've got it. But out there...I know you don't like him, but Raven will be a good ally to you."

I grimaced and patted him on the shoulder, so he'd let me down. "We shall see, Loch. Be safe. Watch the borders like a hawk. If this entity was willing to stir up the vampires, who knows what else she might do."

"If she is going to go after anyone," Sienna said softly, "it will be you now as you search for another of the keys."

A chill swept through me and I nodded. "I'll be careful." I took a step back and bumped into a solid body that I'd not even realized was there.

Raven grabbed my arms, turned me and set me on the plank. "Time to go. Wind is changing."

"Hey!" I barked but he was all but shoving me up the plank. "Do you not say goodbye to your friends?"

We were on deck when he finally stopped and looked out over the beach. "Fare thee well, fine friends. May the gods show us boon that we may dine together again someday!"

The werewolves on deck aside from Hamish, who had a clear distaste for Raven for which I couldn't fault him, laughed at his over-the-top words.

I did not.

"You mock the emotions shared between me and my family?"

Raven shot me a look. "Not at all. But I have said goodbye too many times to those I loved, only to see them dead on the other side. So now it is a casual thing."

Nicholas joined us as the boat was pulled out into the harbor, the kraken's tentacles wrapped around the bow. "So, it is a superstitious thing then?"

"Something like that," Raven said as he lifted his hand, not in a wave, but in a hang loose symbol. Surprisingly, Dominic and Lochlin flashed the same hand motion back.

"Hang loose?" Nicholas asked.

"Not for us." Raven stepped back from the deck and did not elaborate.

I blinked, surprised by the seriousness of him, so swiftly following the fool's antics. The wolf perked up inside of me, her curiosity more like that of a cat. What was beneath all the laughing and teasing? A monster? A battle-hardened warrior? Something else?

I shook my head. I did not need to be musing about Raven.

"I have something for each of you," I said. "A gift."

That paused Raven in his steps. "Please tell me it is a view of those luscious brea—"

Hamish was on him in a flash, cutting him off before he could finish the word. "Do not speak of my lady so!"

Raven dodged the werewolf with ease so that Hamish stumbled to the edge of the boat. "They would be luscious, though. I think she binds them to keep them out of her way for fighting."

How the fuck did he know that?

Raven's eyes fairly twinkled in the light of the crescent moon. "I have an eye for breasts."

Nicholas snorted. "That will surely be useful on our quest."

Raven shot a look at him. "You'd be surprised. But tell me, young Nicholas, because I've been asking myself since the General selected you...What talents have *you* been hiding?"

Nicholas had seemed fairly quiet since I'd known him.

I'd assumed it was a lack of confidence. Perhaps it was something more deadly.

It was as if something was turned off in the younger man as he schooled his features. Raven moved closer, and it was like watching a panther emerge from the shadows stalking its prey; his attention was so fully on Nicholas that I was not sure he saw anything else, and in such a way that even on the periphery of it, had my heart racing. His fangs extended from behind his lips. "What. Are. You. Capable. Of?"

This Raven was not the fool. This was a Raven to be feared.

I snapped my fingers in front of his face, knowing I had to change the direction of his intensity.

"Enough! To the gift I have for each of you."

That pulled Raven's turquoise colored eyes to me and, for a moment, he didn't hide the darkness behind them. If I hadn't been staring so intently at him, I would have missed it. I stared right back until the darkness settled.

He gave me a slow wink and a smile crossed his face. "Gifts, then."

As if he knew I was stopping him from pestering poor Nicholas. "Hamish, bring me the inlaid box from the captain's quarters. The one with the daggers."

Raven's dark eyebrows shot up. "I already have a dagger. Two to be exact. I like keeping my weapons in pairs just in case I was...relieved of one of them."

Nicholas moved so that he was on my other side, effectively putting me between him and Raven.

"Thank you, Diana."

Hamish brought me the box and gave Raven a dirty look when he did. "Should throw him overboard, let the kraken have him."

I took the box and forced myself not to sigh. "I did try to get him to remain behind, but it seems he has a sense of honor to Dominic and Will. And I doubt the kraken would eat him. Likely would just spit him back out."

Hamish laughed. "Good point."

Flipping open the box I held it first to Raven, then to Nicholas. "They are identical in weight and in purpose—to a degree." I pulled a third blade out, from under a light cloth in the box. "Those two you hold will keep you safe from the sun, reflecting the light so that you can walk freely with me."

"And the one you have?" Raven asked.

"To keep me from shifting when the full moon hits," I said. "We thought it prudent to keep me from feasting on any of the non-wolf members of our little crew."

Nicholas swallowed hard, trying not to show his discomfort and failing miserably. He was still so young. And yet Dominic had assured me that the gift he had been blessed with would help our cause greatly. "Thank you."

As for Raven...his smile was slow. "I'm not sure I'd mind you feasting on me, Your Majesty."

"Goddess," Hamish whispered. "He won't stop, will he?"

"Unlikely," I said and snapped the box shut, choosing not to think about the image that just flitted through me. No. I would not think about Raven as anything but a soldier in my command. Certainly not anything to do with him outside of this quest.

Certainly not Raven naked underneath me.

I sucked in a sharp breath and strode to the front of the ship so the ocean air could drag some of the heat away from me. The kraken splashed and kept pace with us and I made myself stand there until the spray had cooled my skin, wishing it could cool the images I struggled to banish.

Two days we traveled before the kraken turned back and left us to our own devices, just as Sienna had said.

Two days of Raven's innuendos and flirting.

Two days before we realized we had a stowaway.

She was dragged out of the storage room by Yessop, one of the crew. The young werewolf didn't know who she was. "Look at what I found eating all our rations! I thought we had a rat!"

The Oracle looked as ragged as ever, a loaf of bread in one hand, half gnawed. "Pup, you'd better let go of me!"

She wobbled toward me. I carefully grabbed hold of her arms. "Myrr! What in all the hells of all the worlds are you doing here?"

"Food!" She grinned. "There is so much food on the mainland, mountains of it. Things I've never tried! Tables spread out in lines so long you could never eat it all! And have you heard of a mukbang?" She let out a blissful sigh. "Figured this was the best way for me to do a tour of the world—with my own people."

Her own people. I closed my eyes and resisted the urge to pinch the bridge of my nose. This couldn't be happening. It couldn't be. The last thing I needed was Myrr and her added craziness.

"Hamish, turn us around, we're taking her back."

"I don't think you want to do that." Hamish sounded sheepish.

"Why?" I barked. "Because she's the Oracle?"

He cleared his throat even as young Yessop yelped and fell to his knees, babbling an apology. "No. We've got a raging storm behind us. I think it's why the kraken headed back to deep water."

I spun around to see storm clouds rolling behind us, the shapes and colors within it anything but natural. My heart clenched because I knew what we were facing.

"The weather, it's crazy," Nicholas whispered.

Apparently no one else saw what I saw though. No one else understood just how bad this was.

But I was wrong.

One other person saw it.

"That's no natural storm," Raven snarled. "That's demon driven. We need to find shelter on an island and lock this boat down unless we can outrun it. Now!"

Hamish didn't wait to hear it from my lips. "We have the wind at our backs."

"Get the engine going too!" I yelled.

Because there were no islands close, we had little choice. We had to outrun the storm.

In minutes there was a rumble below us and we were picking up speed, staying just ahead of the storm, the edges of it licking at our asses. I held my ground, staring at the clouds as they seemingly chased us down.

The wings within them.

The beasts that evolved and morphed with each turn of the clouds.

Flashes of light and dark, lightning of impossible colors.

And as suddenly as it had come on, the storm shifted direction, heading east, away from us.

"Don't slow," I said. "Keep up this pace tonight. We'll set a watch, I'll take the first."

Myrr had taken over the captain's quarters, so it wasn't like I had a bed to go to anyway.

I paced the deck, mulling over the meaning of the demon storm. Wondering if it had anything to do with us. Or possibly to do with the dark entity who'd tried to kill Sienna.

The Alpha Territories had been strong together all those years before, how could we possibly make them strong again? Were the keys truly the way to healing the Veil? To bringing our worlds back into balance? I wasn't sure what the answer was, and I was no closer to an answer or solution by the time my replacement came up.

Yessop took over my position and I grabbed a blanket, throwing it on the deck. Good enough for me, I'd slept on worse.

What I was surprised to see was Raven emerge from below deck. Unaware of my presence, he strode to the edge of the boat with such energy that I thought perhaps he might hurl himself into the water. But no, he stood, the wind pulling at his hair and shirt, rippling it around his upper body. He looked to his hand and then threw whatever he'd been holding into the sea.

I watched in puzzled silence as he turned and made his way back down below deck.

What the hell was that all about?

My wolf pushed me to my feet, and I was to the railing where he'd stood, gripping the edge as I stared out into the black, swirling water. There, just a few feet behind and trailing faster was a...piece of paper?

Damn my curiosity. I wanted to leap over and grab it, but that was ridiculous. For all I knew it could have been a goodbye from a lover. Or it could be something as simple as a to do list.

But I knew in my heart it was neither.

A wave splashed and the paper was sucked under the water—I stared hard, not sure I was seeing what I thought I was seeing.

But when the young mer-girl shot out of the water to grab at the edge of the boat, and pull herself up to the railing, I knew I was not losing my mind.

"Sorry for spying but good thing I was. Your mate dropped this." She smiled, flashing perfect teeth in her pale, almost pearlescent face. She shoved the sopping wet piece of paper into my hand.

"Oh, he's not my mate." I crouched so I could see her more easily through the railing. She had long, green hair the color of emeralds, and her eyes were like quicksilver. "Are you going to get in trouble for talking to me?"

She grinned wider. "Trouble is my middle name. But my first name is Xefia." She paused and then cocked her head. "I have to go! They're calling me." And with that she flipped backward and was gone in a splash.

Young, she was so very young. Still, she'd have had it hammered into her head since birth. *Don't talk to anyone above water.* She was just a little rebel at heart. I couldn't help but smile a little.

Xefia was trouble indeed.

The wet paper in my hand called to me and I smoothed it out. The words were not a man's handwriting, but I recognized it nonetheless. The Oracle had written this.

For Raven?

Your salvation lies in the Alpha Territories.

Was that the reason he'd returned? Why he'd been so hesitant to come on this journey? Had he thrown the note away because he already knew what it meant, or because he no longer believed in the prophecy?

Whatever the case, the whole thing left me with a nugget of doubt in my belly. Dominic might trust this man, but the proof was in my hand.

Raven had a secret that he'd chosen not to share...

Was it the only one?

CHAPTER 5

Raven

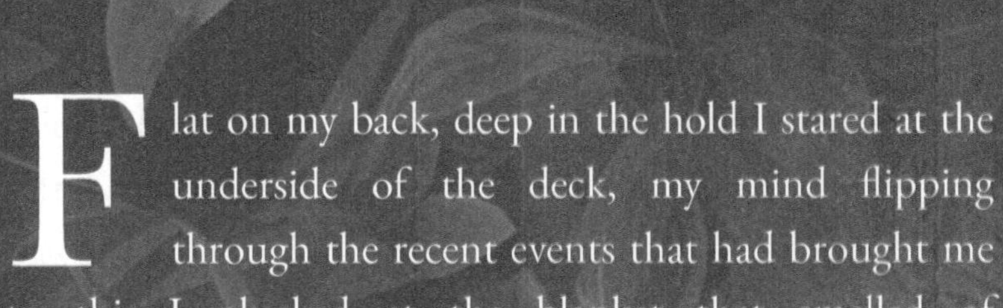

Flat on my back, deep in the hold I stared at the underside of the deck, my mind flipping through the recent events that had brought me to this...I plucked at the blanket that smelled of fish...destination.

Fucking Myrr. I'd just been minding my own business, pretending not to notice the subtle changes in Seattle's weather patterns. The near ever-present drizzle had stopped, and it was full sun, to my chagrin, or full downpour. People commented on it, but like frogs sitting motionless in a pot of water beginning to boil, they didn't really react beyond idle chit chat. "Weird weather lately, huh?"

I'd been no different. Then, I'd gone to the auction and saw Dominic. He'd told me things had been a little off in the Territories as well. A little voice inside me had bleated out a warning.

Something fucky this way comes.

But I'd dulled my concern with absinthe...buried my worries deep in the womb of the next willing female.

Then I got the note from the Oracle.

Your salvation lies in the Alpha Territories.

It was never a question of whether to go back to the Vampire Territory. Dom might mock the gifts of the Oracle, but as odd as the little woman was, she'd never been a joke to me. As a younger lad, I'd seen first-hand the terrible proof of her power...

I shoved that memory away before it could take hold, focusing on the present. And, presently, after going all the way to the Territories per my "destiny", I was on my way back to the human realm I'd only just left months before. Had something happened that changed my fate? I'd tried to ask Myrr before we'd left the keep, but she just shrugged.

"What do I look like, a vending machine? I can only tell you what I know when I know it, Beefcake."

Then, she proceeded to pick my brain about vending machines for the next ten minutes. Could they dispense hot food? Were they everywhere? It should've been a clue that she was mildly obsessed with going to the mainland. Unfortunately, I wasn't an oracle, because I definitely hadn't foreseen her stowing away.

But now that she was here, maybe I could try again. And this time, maybe I'd ask her what I truly wanted to know. The question that had haunted me for most of my life.

Was salvation still in the cards for me?

I doubted it. In fact, until the note had arrived, I'd never even considered it. Not after all I'd seen and done. But I couldn't deny the tiny ember of hope Myrr's words had lit in my belly when I'd first read her letter.

That was gone now.

And, in the dark of night, alone in this shitty little cot, I had to admit its absence left me feeling a little cold inside.

"Cry about it, you wimpy twat," I muttered under my breath as I shifted restlessly until I found a comfortable position. Then, I lay perfectly still, willing my brain to stop churning. Instructing my muscles to relax, one by one. Letting the rocking of the boat lull me into a sense of calm.

A gentle scratching pricked at my ears just as sleep was about to free me from my thoughts. It was barely audible, even to my own hypersensitive ears, due to the endless crashing of waves, and I cursed myself for being so on edge. Groaning softly, I rolled onto my side. Probably just Nicholas walking around on his watch.

Either way, I was starting to wonder whether or not this whole sleeping thing was going to work out. I brought my focus back to the sound of the waves, letting out a long, calming breath.

Thunk.

I sprang to my feet, and cursed myself inwardly as I strode toward the door, pausing to strap my swords around my waist. Then, I crept out of the room still barefoot, vampire stealth engaged, careful not to wake the others.

"Nicholas?" I called softly. If I wasn't going to be able to rest anyway, I might as well take over his watch early. I strode toward the sound of movement a few dozen feet away, calling for him again.

Click. A blinding flash of white light obliterated my vision in an instant, accompanied by a *BOOM* that shook the world. My knees thudded against wood as I dropped to the deck, ears thrumming with pain, eyes watering. I rolled to the side on instinct alone, hardly able to think through the all-out attack on my senses. The wooden boards beneath my feet rumbled softly with footsteps, and I could just barely make out a series of shouts over the horrible ringing in my ears.

I blinked furiously, whipping my blade from my belt just in time to block the first man's attack. I sprang forward, and my hand found his throat just before he could slip out of range. I snarled, bloodlust fully consuming me as I ripped out his windpipe. A shape blurred from behind him, and I had only just begun to move when a blade tore directly through the still-living man's stomach, aimed right at my chest.

Pain screamed through my shoulder as it absorbed the blow, and I spat a curse as I rolled to the side.

Vanators.

Vampire hunters.

They were vicious fighters and gave no quarter because they thought of us as creatures, without a soul or an ounce of humanity. To make matters worse, many I'd tangled with in the past had even been able to resist my mind control. It was said that four out of every five people who enlisted would be killed in the brutal training process. And the one that was left? They became something just a little more than human. Zealous hatred was a powerful drug.

Fresh rage rolled through me as I caught sight of the smoldering ruin that had once been the Captain's Quarters. That explained the explosion. Day three and already I'd failed Dominic.

Failed *Diana*.

No. I shoved the horror aside and forced myself to think. No, surely, she'd sensed something was amiss and was able to save herself...

I called for her, but there was no time to search, as another Vanator was upon me.

I bared my fangs, ripping my second blade from its sheath as I met him head on. I lunged forward, but, in trademark Vanator style, he'd begun to dodge in the same moment I'd chosen my attack, if not earlier. My second blade wooshed over his ducking head, and I sprang backward on instinct as the blade of a second attacker sliced the air where my throat had been a moment earlier.

They typically fought in threes, and relied heavily on teamwork, similar to a pride of lions. The fact that I'd killed the first of their trio meant little; they almost always put the least skilled and most disposable in front. The two that were left were a different beast entirely. It wasn't that he'd seen my parry coming. He'd predicted what my next move would be and moved *before* he'd seen it. And it wasn't some preternatural power either, just well drilled reflexes and countless hours of training.

I glanced behind them to see Nicholas was fending off a trio of his own and felt a wave of relief as a door burst open to my left.

"To Nicholas!" I shouted, directing the werewolves.

"Confident, are we?" the nearest Vanator taunted, advancing.

I sprang forward, sweeping at his legs. Metal crashed into wood as he leapt just over the blade, ignoring my second sword as he descended on me with an attack of his own. The second Vanator appeared at his side just in time to block for him, but I released my grip in the same moment, smashing my palm squarely into the first man's jaw. The sickening crunch of bone split the air, and his head snapped to the side at an awkward angle as his sword clattered to the ground.

The scent of blood was heavy on the air, and I let out a bestial growl as I let him fall, sidestepping a thrust from the final Vanator. A female this time, which was fine by me. I closed in on her, baring my fangs, and, to her credit, she did not retreat.

Managing to block the first strike, she sprang forward, leaving her sword behind as her hand shot toward her waist. I took a step back on instinct, only to feel a vice-like pressure on my ankle.

The fallen Vanator?

My attention drifted for the briefest of moments, and I looked back up to see a massive wooden stake hurtling directly toward my chest. I whipped my arm awkwardly to the side and a second later pain spiked through me as the sharpened chunk of wood caught me in the tricep. I tore free of the fallen man's grip, kicking him clear across the deck in a heap.

The final Vanator in my sights stared up at me in defiance as she whipped a small dagger from her belt. I closed in on her, bloodlust raging hot now.

A wolfish howl split the night sky a moment before Diana leapt down from the upper deck, descending on the already-struggling Vanators that the others had been fighting.

Thank the gods. She was alive.

I clenched a fist, letting out a breath.

"Looks like it's your lucky day," I muttered to the female in front of me as she lunged forward. I dodged a quick slice from her dagger as I leapt toward her, managing to grab both wrists in a single motion. She struggled against me, but I got them behind her back easy enough. As tempting as it was to drink her dry right there, I held back. She'd be a useful source of information and potentially of blood if need be. Besides, there'd be something unsporting about killing her now, especially since the others didn't need my help to clean up the rest of the Vanators.

They were expert Vampire-hunters, but their training was specialized for fighting us—not werewolves. Diana made quick work of the remaining two. By the time all was said and done, we had three Vanators out of the original nine who'd come aboard tied up, with the others lying dead on the deck.

I stepped up to Diana. "How'd you survive an explosion like that?" I eyed her up and down, noting that she was unscathed.

"Myrr took the captain's quarters," she said, shuddering slightly as she glanced at the burning hole in our ship where the captain's quarters had been. "If they'd come just twenty minutes sooner...Luckily, she got hungry and went into the galley to whip up a cheeseboard." She shook her head, her expression hardening. "But it was too close for comfort."

"Couple close calls today," I said, flashing the back of my arm and nodding toward the female Vanator. "The bitch tried to stake me."

Diana glanced at her ruined cabin once again, then spun toward the Vanators. "Where's your ship?"

She got no reply other than a glob of spit that would've caught her in the cheek if she hadn't dodged.

"Over that way," Nicholas said, jabbing his finger toward the back of the ship.

I followed his finger, squinting to see a ship in the distance that couldn't have been much smaller than ours. "We going to take it?"

She nodded curtly, then turned to address everyone at once, "We don't know if the underside of this ship was compromised in the explosion. Tend to your wounds and get our supplies ready to move."

"I'll board first and do a sweep to be sure that was the lot of them."

"I'll come with," Nicholas murmured.

I grunted, the pain in my arm flaring. I'd rather have taken a blade. Wood doused in holy water stung like nothing else. It would heal up in a few days, and was little more than an inconvenience, but something strange had happened back there. If I'd been a few milliseconds slower...

She'd almost gotten the drop on me.

But how? No Vanator had ever gotten that close to killing me.

I made my way over to the corpse of the Vanator who'd grabbed my ankles when I thought he was dead.

I pressed at his neck and jaw, finding nothing but shattered bone. No human I'd ever seen could've survived such a wound, even for a short time. Vanator or no. Maybe some of the damage had come later, from me kicking him across the ship? I scrubbed a hand over my face, staring at the massive black bruise that'd formed on his jaw. Then, I leaned in, something just below the bruise catching my eye. A tattoo? It was circular, spiraling outward with the outer final spiral seeming to erupt in thorns. My finger brushed against it and it was like touching dry ice. I jerked my hand back and the mark faded.

What the hell was that about? A new Vanator trick no doubt.

"Get that wound wrapped and let's get a move on," Diana called from behind me.

"Not sure a wrap will do much for him at this point. He's definitely dead," I said, turning to shoot her a wink.

She rolled her eyes, but turned away from me without a response, heading toward the helm. And I'd be damned if it wasn't nice to watch her walk away.

It had been too close. Despite the jokes, the fight had

shaken me to my core. I'd assumed any trouble would come once we'd hit the mainland, and I'd let my guard down. I was going to have to step it up. Way up. Because I refused to have this woman's blood on my hands...unless it came by way of the puncture wounds in her neck as I—

Pain jolted up my arm as I shifted my wounded arm. I let out a snarl and headed for the cabin.

Focus, you fucking ingrate.

First things first; secure the new ship. Second, prepare to debrief the prisoners. The surviving Vanators weren't very talkative just yet, but I *would* find out what had happened here tonight...

Or they would die with me trying.

CHAPTER 6

Diana

I tossed my knapsack from the deck of our damaged ship onto that of our new one just as the first blush of morning touched the sky. We'd been back and forth a dozen times in the wee hours, first boarding the Vanator's sleek vessel and ensuring we weren't stepping into some elaborate trap. Then, once we realized the Vanators on our ship had been acting as crew as well, we moved our supplies, weaponry and crew over.

Now, all that remained were the prisoners we'd taken alive and had left in our original ship's hold to ponder their circumstances while we worked. I'd left Nicholas and Raven to check in on them and start the interrogation, but I'd never been good at delegating. It had only been a few minutes and I was starting to get a little twitchy. I had no taste for torture, but I hated being out of the loop even more. A queen's reign relied on her being on top of things, after all.

Maybe a quick check in to see how it was going...

"Why don't you pick a cabin, get settled and get some rest?" I called to Myrr, who stood with the rest of our crew on the Vanator ship, waiting for me to join her. "We'll be over shortly."

She scowled but then nodded. "Mayhap I should check out the galley and see what they've got for vittles first, though. Fighting makes me hungry."

Far be it from me to point out that she had not, in fact, done a lick of fighting. So long as she stayed out from underfoot, I didn't really care where she did it.

"Sure, good idea. Be over in two shakes."

She toddled off, and I wheeled around and headed down the steps to the underbelly of the ship. Once I'd descended the second flight of stairs, I stepped into about four inches of icy water and winced.

"Well, fuck me..."

"I'd normally be game, but I'm afraid even I'd have a hard time doing it with Nicholas watching. He's a young pup, after all, and I'm not sure he's seen it done the way I do it."

I turned to find Raven standing in the doorway of the hold, body facing the room, but his head turned toward me.

"Do you ever turn it off, Raven?" I asked with a

disgusted shake of my head that I hope looked genuine. Because in fact, I was wholly distracted trying to imagine exactly how he did do it and what would've made it so bloody special.

"I've seen plenty of sex before, and even taken part in my fair share, I'll have you know," Nicholas said, pushing his way past Raven out of the hold. "But that's neither here nor there. We have a bit of a situation, Your Majesty."

"Other than lollygagging on a slowly sinking ship, you mean?" I shot back, the chill of the water finally seeping through the thick leather of my boots.

"Indeed," he said with a clipped nod. It was only then that I realized he was looking a little green around the gills. He stepped back to make space and swept his arm, gesturing for me to enter the room. A sense of foreboding swept over me, leaving chills in its wake as I moved closer and craned my neck to look past him.

I'd expected to see a trio of possibly bloodied but definitely emotionally defeated Vanators lined up against the wall. What I found was three dead bodies hanging from the ceiling, rocking gently to and fro with the motion of the waves.

What the hell?

I instantly turned to Raven. "Did you do this?"

He rolled his eyes. "What possible reason would I have to do such a thing? You must truly think me an idiot."

I was starting to doubt that more and more, actually, but I wasn't about to tell him that.

"I don't think of you at all," I said, lying through my teeth. "And up until several weeks ago, you were a total stranger to me. So spare me the pearl-clutching over my questioning your honor and tell me what the fuck happened here."

He'd fought well, to be sure. But now that I knew he for sure was keeping secrets—the note had said he needed salvation, and I kept wondering from what—the little trust I'd had in him had vanished.

One step forward, two steps back...

"We came down to have a chat with them and see if we could get them to tell us how they'd known we were coming. If there were others in their organization who knew of our travels to the human realm," Nicholas began, but Raven stopped him with a raised hand.

"Clearly they were instructed to kill themselves if they were captured rather than be questioned and potentially give up their plans. Which means this wasn't a lucky run-in on their part, and this isn't over. This was the first in a planned series of attacks that likely won't stop until they achieve their goal, whatever that might be."

One of the bodies swayed, turning until the face of its owner came into full view, lit by moonlight streaming through a tiny porthole. Now that the heat of battle had passed, I realized how young he looked. Too young to have been indoctrinated into a cult of hate, that was for sure. As much as I understood the hatred of vampires, and had even taken to it myself at times despite my own blood being of the mixed variety, dedicating your own children's lives to such a cause seemed cruel.

I shoved back the sudden rush of pity. He'd chosen this life. He'd come onto our ship and tried to kill us. We'd done nothing wrong. And still...

"Do they always fight like that?" I asked, thinking back to the hand-to-hand combat. It had been vicious and, even though I'd emerged the victor, there had been an edge to the fighting that seemed almost uncanny. Desperate, eyes shining with something like a fever. "Could they have been struck by lunacy maybe?"

Since the Veil had fallen, we'd have several of our own descend into madness.

"Could be," he said, nodding slowly. "They've always been great fighters, and zealous to boot. But they're also known to retreat when they've no chance to win. They would die for the cause, to be sure. But they would rather choose to fight another day than risk diminishing their numbers needlessly. Which makes this triple suicide noteworthy, in my opinion."

The whole thing was strange. Had someone alerted them to our arrival? Or had we been marked somehow, despite the gemstones' powers that were supposed to keep our Otherly presence undetectable?

The thought was chilling. We were going to have to be extra cautious going forward.

I tried to put more of the pieces of the puzzle together, but my exhausted brain couldn't seem to make sense of anything right now. Maybe Myrr had been right after all. Food, a hot bath, and some sleep, in precisely that order.

I shot a glance down at the water swirling around my ankles and rising at a steady clip. The more weight the hull took on, the faster it would sink.

"Cut them down and close the door. The ship will be at the bottom of the ocean before full daylight. Then come join me on the Vanator ship. I'll put two of the crew on watch so we can all get some rest."

Something told me we were going to need our strength again...and soon.

I turned and made my way back to our newly acquired vessel, leaping onto the deck with a sigh. We hadn't even gotten to Isla Naranja and this whole mission was already turning into a proper clusterfuck. I found myself sincerely wishing I'd considered taking Lochlin instead of letting Dom browbeat me into allowing Raven to come. Sure, that would have meant selecting someone to watch over our clans, which I was loath to do in these turbulent times. But at least I wouldn't have to watch my back...and my front, both of which *Raven* seemed to spend a lot of time doing.

My cheeks flamed as I recalled just one of his wholly inappropriate remarks.

How had he known my breasts were bound, anyway? Literally no one had ever known, and it was a practice I'd started in my teen years. Yes, partly for practical reasons. But also because I knew I would be taken less seriously as a contender to rule if I spent my days bouncing around the keep.

Shame had me gnawing on my bottom lip as I jogged down the steps toward the galley.

I was a fucking queen, for gods' sake. How had I allowed myself to buy into that type of nonsense? An excess of breast tissue had exactly zero impact on my ability to rule. Yet I knew I'd made the correct decision. Because men were men, no matter the species. And all it took to distract them from the crux of any matter was a great pair of tits. That wasn't my fault. It was society as a whole.

Now that the Veil had come down, and all hell was breaking loose lately, maybe it was time for a new era. A no fucks given era. An era of freeing the titties...at least when I wasn't going to battle, in any case.

"I'm doing it," I muttered. "Once we're finished here, I'm taking off these bindings and I don't care who looks."

"Do it. What you've got going on there is positively barbaric, if you ask me."

I whipped my head around to find Myrr staring at me

from her perch on a high back stool by the table. She had a steaming bowl of something that smelled amazing in front of her and a serving spoon in hand.

"I-I figured you'd be in bed by now."

"I would've been, except after I ate a stale loaf of bread, I found this pot of lemon chicken soup. Diana, it has orzo in it," she whispered before slurping up a heaping mouthful from her way too big for the job spoon.

I padded over to the cabinet and snagged myself a human sized spoon and a tin bowl, filling it with the fragrant soup before joining Myrr at the table.

For a few minutes, we ate in silence, punctuated by low sounds of pleasure and more slurping from the Oracle. Once my belly was warm and full, my feet seemed even colder by comparison.

"I'm going to see what they have in the way of hot water for a bath."

She nodded as she pushed her bowl away with a satisfied sigh.

"And I'm going to sleep until Isla Naranja. I don't foresee any more trouble along the way."

I paused and narrowed my eyes at her.

"Any more trouble? Did you foresee the Vanators attacking us?"

"I did."

I took a full ten seconds to reign in my flaring temper

before replying. "And you didn't think to mention that why?"

She shrugged one sloping shoulder. "Because I knew we'd suffer no losses, and it was part of our journey. A necessary piece of the puzzle, if you will."

As much as I was relieved we would make it to shore without further incident, this whole unreliable oracle stuff was getting old fast. I had a fellowship of three traveling companions, and could trust exactly none of them one hundred percent.

I pinned the old woman with a glare.

"In the future, if you could warn me regardless of your thoughts on whether it's need to know or not, I'd really appreciate it."

She hopped off the chair and hobbled toward the door.

"We'll see."

She was almost out of the galley when I called to her.

"Myrr?"

"Yes, dear?" she replied, turning to face me.

"You wrote a note. I believe it was meant for Raven." I studied her expression carefully, but it gave away nothing. "Something about his salvation being in the Territories. What was that about?"

She shook her head and frowned. "You're a nosy one, aren't you? I wonder if you'd be as keen for me to speak so freely if it was your prophecy in question instead of Beefcake's?"

The gentle barb struck home and I winced.

"Fair enough. So long as it doesn't put our mission in danger."

"It does not," she conceded as she made her way out the door. "But I can't say the same for your heart."

What the actual fuck did that mean?

"Myrr?" I leapt from the chair and stalked after her. "What is that supposed to mean?"

"Nothing dear. Not a prophecy, just the ramblings of an old woman with an eye for sexual tension. The way he looks at you...like you're a hot bowl of that soup we just ate and he's got a hankering for soup. It does my withered nether parts good to see all those young hormones churning."

That visual had me stopping in my tracks as my soup threatened to make a reappearance.

"Good night, dear," she called over her shoulder. "See you on Isla Naranja."

I shuddered and headed back into the galley. I took out two more bowls and served them up for Nicholas and Raven, and then put the remainder of the food away. Then, I grabbed my knapsack and went in search of a cabin. Their ship was much more well-appointed than ours, and I struck gold on my third try, finding the empty captain's chambers.

A massive, claw-footed tub sat in the center, firmly in place if the metal tie downs had anything to say about it. I let out a groan.

Score.

My boots were off in record time, and I was yanking at my pants' zipper even as I crossed the room. Ten minutes later, I was up to my neck in water so steamy that it stung my skin. For a while, I just lay there, eyes closed, trying not to think at all. It was only when an image of that teenaged Vanator hanging by his neck in the ship's hold flickered into my head that I blinked and sat up. The move sent water sloshing over the sides of the tub and I mumbled a curse.

"Don't think about it. Just think about getting to Isla Naranja, making short work of that bastard Maverick, then getting the hell back home."

My gaze caught on the splotch of dried blood on my wrist, and I reached for the massive block of soap seated in a tray beside me. It smelled like bergamot and sandalwood —typical man—but I didn't care. I scrubbed my skin raw and then tugged my hair from the confines of its tight braid. The pressure in my scalp released and I hissed. It was almost as good as taking off my bindings. I lathered up my hands, closed my eyes, and slid down low, until I was fully submerged in the steamy water. Quick scrub of my hair followed by a fresh change of clothes; I'd be a new wolf. Once the deed was done, I let my head break the surface again only to find myself staring into the turquoise eyes of Raven.

My pulse stuttered as I tried to say something, but all that came out was a muffled squeak.

He jerked back, looking almost as surprised as I was. "Bloody fuck, Your Majesty. I smelled the soap and hoped to take a—Gods, I am so sorry—"

He broke off, his gaze drifting lower. His throat working even as his nostrils flared.

I didn't have to look down to know that my breasts were bobbing like two, creamy buoys. I covered them, one in each hand, and aimed a death stare at Raven.

"What the hell are you doing in here? Have you ever heard of knocking?"

"I knocked," he said, his voice thick and husky. "I also called out a hello from the door just to make sure no one was in here..."

And I was underwater, completely oblivious.

Not his fault. But that didn't stop me turning my embarrassment-fueled fury his way.

"Well, you see me now, so what are you still doing here?" I snapped.

"As I said, I do apologize, but fucking hell, Diana." He held up a hand and tore his gaze away, giving me his back. "Why would you ever hide yourself like that? I may have given you the excuse, but don't try to feed me some line about fighting. Scarlett did just fine as a female with breasts, and Sienna more than holds her own on the battlefield."

I don't know what made me answer him honestly, but the words were coming from my mouth before I could stop them.

"Because men like you would never take me seriously as a leader, Raven, as was evidenced by the way you spoke to me the other day. That's why."

He let out a low snarl. "Your clansmen respect you because you're a badass...dare I say it? A badass bitch, and a fair, brave, and honest leader. Your tits or lack thereof have nothing to do with it. And for the few that would consider the beautiful bounty of your femininity to be a weakness?" He shrugged his broad shoulders and let out a snort. "You don't need to earn their respect and likely never would truly have it anyway. Those are not males of worth. The way I spoke to you...well, it's the way I speak to everyone. Sort of my trademark, if you will. I mean nothing by it, and I would not be here fighting by your side if I didn't believe all the things I said about you, friendship with your brother or no."

I was desperate for some wiseass comeback, but I was fresh out. And even if I wasn't, I doubted I could get it out past the lump in my throat.

"I'll leave you to your bath, then." He made his way toward the door and opened it and paused. "But for the record, I was right. They're absolutely luscious."

He exited and closed the door behind him, the boot I'd hurled at him bouncing harmlessly to the floor.

I needed to hold onto the fury inside me and wield it like a shield. Because just beneath it was an attraction like nothing I'd ever felt. And if I wasn't careful, it could turn into something that would make me stupid and vulnerable, just like I'd been with Maverick.

"Never again," I whispered, sinking back into the rapidly cooling water.

Never again.

CHAPTER 7

Raven

I couldn't shake the image of Diana in the tub, slick, soapy, steam rising around her as she sat up. It stuck with me all through the next day while she hid from sight.

Breasts that had so very obviously been bound, finally free of their constraints. As much as I'd enjoyed the view, I'd noticed the marks where the binding had bit into her chest, along the top of her breasts.

All because she'd damn well known she wouldn't have been taken seriously.

While vampires were notoriously lecherous in their own way, powerful females were common. In the werewolf world, it was different. The thing that Diana didn't want to say was that, in that world, women were expected to mate. To produce heirs. To take care of hearth and home.

There had never been a queen before Diana. From now until there was another, she would be the example. If she succeeded, it would change the power dynamics in their territory forever. Little girl cubs could look to her and imagine themselves Queen some day. The tide of women in positions of power would rise. Minds would change, hearts would be won over.

And if she failed?

It could be a thousand years before another woman was afforded a chance to prove herself. The weight of that burden was far heavier than that of those glorious breasts, to be certain.

I stood at the railing of the boat, watching the waves dance, occasionally catching a glimpse of a fin or the white underbelly of a fish.

"You got a new boat!"

I blinked and looked down to find a small set of hands clutching the slick edge of the ship. Crouching, I looked the young mermaid in the eyes. Silver, like fog on a winter's night, but far more liquid.

Mercury.

"Well, hello beautiful." I smiled. "You are braving our world?"

Her grin was a flash of white teeth, almost as sharp as my own. "Oh, it's not my first visit above. Where are you going? Not very often I see boats coming this direction. Usually they go over the chumming waters and that's it. You know, we rescue people when they're tossed overboard. Do you mind if I just keep following you along, is that pretty lady with the eyes like mine who I gave the piece of paper to, is she someone important, because it seems like she would be someone important? My name is Xefia, what's your name?"

Her words were fast, with almost no beats between each one as if she knew she only had a little time. So I did her the favor and spoke just as quickly in return. "We are going to Isla Naranja, I didn't know you saved people from the chumming waters, that's interesting, you can follow along if you like, I don't rule the water, and the lady is no one important, although I agree, she is very pretty. My name is Raven, and I'm a vampire from Seattle."

Her mouth dropped open wide. "A VAMPIRE?"

And then she was gone, flipping off the edge of the boat like I'd electrocuted her.

I stood slowly and wondered at the young supernatural. She was awfully brave to be reaching out to someone on a boat.

And she'd already spoken with Diana...the pieces clicked together rapidly. The little mermaid Xefia had given Diana my note from the Oracle.

But had Xefia fished it from the water on her own, or

had Diana instructed her to get it for her? Not that it mattered. The note was cryptic even to me, and I was the one it had been intended for.

"I'll relieve you," Hamish grunted at me.

I turned and he made sure to get in my way, just enough that I had to choose to step around him or go through him. I stopped so we were almost chest to chest, and smiled down at the burly werewolf.

"Hamish, this is getting tiresome. Are you sure you really want to play this game with me?"

He made the mistake of looking directly into my eyes. "I don't play games."

Here's the thing. I was better than most vampires when it came to taking someone else's will. Particularly if they didn't know that I was capable and didn't take measures to ensure against it. I held his gaze and willed him to kneel. He never looked away as he dropped to one knee, then the other.

"Hands too, if you please. All fours," I said, my tone light. Hamish blinked rapidly but couldn't look away, not now. Perhaps if he'd fought my magic in the first moment...but he'd been stupid.

So on hands and knees, he stared up at me, his mouth working, no sound coming out.

"You see?" I crouched so we were eye to eye. "I do play games. But the one I play will leave you in the rather...

awkward situation of having to recognize the apex predator here. And I can promise it isn't you."

Fury rolled off him in waves, but I had him locked in place. I snapped my fingers, his eyes rolled back in his head and he slumped to the ground. Stepping around him, I withdrew my magic so he would wake up as I walked away.

"Making friends, are we?" Nicholas asked from the shadow of the door that led below deck.

"Nicholas. Are we going to have a problem as well?"

The younger vampire shook his head. "I know my place, Raven. I know the stories that are whispered about you."

Now that was intriguing.

"What stories are those?" I motioned for him to follow me to the front of the boat. He was here for a reason; of that I was certain. He was a decent fighter, although there were others far better suited and more seasoned...Then again, after Dominic's second in command Scarlett had betrayed him, the General valued trust now more than ever. And, for whatever reason, he believed young Nicholas of Southwind to be trustworthy. Maybe that had been reason enough to send him.

And maybe not.

But I was going to find out.

Nicholas though, he was a sight smarter than Hamish. He kept his eyes lowered as he replied to my question.

"There is talk that you were cast out of the Territories long ago for killing one of the high lords when you were a young boy. That your power is, I suppose *was*, second only to the king himself. That you ruled Seattle as a kingdom of your own and were on your way to ruling all of North America."

"Well, except for the killing of the high lord, the rest is incorrect," I replied with a low chuckle.

Nicholas snapped his head up but quickly looked away. "You killed a high lord?"

Even that wasn't quite right, but seeing as we were standing on a boat with nothing else to do, I would indulge him. Also...judging by the strong smell of sandalwood wafting my way, Diana was just behind us, listening in.

"The high lord was young as well, and so we knew of each other. It was my first visit back to the Territories. I caught him...planning to relieve a friend of mine of his head. I took exception to that, and beat him to it. A proper duel though, so even though I killed him, there were no repercussions."

The memory was sharp inside me.

"The friend was Dominic, wasn't it?" Nicholas asked.

"Yes." That was the first kill I'd made. And one that I still regretted. We'd all been young and stupid. There was no way I could have known Reggie would have been stopped. He'd been friends with Edmund, so it was hard to say.

Nicholas blew out a breath, his hand brushing against my bare forearm as he turned.

He stumbled back as if I'd burnt him, eyes widening in shock. "Holy shit."

I stared at him, a sense of unrest rolling through me. "What do you mean, holy shit?"

"Nothing. I—" Nicholas shook his head. "Don't kill me. I didn't mean it. I can't always control it."

I tipped my head to the side and tried to catch his gaze. "Why would I kill—"

And then it hit me like a ton of bricks off the top of a ten-story building. The air whooshed out of me in one fell swoop.

Mind reader.

Of course he was.

I took a step back and then another until we were at opposite sides of the boat.

"Dominic, you prick," I growled. Oh, my old friend had aimed true with this one. How many times had I told him the only vampire power that truly terrified me was mind reading? That one place that anyone should be safe was in their own head. And mine was a dark, brooding cavern, filled with cobweb-covered hidey holes of secrets and fury and, yes, sadness.

Fucking Dominic.

"I hate it," Nicholas breathed. "I...wish I didn't have it. But I didn't mean to see...I don't always—I can't always control..."

I held up a hand stopping him. "Be quiet. Diana knows?"

"Not yet." He shook his head. "She knows it's something along those lines. Something that would be helpful during interrogations, but Dominic felt it would be better to share on a need-to-know basis. If we found Maverick was feeling uncooperative and we couldn't change his mind, then I could employ my...methods."

I drew in a slow breath, and all I tasted was his rancid fear. "We used to kill your kind. How did you keep it from Edmund?"

Nicholas swallowed hard. "My mother kept me close to home. Told everyone I was scrawny. Too scrawny to play with the others my age."

A hard thing for a young buck to take. "And when you bed women? What happens then?"

I heard the subtle intake of Diana's breath. But Nicholas didn't seem to take note of it.

"I...don't...not with women."

I shrugged. "With your chosen partners then. How do you control it?"

He closed his eyes. "I can't. It makes things...difficult."

I couldn't even imagine. It must've been awful. And still...

"Keep your hands away from me. If you touch me without my permission, I will remove your head from your shoulders." I glared at him. "Understood?"

"I think not," Diana snapped as she finally stepped into view. Breasts bound tight again, but I knew what was under there now.

Clearly, she'd only heard bits and pieces of our conversation over the whipping winds. I turned to her and smiled, perusing her slowly. "Frostbite. Missed me, did you?"

"You homophobic prick!" Diana snapped. "How dare you—"

Nicholas cut her off. "No, it's not like that. Diana...he doesn't want me to touch him because...I can...read minds. If I touch someone. That's why Dominic sent me."

Her feet stalled out and her eyes shot from me to Nicholas. "Truly?"

He nodded.

She eyed him thoughtfully and then stuck out her arm. "Take my hand, then."

Now I would have done no such thing, yet she seemed to have no fear of what Nicholas might see. And her response was immediate.

Nicholas reached out and took her hand. For a moment, he just stood there, fingers laced with hers. Then, he looked up at her.

"Do you mind if I share?"

Her brows collapsed but then she nodded. "Alright..."

"This is the other part of it—something only I can do that I know of." Nicholas kept Diana's hand in his and turned his other palm up. A small scene began to play out on his palm like a play on a tiny stage. From Diana's point of view as she fought a female demon, black wings and deep forest all around her, Diana under the demon while the life was choked out of her. Suddenly, the demon stiffened and fell to the side. Behind the demon was a man with long dark brown hair, earrings on one side, scars across his chest where his shirt gaped.

He motioned at Diana then dropped to his knees.

Diana dragged her hand from Nicholas then and the vision shimmered and disappeared. "That is a very useful gift, Nicholas."

"I will keep my hands to myself, you have my word on this. And I have gloves if I feel it coming on." Nicholas ducked his head.

Much as I was riled up by the young vampire and his gift—because as far as I was concerned the last thing I wanted was someone digging around in my head—the scene was important, I was sure of it. Diana did nothing by accident.

"The demon and the man, who were they?"

She nodded. "The demon, I have no idea who she was. The man is Maverick. Of course, he is human, and so much younger there. But at least now you have something to go on as far as what he looks like."

She glanced at me and her face immediately flushed and I knew she was thinking back to the night before and my view of her naked body. The image had practically been burned into my retinas, and I could feel myself hardening.

With obvious effort she pulled herself together. And continued. "He will have aged. Might have cut his hair. It likely will be gray, or even white. But that won't matter to a degree. Once we get close, I will be able to pick up his scent."

My eyebrows shot up. "That simple?"

"There is no way he will escape, not once we are on his scent." She said with such confidence that I'll be damned if I didn't believe her.

I looked ahead to Isla Naranja, the mountains soaring along the northern edge of it, the white sandy beach. It was as I remembered it, a paradise tucked away from the world.

"What's the plan once we reach shore?" I asked. "Find a nice little hotel room, strip ourselves naked—"

Diana whipped her head to glare at me. If looks could reflect their owners' true intentions, I'd be buried six feet under a block of ice.

A distant part of my mind wondered what it would take to thaw said ice...

Diana flipped her own dagger, catching it by the hilt. "Plan A is for me to go to shore and track him. Assuming I find him, I will bring him back with me to the boat and we will return to the Alpha Territories, leaving before the sun has set."

For once, it wasn't me scoffing. Nicholas snorted which drew her eyes to the young vampire. He cleared his throat.

"Apologies, Diana. But...that is not prudent. Nor is it safe. Because if it was going to be that easy, Dominic never would have sent us to help you."

So the young one had some spine in there despite his mother's efforts to ensure he never had a chance to develop one. Good.

"I'm not saying you can't help. I just want to start by taking the path of least resistance. No one will be put on guard if a lone woman shows up in town. If we go in with the entire group, there is no way that we can hide the fact that we don't belong." Diana said, her voice even and calm, though I could hear the heat behind it. "We draw closer to the full moon. My crew does not have the luxury of holding a dagger to keep their wolves at bay."

My eyebrows shot up. "And they came anyway?"

Her eyes were back on me, though her tone was sweet and sharp. "We could not bring more vampires either, for fear they'd set the ship on fire at the first sign of daylight. There were no others."

“Humans,” Nicholas pointed out.

I chuckled. “You do realize she’ll stake us both before this is over if you keep up pointing out the obvious to her?”

Nicholas shrugged. “I am a diplomat. There are times that we have to consider more than our personal wants and needs. As a great leader, Diana knows this well.”

It was like he’d taken the wind right out of her sails. Curious. “Nicholas, you are correct. We will dock, and settle Myrr and the crew on land. I will take one of you—”

“You will take me,” I corrected her. “I will go with you to find the thief.”

Her jaw flexed and she nodded. “Fine. Unless you would argue the choice, Nicholas?”

Weird, she looked so hopeful...

“Not for a minute. Raven is the proper choice for this task.” He bowed at the waist and inched around us. “I will get Myrr ready.”

He left and I turned to Diana, only to find her all but fleeing back the way she’d come.

“Be ready, Raven. The minute the boat docks I will be on dry land, with or without you.”

It was my turn to bow at the waist. “As always, I am yours to command, Frostbite.”

We docked less than an hour later, and true to her word Diana was off the boat before the vessel was even tied to the moorings.

I leapt out after her, less than a step behind. The smell of salt and filth tangled its way through the air, as if to gag a person.

Diana was a few steps ahead of me, but I caught up to her easily. "So eager you are to find this thief?" I asked. "Or eager to reunite with him?"

She didn't stiffen. "I have no love for Maverick. And as I pointed out, he'll be an old man now. Sixty years have passed. He was in his thirties perhaps, when I knew him. For all we know, it won't even be Maverick. It could be a descendant of his that has the crimson stone. Not that it matters, we need it and that is all there is to know."

I tucked my hands in my pockets and walked as casually as I could. "Well, I'd like to know if you fucked him."

Her feet slammed to a stop and I kept on walking, knowing she'd catch up.

"What?"

"Well, it's obvious from the little I know that he pulled a fast one on you. So, he's a charmer. It explains why you hate me." I turned and winked at her. "Although, to be fair, I wouldn't have stolen anything but your heart. To take both is adding insult to injury."

She rolled her eyes and then rushed to catch up to me, but I put a hand on her arm. "Loosen up. You look like you're marching into battle, and we need to not let people know we are here for a fight. Understand? The demons that rule this part of—"

"Demons?" she hissed. "Shit...Are you certain? That was not on my team's research when they'd scoped the area. It had been all human, all the way through!"

"Well, the last time I was here, that was the case. I've not heard of any changes, and that was perhaps twenty years ago." I took her hand and settled it into the crook of my arm, as if we were on vacation, strolling the streets. "Look casual, Diana. It will get us further here. They don't like law, they don't like rules, and you werewolves are all about keeping your boxes ticked and your t's crossed."

She snorted, but I felt her relax at my side, her gait slow and measured now. "How did you know he... fooled me?"

That made me smile. "Do you know how many hearts I've broken? Charmed? I've seen the rage of a woman who's been...loved and left behind. It's a very specific look to the eye, to the angle of the jaw. Not that I think you'd care for him now—"

"Definitely not," she agreed. "But you're right. I cannot help but hate him for tricking me into betraying my father...for taking the gem. For forcing me to come after him. I will take the opportunity to hand him his balls—literally, if the fates shine upon me."

My eyebrows shot up. "Remind me not to break your heart."

"As if I'd give you the chance," she let out a laugh, her eyes softer than before as she glanced up at me through dark lashes. "It's more likely that you'd fall in love with me, and then I'd have to break your heart. Assuming you have one?"

Her daring had me throwing my head back as I chuckled in response. "I do. But you would be the first to break it. The only first I have left in me, to tell you the truth."

She tugged her arm from me as she tried to step away, but I caught her hand and brought it to my lips, kissing the back of it, tasting the essence of her skin, letting my tongue graze its way across her knuckles. Her eyes locked on mine for just a split second, before they darted to something behind me.

I tightened my hold on her and spun, putting myself between her and whatever she'd seen.

A child—a little boy—stood behind us, grubby and thin enough that I could see ribs under the ragged, knee length t-shirt.

I rolled my hand and a coin appeared across my knuckles. "*Vamos.*"

The boy snatched the coin and took off running.

"Why did you do that?" Diana strode forward, the spell broken between us.

"He was most likely there to beg," I said, realizing she was probably unfamiliar with the concept because werewolves didn't allow for their own to go hungry. "I gave him a coin so he didn't have to." I frowned as I stared at the houses around us—or what was left of them. "This place has changed."

"How so?" Diana asked quietly as we stepped around a pile of rubble that had been the front half of a house.

"It was ritzy houses, high end resorts, the best of the best. Where the wealthy and powerful came to blow off steam, party, and network. But this...looks like the slums of such a city." I frowned as I looked around, really looked around. Homes leveled to rubble, piles of ash and rotting roots where trees had stood. "Either this place was bombed or the weather here has been as unpredictable and fierce as it has been in the Territories."

"Weather," Diana said as she led the way. "See the way the salt from the sea corroded everything? And I received reports of wildfires being rampant in the human realm just last week."

"Goddess," I whispered, unable to come up with a quip. Not in that moment. Because it was confirmation that the world was coming apart at the seams, and unless we found a way to stop it...the destruction would only continue.

"This way," Diana said softly, and I felt it then too. As if we were walking through a mass grave, and as soon as I thought it, I could see the body parts. Could smell the decay. I'd been too busy earlier thinking about Diana naked to really process the level of destruction.

Jaw clenched, I made myself pay attention to the damage done. I'd fought it kicking and screaming, but *this* was why we were here. This was the destruction we were trying to put a stop to.

We turned a corner and things changed. Buildings ahead of us were still standing, still had power, still had some people milling about. And the center of it? The Wild Queen Casino.

Diana snorted.

I grinned. "Perhaps fate knew you'd be coming this way?"

Once more I tucked her hand into my arm and held her tight to me. "Let me do the talking. I've been here before, though they've changed the name since then."

"And what was it before?"

I grimaced. "Doesn't matter." And it didn't, mostly because I did not want to invoke bad luck before we went in.

Because it used to be known as The Lost Queen Casino.

The barrel-chested guard at the front crossed his arms and stepped in front. "Private party tonight. Try tomorrow."

I locked eyes with him, stole his will from him and his

desire to stay awake. He was on his back in under five seconds.

"What did you do?" Diana gasped.

"He's alive. He'll sleep. Perhaps he'll dream of large women." I patted the giant man on the head as I walked us through. "If I remember correctly..." I turned to the left where a hallway led to a series of dressing rooms that had been there before, back in the day. "The showgirls and dancers change in those rooms, so there should be plenty of clothes to choose from. Put on a dress...something that shows off your figure."

Her nostrils flared. "What?"

"You do not want to be recognized, correct? Everyone will know what you are if you go in with leather pants and shitkickers looking like a warrior from the wastelands."

Diana frowned, but did as I asked, which surprised me. But I suppose it shouldn't have. She was pragmatic when it came to getting things done.

Five minutes later she emerged and handed me a backpack. "My clothes are in there, along with my blade. Do not lose it."

Of course, if she hadn't been wearing the dark blue, curve hugging dress that showed off not only her amazing breasts now that she'd freed them from the bindings, but her waist-length curls, and softly tanned legs that went on forever, perhaps I would have been able to respond. As it was, all I could think about was the tiny sofa that had previously been in that particular dressing room...

I reached for her instinctively, without thinking of anything *but* her. My eyes flickered shut as I leaned in, fully in the moment and prepared to stay there forever if not for one thing. The sharp stinging slap that caused a burst of stars to explode behind my eyelids.

"Raven, pull yourself together. We have work to do."

It took everything in me to release her, bow at the waist, and harness the need burning through my veins and murmur, "As always, I'm yours to command."

CHAPTER 8

Another time, Raven's words, his presence, the way his turquoise eyes dilated with hunger, I might not have been able to resist him. But here, in the den of a demon, my senses were far too amped up to let a bit of stupid desire get the better of me.

"Are you sufficiently pulled together? Or should I slap you again?" I demanded, half hoping he'd pick the latter.

Raven grunted. "I'm fine. You caught me off guard. I knew you were a beauty, but you've been hiding in the shadows, Diana."

He spread a hand as if to encompass me and I turned away, trying not to be pleased by his comments.

"I have done no such thing. Now let's get this over with."

He tipped his head, charming mask back in place with

a lazy grin and a wink. "Indeed. Think of all the time we'll have on the trip home to get to know one another better. That big captain's bunk of yours is probably feeling empty with only one body in it."

A pair of footsteps were approaching us from the far end of the building, and a waft of demon rolled ahead of it. I looked at Raven, saw the slight flare of his nostrils, felt the tension in his arm.

The laid back, devil-may-care attitude. It was an act, wasn't it? It was all an act; I was fairly certain. I was impressed and somewhat taken aback at the same time. Was he pretending to be attracted to me, too? I shoved the thought aside and tried to refocus. What did it matter to me, anyway? We'd finish this job and I'd hopefully never see his face again. My stomach gave a weird squeeze that I didn't have time to examine as a demon appeared in the doorway ahead of us.

Dressed in dark slacks and a colorful Hawaiian shirt, he looked every inch the over indulgent gambler, right down to the gold chains hanging from his neck. The aura around him though, I could see through it. Right to the dark gray wings tucked tightly behind him. "I'm sorry, we have a private party—" He cut off when he locked eyes on my companion. "Ah! Raven...it's been a very long time, old friend. We weren't expecting you."

"Is anyone ever?" I laughed and batted my eyelashes at

the vampire on my left. "He does like to keep things exciting."

Raven joined the charade. "My date is correct. I happened to be in the area, thought I'd pop in for a game. Unless of course you'd prefer I spent my money elsewhere, Raphael."

The demon's throat worked but he nodded and forced a smile. "Just Raph, and you know it. Fine, come in. Though Gabe is in the middle of a game, I'm sure he'd see you after for a round or two of darts."

Raven gave a long-suffering sigh. "I suppose darts will have to do."

They went back and forth, talking about this and that and nothing. But all I could think about was the fact that the demons mentioned so far both had the names typically reserved for angels. An inside joke? Or something else?

Malach was the leader of the Angels in the Alpha Territories, and I owed him now for allowing us to cross his lands and battle Edmund. That being said, I didn't know anything about these demons, something I intended to change.

"Your companion is a werewolf, yes?" Raph glanced back at me as he spoke.

I nodded. "I am."

"Not many shifters left on the mainland."

I shrugged. "A few of us are survivors."

Raph laughed. "You'd have to be, with the Vanators locking you up in cages and testing on you these days."

His words shot a shock of horror through me.

"What did you just say?"

Raph shrugged, as if my reaction meant nothing to him. "I assumed you knew. There weren't many shifters left once they'd been recalled to the Territories, mostly those who come and go for trading or to the auctions. The tides have turned with the weather, though, and any wolves who remained...well, let's just say that the Vanators have grown bold lately." His eyes, swirling with darkness as if black smoke curled within them, watched me. "I thought you of all people would know, given your lofty position..."

Raven moved so fast, even I didn't see it. He was at my side one second and the next Raph was pinned to the wall by his throat, the crimson inset dagger pressed hard to Raph's chest.

"Who knows?"

"Lucifer's tits, man," Raph tried to squirm but that only made the blade dig harder. He kept his hands up. "Just me. I remembered her from the last time I went to the Territories decades ago."

"You will say nothing," Raven growled. "We are hunting, not a demon, but a thief. Not a word, Raph."

He dropped the demon but to his credit, Raph didn't shrink away from Raven. "Untwist your panties, man.

The only other who might recognize her is Gabe. I'll warn him to keep it under wraps if he does."

"Do that," Raven growled.

Fucking *growled* and the sound had me squirming as if it circled my damn clit and vibrated against it. Which was a big reaction for a growl, even for me unless...

Moon goddess no...not now.

Please not now.

I struggled to breathe through the sudden heat roaring through my veins, like a human's menopausal core temperature increase, only mine had nothing to do with being too old and everything to do with being a wolf in need of a sound, hard fucking.

"What is that scent? Of all that is unholy," Raph groaned and stared at me. "Satan's taint, this is not good. We can't take her in back like that."

I breathed through the first roar of hormones that told me I should take both men and fuck their brains out. A werewolf heat was no small thing and it came on randomly...lucky me.

"I'll be fine. Get me a cold drink. I can breathe through this."

Raph let out a pained laugh. "Yeah but can the rest of us? You're throwing off take-me-now hormones like a deadly tsunami that even I'd take a chance on."

Raven snarled. "Touch her, and I'll make you eat your own heart."

That did it. My inner wolf liked those words far, far too much, the possession in them, and his willingness to kill for me.

My nipples tingled, blood rushed to pool between my thighs as I struggled not to climax right there, Raven's words sinking into me like hands dragging through my hair, pulling my back into a perfect arch so he could bite my neck as he fucked me from behind.

I bit back a howl.

No, I could do this. It wasn't the first time a heat had come on unexpectedly. I could shut this down—I had to.

I closed my eyes and thought of Maverick, and his betrayal, of the absolute disgust I had for him. That cooled my blood some. I thought of my family waiting for me, of the destruction of this world and ours. Of the little beggar boy in the street and the horrors he'd have witnessed. Eyes full of hunger and fear. Of my father and the quest he set out for me.

Everything slowed, my breathing, my blood, and finally, I opened my eyes.

"A glass of water," I croaked. "I'll be fine."

Raph stared hard at me, eyebrows to his hairline. "Impressive."

Raven once more stepped between us, his broad back to me.

"Water, now."

"Prickly today, are we?" Raph chuckled and left the

room, back only a moment later with a bottle of water which he handed off to Raven, who handed it to me.

"Nah, but you remember Dominic? He'll have my balls if I let anything happen to this particular woman." His eyes swept over me while he was half turned from the demon at his back. "I'm rather fond of my balls." His words were light, but his eyes were not.

They were searching me for signs of my condition. I waved my fingers at him, motioning for him to move. "I'm fine. Let's go."

I was not about to have a discussion regarding my heat cycles. Unlike other werewolves, maybe because I was made and not born one, mine had always been erratic. This was just shitty timing, that was all.

"Okay, let's go." Raven took me at my word though I noted he didn't take my hand again. "It's obvious just being in my presence for the past couple of days has finally gotten to you. Don't feel bad. It happens to all the ladies."

I rolled my eyes. "Or perhaps it was your friend there that sent me into heat. Raphael, is it?"

Raphael let out a nervous laugh and ruffled his wings a little. "Please don't get me killed because you want to tease that one. Come on, I'll take you to the games room."

We followed Raphael through the casino. The Wild Queen indeed. There was magic here, I could feel it thrumming under my skin and perhaps that was what had set me off. No matter the reason, I had my heat under control.

For now.

I barely saw the walls, the large rooms around us. We passed through them, but they were a blur of light, sound and scents that I cataloged distantly knowing it was the best I could do. Mostly human, a few more demons, no other supernaturals that I could pick up on.

The room Raphael took us to was behind a large pair of double doors, with a carving worked deeply into the wood. An angel falling from the sky, wings tattered, feathers floating all around. Carved on the bottom of the door was what looked like stacks of wings, the same as the angel wore above, as if they'd been chopped off.

Feathers.

Not the leathery wings that Raphael sported.

The demon didn't slow, just put his hands on the big doors and pushed inward. The room beyond was dim, smoke circling the ceiling and coating the air so picking up scents was tough.

Raven stepped ahead of me, setting my backpack down at the door. "Gabe, I know it's been a while, but how could you hold a tournament and not invite me? Do I mean so little to you now?"

A man—no demon—leaned back in his chair as he surveyed us. He had snowy, white hair that fell well past his shoulders. His eyes were a deep blue, like the night sky right before the sun rose in the morning. Cobalt.

"Well perhaps if you were home when I sent the invite, you'd have known. But my understanding is, you've been gallivanting. Picking up women," He nodded my way casually, but I felt him perusing me.

"Well can you blame me? Seattle is dreary this time of year." He sat himself down at the table and pulled a pouch from his hip. "I can see you're done this round. Deal me in."

Gabe sighed. "Fine. We were just about to start a new hand."

I stepped behind him, a perfect choreography as if we'd planned this all along. I dared to let my hand rest on his shoulder as my eyes adjusted to the dim light.

"Candles?" Raven commented as he glanced at his cards. "Going for some ambience, Gabe?"

Gabe squinted at his own cards, then threw in a chip. "Power is sketchy. No one trusts anyone here enough to have the lights go out and not lose a chip."

Chuckles rippled around the room.

One of the chairs was empty, but a jacket hung on the back, and a small pile of poker chips sat before it.

"Who am I playing with tonight?" Raven drawled. "I like to know whose money I'm taking."

Gabe did introductions.

To Raven's right were two demons named Matthew

and Mark. To his immediate left was a human named Steve who looked a miserable sort.

"On the left of Steve—and the empty seat is Maverick. He just went up to his room to get some more cash."

Raven snaked a hand around my waist causing me to stumble more fully into the dim light.

Shit.

I kept my eyes down and let my hair cascade forward, as if I were shy. Nervous. Truth was, I was trying not to spiral into a rage. Maverick was here. In this very hotel. What was going to happen when he walked in and saw me? Maybe he would stand there in total shock and stare. Or maybe he'd take off running. Then again, there was also a very real chance he wouldn't recognize me at all.

Just because Mav had left an indelible scar on me didn't mean I'd done the same. I was probably just another mark he'd fooled and forgotten.

But as much as my thoughts should've been consumed with planning my response to every possibility, Raven's hand was still tight around my waist, and it took all I had not to curl around, straddle him from the front, and grind away until we both—

Around us the building shook suddenly and everyone froze.

"Fucking storms," Gabe growled. "And this, Raven, is exactly why we use the candles."

The storm hadn't even been on the horizon when

we'd come in, but within minutes it was raging, pulsing against the building and making the very timbers of it shake. And it was a good thing. It had given me the jolt I needed to get control of my traitorous hormones yet again. I just hoped that Nicholas and Myrr had found a place to stay before the storm hit.

"So what's been happening since the last time I saw you?" Raven asked. "Business okay despite the weather?"

The discussion between the men flowed back and forth. Gabe and Raven seemingly catching up, yet I heard the questions and knew Raven was gently prying. I struggled to keep up, Raven's scent suddenly seeming that much more delicious. My cheeks flamed, and I found myself absently tracing the muscles in his shoulder, wondering if he could handle my wolf at her worst...

Knowing he could.

I swallowed a moan and tuned back into the conversation through the rush of blood pounding in my ears.

Apparently, from what I could glean, Maverick had been in town more than a few weeks. He'd been here for months. Doing well enough at the poker tables that Gabe had finally let him play with the big boys. It surprised me that he was willing to sit at a table with demons until...

"He was a Territory slave at one point," Raph said quietly. "Which means we have something in common with him. A hatred of the Ranks."

Ranks being how Malach and his Fallen angels, along

with the demons in the Territories divided themselves. Right down to the humans they enslaved.

"And what of you, Raven? What brings you back to Isla Naranja?" Gabe asked, cocking his head and studying us both with something sharper than easy curiosity.

Gabriel was no fool. He knew we were here for a reason, and I hoped Raven knew it too. Lying now would be a mistake.

"Weirdly enough, we came looking for the man you mentioned...this Maverick. He...has something of mine. We just want to talk to him about how best to get it returned to me."

A partial truth, calmly delivered. Well done out of Raven, even I had to admit.

The lights flickered suddenly and a door creaked behind me. Before I could turn and see, it slammed shut hard enough to rattle the walls.

"Who was that?" Raven demanded, all but upending me off his lap as he stood.

"I think it was Maverick," Gabe muttered, brow caging into a frown.

We both sprinted for the door, only to find Gabe had magically reached it before we did.

Fucking demons.

"What the hell do you think you're doing, Raven?"

If it had been anyone else, I'd have let the adrenaline take over and fought my way right through him to get to

Mav. But something about the fierce light in the demon's eyes gave me pause.

"I've already explained. That man stole something and it's imperative we get it back. I'm going to need you to move, Gabe. Or I'll have to move you."

Annnd, apparently, Raven had fewer qualms than I did about going toe-to-toe with this particular demon. Confident or foolhardy, I wasn't sure, and I wasn't about to blow our entire mission by finding out.

"Please, Gabe. If he's been here for months, surely you know his ethics are...questionable. Lives depend on us getting back what he took. Can we just follow him so we can talk about it?"

Gabe's eyes narrowed but he took a conciliatory step back. "He's been known to run a con or two on some of the less likable fat cats that come here, and I've turned a blind eye, so I don't doubt your story. But we have a zero-tolerance policy for the kind of trouble you're itching to start here, Raven. We pride ourselves on the reputation of being... better...less barbaric than my brother Malach and his counterparts in the Territories. Raph will go track Maverick down and come back here immediately afterward with him in tow so we can all talk about this together. Good enough?"

I wanted to argue, but I also recognized the need for compromise. This wasn't my establishment, or my territory. I held no power here, unless I wanted to fight for it.

While I had no qualms about getting my hands dirty, as I'd said to Gabe, I had other people's lives resting on my shoulders. If this could be done quickly and quietly, without bloodshed, the more the better.

I almost thanked the demon. Almost. But he was still a demon. Instead, I gave him a nod. "That will do."

Raph headed out the doors we came through only half an hour before. The lights in the room flickered, plunging it into an even gloomier darkness. The wind outside rattled the building again as we took our seats.

"Gentleman, take your chips and head down to the roulette table for a time. We have some personal matters to attend to. I'll call down to the bar and let them know, cognacs on me." Gabe's smile was wide, but his tone brooked no argument, and the men gathered their chips and dispersed without issue.

"You want to tell me a little more about whatever it is you have going on here, Rave?" Gabe asked the second we were alone.

Raven shot me a glance, and I shrugged. But before we could launch into an explanation, Raph came barreling back into the room, his face pale.

"Mother fucker leapt out the damn window!"

My stomach dropped as Raven grabbed the demon by the shirt.

"Show us," Raven snarled.

"I'll circle around front and try to stop him from leaving the property!"

The rest of us sprinted down the hall and up the stairs double-time, but I didn't need Raphael to show me which room was Maverick's. The door was still ajar and it was coated in his scent. The window was open and the rain lashed the interior of the room, as if the entire storm was trying to shove itself inside. I leaned out the window, and knew before I even circled around outside what I'd find.

Nothing.

His trail would be washed away in the storm, scent dispersed, the rain soaking everything.

Raphael stuck his head out the window. "See! There's no way he could have climbed down, which means he jumped."

We left the room, circled around the casino, and checked under Maverick's window.

There was an already washed-out pair of footprints where he'd landed in the mud of the garden up against the building, but the path quickly turned to stone after that.

The rain hammered at us, soaking us through as we searched the immediate area.

Anger snapped through me. "Raven, are you getting anything?"

He lifted his head and stared out into the dark. "I should be able to see him still, the land slopes here, but has a long view, but he's gone. How the hell did he put so much distance between us?"

That was the question of the day.

Gabe met us at the entrance of the casino, full of apologies. "I'm so sorry, Diana. He got away. He's never shown any sign of being anything but human, there was no way we could've foreseen that he could leap out a fifth-story window like that." He raked a hand through his long hair. "He must've heard Raven talking and got spooked... Look, the seas are impassable in this storm. He isn't getting off the island any time soon. Stay the night. Regroup and I'll get some of my team to help you in the morning. It's the least I can do—"

"And he knows better than to deny me a room and some food!" Myrr snapped from a table just to the left of us.

I closed my eyes and fought the snarl that rose to my lips.

The confounded old woman was going to be the death of me.

"Myrr, you and Nicholas are not supposed to be here. You were supposed to find a place to stay."

"And so we did." She grabbed a pair of dice and threw them across the table. "Snake eyes!" she yelled. As the dice slowed, they came to rest on a six and a three. "Damn."

"I apologize, Diana." Nicholas cleared his throat. "I tried to get her to come back to the bed and breakfast we secured, but she refused, so I followed her. She walked until the storm was on us, and we were here. I had no idea you were here also."

Gabe looked at the four of us, one brow raised. "Your hunting party, I assume?"

I shot him a sharp look. "With the exception of Myrr, yes."

"I'm just here for the food." She walked over to Gabe and jammed him in the belly with a pointy finger. "You do have a casino buffet, do you not?"

Gabe grunted. "Follow Raph, he'll get you to the food, you crazy old bird."

She gave a caw and flapped her arms like they were wings, 'flying' after Raphael with Nicholas close behind. Gabe sighed. "She's a pain in the ass still?"

Raven barked a laugh. "What do you think?"

"Still," Gabe muttered. "Look, there's no point in them going back out into this." He rolled his hand and a key appeared in his palm like magic. "Take the big suite, you can all stay together."

Raven scooped the key, offered a clipped nod of thanks, and we were headed to the room. "I grabbed your bag," he said. "So you can change."

I nodded, taking it from him, anger and frustration coursing through me. "He still smelled human. There is no Territory blood in him that I can sense. How is he leaping out of fifth floor windows and surviving?"

Truth be told, I'd wanted him to be old and nearing the end of his life. To be nothing like the man my heart had fallen for all those years ago. Instead, he was hiding some superhero shit, and that made him even more dangerous than before.

The room that Gabe had given us was a two bedroom suite, with a kitchen and two bathrooms. Raven stood in the kitchen area.

"Could he be like Sienna?" Raven stripped off his wet shirt, revealing a pale expanse of muscles, a few scars and a dark tattoo of a twisted tree, the roots reaching down toward hard cut abs.

My wolf reawakened and let out a low growl. It was difficult not to leap on him, nevermind not to stare, so I turned my back on him.

"I, uh, I doubt it. What are the chances we are chasing another person who has a key inside of them? And I guarantee you he was no healer. Not like Sienna."

"But would they all be like her?" Raven mused.

"I wish I knew," I replied, a familiar thrum beginning to beat through my belly. My wolf was back, and if I was a guessing girl, she wasn't going to be denied again. Sweat broke out on my upper lip. "I-I'm going to shower."

"Need any help?" Raven asked, cocking his head and eyeing me long and hard. "I can kiss your booboo, so to speak..."

That same heat coursed up and through me, fresh and

hot as if I'd never tamped it down. I wanted to tell him to fuck off. To tell him I was not now and would never be interested. My wolf though, she had other ideas. Barefoot, I padded across the floor to him until we were close enough that I could have reached out and trailed my fingers across his chest and those lean abs.

Slowly, I lifted my eyes to his. Dominic had warned me that Raven could will people to bend to him, and yet... he'd never tried it with me.

"And what would you do, vampire, if I said yes?"

I watched his eyes darken, until there was nothing left of the color. "Is that a challenge, Frostbite?"

A shiver rolled through me as my nipples tightened, the heat almost more than I could bear. Fuck, I had to get a hold on this or I'd be regretting my life decisions in the morning.

I should have stepped back, but instead I stepped forward. Breathed his scent in, letting it roll through me. "You never listen. Would you do as you're told this time?"

His hands never left his sides, but his head lowered to mine, lips tracing along my cheek to settle at my ear where he teased at the lobe as if it were my clit, rolling and sucking at it, flicking it with his tongue. His voice was thick with desire as he drew back.

"As always, I am yours to command."

The air between us stilled as I rolled up onto my tiptoes and reached for him.

"Jackpot!" a voice called as the door banged open. A second later, Myrr wobbled in, a plate in each hand. "Look at this spread. It's a smorgasbord down there!"

I stumbled back away from Raven, legs weak from a mix of need and relief. That had been far too close.

I managed to find my tongue and turned to find Nicholas also laden with plates, kicking the door closed behind them.

"Did you want to eat, Diana? We've brought plenty."

"I'm alright for now. I'm actually going to take a shower."

Raven laughed softly and bent low, speaking for my ears only. "Think of me, Diana. That should help..."

I strode away from him as my wolf howled inside of me to turn around and beg him to help me find a release.

As it turned out, he wasn't wrong. A few minutes later, I stood in the shower, my body aching with need. It took very little thinking of Raven touching me, of his hands on my body instead of my own to send me over the edge, and leave me a quivering mess, aching for more.

Moon goddess, I was so screwed if we did not find Maverick soon, and get back to the Territories.

I had to get away from Raven.

The sooner the better.

CHAPTER 9
Raven

"Fuck."

My snarl was drowned out by the sound of rattling chains and the punching bag I'd been taking my frustrations out on exploding into a shower of fluff and leather.

"Oh, for Lucifer's sake. Can you not, please?"

Gabe's dry request came from over my shoulder and I turned to find him shaking his head at me.

"This gym is for paying guests. It's a battle to get them in here as it is, what with the apocalypse on the horizon. Now I've got to order a new heavy bag and with the seas so unpredictable, it's going to take a month to get it delivered."

"Hang on," I said, pretending to search my pockets before shrugging. "Out of luck. Seems I've misplaced my violin."

"I know you're pissed, Raven. But I swear to you," the demon moved closer, meeting my gaze unflinchingly, "Me and mine are not in league with Maverick. No one was more shocked than Raphael when the man hurled himself out of the window, I can promise you that. He was sure he'd find him in a twisted pile of blood and limbs. And, frankly, he's worried that you're going to do to him what you did to that bag."

"I still might," I conceded, pissed that I'd destroyed the only decent outlet for my fury in this sad excuse for a gym, filled with Stairmasters and treadmills. Fact was, as angry as I'd been at Raph, and at Gabe for vouching for him, most of my ire was reserved for myself.

I'd fucked up.

I'd let Diana take the reins and attempt to handle this delicately, like a politician. I should've stepped in and done what I'd come here to do. Human or no, Maverick was known to be a slippery bastard. The Raven of old would've shoved Gabe aside and ran Maverick down like a dog. But I wasn't myself and hadn't been since we'd left the Territories. Diana's...situation had only made things worse. Between the frustration of having fucked up royally and spending the night hard as stone with the only outlet that would do in the next room pleasuring herself, I was a right miserable prick. Add to that, losing the entire morning to dozens of miniature tornadoes of all things, we were stuck in this place until the weather broke.

Maybe if you start acting like the security detail you were sent to be instead of a lovesick schoolboy out to impress, you wouldn't be in this position.

Sometimes being charged with someone's life meant making the unpopular decision. I was going to have to start putting my foot down. If Diana got mad, so be it.

Just the thought of her, dark hair wild around her shoulders, eyes flashing with anger and heat–

"Fuck!" I snarled again.

"I have plenty of women who would love to serve you, Raven. One in particular has long, dark hair, and light blue eyes...albeit not like quicksilver—"

"Pass. There's not another gym in this shithole, is there?"

"As a matter of fact, there is. I was just headed there myself. I'll even help you work out your frustrations. But you have to promise to behave. This stuff isn't cheap."

I grunted in some facsimile of agreement, and let him lead me out of the room and down the hall. It wasn't until we had skipped down two flights of stairs that I realized we were headed for the basement.

My fangs instantly snapped from my gums as I slowed, suddenly hyper aware of my surroundings.

"Gabe, I've been nice so far, but I can promise you. You don't want this."

"Relax there, tiger," he said, tossing a grin over his shoulder as he reached the bottom of the steps and shoved the door there open. "This isn't an ambush or something. Dominic would have my head on a platter. Do you honestly think I want to start a war with the bloodsuckers right now? Come on."

He stepped into the room and I followed, still on high alert but also knowing in my gut he was right. It wouldn't make any sense for him to attack me, even if he did have a small chance in hell of prevailing.

I headed through the door and stopped short in surprise. It wasn't a gym, per se. It was a boxing ring surrounded by a hundred or more seats for spectators.

"Can't have a casino without sports betting. And humans love nothing more than watching us supernaturals beating the shit out of each other." He turned, cobalt eyes twinkling in challenge as he cracked his knuckles. "What do you think, Vampire?"

"I think I'm going to enjoy this."

For the next hour, Gabe and I did indeed beat the shit out of one another. And, by the end of it, my ribs felt like someone had taken a sledgehammer to them. I made a mental note to drink some more of my rationed blood before we went on the hunt for Maverick.

"One good thing," Gabe managed through labored breaths as we sat side by side on the floor, recovering. "At least we know he couldn't have gotten too far in this weather...assuming he's survived this long out there, that is."

"His type is wily. He'll have holed up somewhere." And luckily we had a way to find him. If we could just get out there and start the search...

"I want to help you, Raven," Gabe said. "I have resources. But I need to make sure we're on the right side of things. We've finally earned a good reputation here, and I won't have that tarnished."

The irony of this coming from a literal demon wasn't lost on me, but I knew what he meant. "I know there have been some transgressions in the past. Now that Edmund the Vile is dead and we have a new King, you won't see any of us loyal to the crown on the wrong side of things going forward."

He ran a towel over the back of his neck. "Can you give me a little more to go on? What did Maverick steal? And what is its significance?"

I pondered the question long and hard, but another voice chimed in before I could answer.

"It's a gemstone."

My pulse instantly kicked into high gear as I looked up to find Diana framed in the doorway.

"I am the rightful heir and owner, and Maverick took it from me. I need it back so we can save the world. Yours and ours."

She wore a cable-knit sweater that looked far too large

for her and her arms were folded over her chest, covering what I was certain were her unbound breasts.

"Your Majesty," Gabe said by way of greeting.

"Gabriel." She turned her gaze on me, and I could see the pulse in her neck leap as she did. "Raven." She wet her full lips and I realized I'd been staring at them. "The weather has turned. It's still raining, but the winds have slowed. We need to get out there before his trail is well and truly lost."

Gabe stood and wrapped the sweat-soaked towel he'd been holding around the back of his neck as he studied Diana.

"This gem has the power to save the worlds, you say. Care to elaborate?"

Her smile held no hint of humor. "I'd love to, but that's all we've got. That's the trouble with prophecies. They're always veiled in secrecy and double-talk, aren't they?"

Gabe cocked his head as he narrowed his eyes.

"Myrr?"

I rose to join them. "The one and only."

Gabe's jaw flexed as he nodded. "Then I'm at your service. Whatever you need, say the word. Hell-hounds for tracking, boots on the ground. If Mav holds the key to saving the world, then we'll get his ass. This is my island. There's nowhere he can hide that I cannot find him."

The demon's sudden passion for our cause had Diana

and I exchanging glances. I considered pressing him on it, but opted to stay silent.

Fact of the matter was, I didn't care why Gabe was all in. I only cared that he was.

"We accept your offer of assistance, and—"

Diana held up a hand, frowning. "Don't be hasty, Raven. As much as I appreciate the room and the meals, last time we allowed Gabriel to be in charge, our quarry made a break for it and leapt out a fucking window. In fact, that's why we're in this position now." She turned to face the demon. "Thank you for the offer, but with all due respect, we'll take it from here."

I steeled myself for battle, sure to be far bloodier than the one between Gabe and I had just been.

"Disagree, Your Majesty. I haven't been to Naranja in a long time, and the landscape has changed entirely. Yesterday was the first time you ever set eyes on this place. Gabe has dogs, he has knowledge, and resources—"

She wheeled on me, eyes flashing with fury. "His dogs are more formidable trackers than I?" she snorted. "Don't insult me. And we've no need for knowledge of this island. I can scent track him just fine." She turned her attention back to Gabe. "Thank you, but no thank you. We'll fill our stomachs one last time, pack up, and be on our way."

"We won't," I said, my tone firm. "You cannot shift this side of the Veil, and you're already struggling with...other issues. We need to be smart here, and that means using the resources at our disposal." She glared at me and I held her gaze, dropping my voice low as I touched her mind with my own with the lightest of pressure. A warning shot as opposed to an assault. "Don't make me make you, Diana."

She drew back like I'd hit her between the eyes with a brick. "You would dare? You motherfucker." She let out a laugh that was more like a snarl, and I knew I'd pushed her too far. "What happened to 'I am yours to command, my Queen?' This is insubordination in the midst of battle. Tell me why I shouldn't kill you on the spot?"

The blood started pumping in my veins, adrenaline soaring as I scented her wolf clawing to come out. My methods had been flawed, but I still needed her to fall in line, and I wasn't about to back down now.

My lips curled into a lethal smile that had caused more than one man to soil himself. "The arena awaits, Frostbite," I said, waving a hand at the boxing ring. "Let's see you try. Whoever wins gets to make the decision. What say you?"

"Alright, let's all just take a second," Gabe interjected, literally stepping between us and breaking the tension that quivered in the air. "As much as I would pay to see this match up, I'm going to need you both to calm down. We may not all agree on how the cake gets baked, but our goal is the same, and bake the cake we must."

He looked down at Diana and shook his head slowly.

"I know you want to do this on your own, but while I cannot bend you to my will, I can insist that you two leave my island. You are a visiting dignitary who I respect, Diana, but you aren't the Queen here. It's my job to protect Isla Naranja and its inhabitants as best I can. Which means not having you lot running rampant around hunting a human guest, thief or no. The optics would be terrible. Raph can stay behind if you don't trust him. But I will be going with the two of you to ensure that this mission is carried out quickly and quietly, or this mission will not go forward at all. You and yours can go wait on a ship in the bay for Maverick to leave and take your chances on the open water. Understood?"

Diana's luscious lips twisted into a sneer. "What I understand is that you males are all the same. You acknowledge my title when it's convenient, but when push comes to shove, you impose your will upon me regardless of it." Her smile could've frozen the now-melting glaciers. "I suppose I have no choice but to accept your kind offer, Gabriel. Let us gather the dogs and go. We've wasted enough time bickering."

She swept from the room, slamming the door behind her.

"Phew," Gabe muttered, his calm facade slipping a little. "She's formidable, that one. But at least we won that battle."

Had we?

Because it certainly didn't feel like it...

I stared at the door and knew that there was far more than just the slab of mahogany separating me from Diana now. I'd made a terrible misstep. One that was likely to cost me.

"Tell me...is she the type to stay angry?" Gabe asked as he flicked off the lights and opened the door.

I pondered the question as we headed upstairs, and my stomach roiled as the answer came to me, clear as day.

"No. She's the type to get even."

CHAPTER 10
Diana

I blinked back the hot tears filling my eyes and willed myself to take a calming breath as I jogged up the steps.

My own father had only seen it once and that was the day he'd made me into a wolf. There was a zero percent chance I was going to let that macho asshole see me cry. No, instead I'd pour my frustration into revenge. Forget about waiting to deliver it ice cold, it would be served steaming hot.

The thought made me feel slightly better and I turned my focus to the task at hand.

This wasn't the way I'd have chosen to do it, but here we were. A queen was nothing if not adaptable to every situation.

By the time Raven and Gabe made it up the stairs to

join me on the main floor, I'd schooled my features into the picture of calm, cool, and collected.

"The dogs are just down the hall here," Gabe said, gesturing to a long corridor.

We followed him to the kennels, the smell of fresh meat growing stronger with every step. I dug my nails into my palm and counted backward from ten. There was something discomforting about trusting dogs to do a job I would've been more than capable of alone if I could just transform into my wolf form.

"Ready?" Gabe asked, stepping up to a door. "Try to be careful, they're well trained but can be a little protective at times," he said, pulling out a key ring.

I nodded absently, chewing at my lower lip.

"We'll be fine," Raven said, "just open the door."

A cacophony of grunts, snarls, and barking filled the hall in an instant as he fiddled with the lock. "I can go inside and calm them down first, if you like, Your Majesty," he said, glancing at me.

It was back to Your Majesty again, was it? But I waved him off with a short laugh. "This is nothing. Try having dinner with the McClaren clan."

Raven nodded. "I've only had the pleasure of meeting them once, and they are some aggressive bastards."

If he thought agreeing with me now was going to help his cause, he was dead wrong. I didn't even glance his way as I swept past him to stand beside Gabe.

The demon yanked the door open and was immediately consumed in a mountain of mostly black fur. The barking came to an abrupt stop as they all vied for a spot on his face to lick.

"Easy, easy," he called, chuckling as he wriggled out of the huddle of enormous dogs.

And one...large, black cat. She wove her way through all the dogs and leapt up into Gabe's arms. One of the big dogs got too close and she swatted, catching its nose and making it yelp.

Apparently, the cat ruled the roost? Unbelievable. I blinked and looked around.

To call the space a kennel was laughable. It was a gorgeous suite, as opulent as the rest of the place, just with more dog-ish sensibilities and less furniture, aside from six dog beds that I was fairly certain were just human-sized mattresses on the floor. Near-empty bowls of raw beef sat in a row on the far end of the room, with a playing area on the other that was filled with bite mark-riddled bones and neon strips of what must have once been tennis balls.

"They just ate a bit ago, it's a good time for tracking with them," Gabe remarked, wading through dogs as he stepped toward a huge storage cabinet.

My gaze drifted onto one of the larger hounds–it was the size of a pony, for fuck's sake–and his head dipped downward as he averted his gaze.

"They seem pretty harmless," I said, reaching tentatively toward him. He tolerated me as I scratched gently at his ear, but seemed a bit on edge.

"They can smell the wolf in you," Gabe said, watching carefully, "But I can promise they aren't harmless, and they've got the best noses of any animal I've ever seen. Wherever Mav is on the island, we will find him."

"Let's grab their leashes or whatever and get moving," Raven cut in, stepping toward Gabe. "Is this where you keep them?" he asked, pushing past Gabe toward a cabinet against the wall.

The explosion of snarls and barks that came next drowned out Gabe's reply, and my heart thumped in my chest, more from surprise than from fear. A few of the dogs rushed at Raven, who took a step forward, fangs emerging.

"Hold!" Gabe's shouted command split the air of the room like an ax, and the dogs obeyed him instantly, coming to a sudden stop just inches away from Raven's face.

"Good choice," Raven said, eyes locked with his nearest attacker. The cat.

She was puffed right up and kept on moving forward, hissing and growling.

"Abyss! I said hold!" Gabe snapped as he got between them and scooped up the cat.

Abyss. Good name for a black cat.

"No sudden movements near me, please. They don't like men much to begin with."

Them and me both, right now.

"Might've been a good thing to mention before we came in here," Raven said.

"I said they were protective," he shot back with a grin as he set Abyss onto the top of a cat tree. "Alright, down to business. I think it's best to take three to start and leave the others. If the weather holds, we can bring out the next three fresh." He let out a sharp whistle and all the dogs sat in a single file line. "Magnus, Athena, and Kevin."

Two of the black dogs stepped forward, followed by the only white hound in the pack.

"Let me guess...Kevin?" I asked.

"How'd you know?"

I studied the dog for a long moment, noting the tuft of fur that stuck straight up on top of his square head, his slightly crossed eyes, and the way his tongue lolled out a little too far. Everything about him was just a little off kilter, and I had to admit, I was charmed.

"He gives off a Kevin vibe."

"That's what I said. Like a super fun frat buddy or something, right?" Gabe said with a wink. "Raph wanted to name him Thor and I was like don't be ridiculous. He's nobody's Thor. But don't underestimate Kevin. He's the heart of the pack, and the bravest creature to ever grace this earth." Gabe reached down and ruffled the hound's head, whispering what a good boy he was.

Abyss sniffed, curled up into a ball and put her back to us. Apparently she did not agree.

Alright, so Gabe had pissed me off before, but maybe he wasn't all bad. Anyone who treated their animals with such affection earned some respect from me right out the gate.

"I don't know. He doesn't look all that smart..." Raven said with a frown.

Kevin's ears dropped back and his lips rolled away from his teeth as he let out a low growl in Raven's direction.

"Neither do you," I observed, tickled by the dog's reaction. "But we're letting you come with us."

That got a laugh out of Gabe, and even Kevin seemed to be grinning, but Raven just shrugged.

"Whatever. Let's get a move on while the weather is cooperating."

The three of us leashed up the hell-hounds whom Gabe deemed best suited for the task and made our way quickly to the ground floor, heading out into the darkness outside. Wind whooshed all around and rain still peppered our clothes, but the weather was noticeably better than it had been. When we got to the spot Maverick had landed when he'd jumped, Gabe leaned down and unleashed the dogs. Then, he tugged a T-shirt from his pocket.

"I got it from the laundry basket in Mav's room," he said, holding it out and snapping his fingers. The hounds stepped forward in unison to snuffle at the shirt, inhaling deeply and tossing it this way and that before stepping back, deep red eyes locked on Gabe as they awaited his next directive.

"They are very well trained," I said, my hopes rising just slightly at the display.

"Magnus. Athena. Kevin. Track!"

The three hell-hounds burst into movement in unison, sniffing at the ground and leading us forward at a rapid pace. They zigzagged some, but always seemed to find their way back onto his trail surprisingly quickly. The only problem was that they were leading us away from the city and directly toward the forest.

I exhaled sharply in annoyance. Until now, I'd been holding out hope that Mav had gone to a friend's or checked into some seedy motel to wait us out. But why would anything go our way?

"Going to be damn hard to track him here," I said, using my own still-keen human nose to take a deep whiff. I could scent Mav, but barely. The smell of rotting vegetation and wet earth mixed with the sea air making it a confusing stew of scents and I knew it was going to be a long day.

“This is why we brought three hounds,” Gabe said. "They can cover loads of ground and we can be prepared when they flush him out."

When, not *if*. I had to admire his confidence.

Athena and Magnus tore off into the forest in a rush of dark fur, barely visible just a few yards away even to my enhanced eyes.

The foliage was dense, the fog thick, and the sky was so dark and stormy, it may as well have been night.

“Don’t lose them," Raven said, breaking into a jog to follow after them.

Gabe and I followed suit, Kevin edging out to take the lead, sniffing the sodden ground as he went. We wove through the woods in a blur, fifty paces behind the massive hell-hounds ahead, and it didn't take long before the thrill of the hunt began to heat my blood. If only I could let my wolf out, we’d—

The rumble of cracking earth split the air, and panic surged through me as I felt the ground shaking beneath my feet.

Earthquake?

The ground directly in front of the hell-hounds cracked and churned, threatening to give way beneath their feet. Two of them dashed to the side just in time, but Kevin had been on a collision course with the spot and was too late to veer off. A hole began to open up beneath him, its gaping maw threatening to swallow him whole.

Without thought, I leapt forward and shoved the beast with everything I had. He rolled away from me in a heap, and I pinwheeled my arms furiously as the ground split beneath my feet.

Adrenaline coursed through me as I scrambled to catch some part of earth, but to no avail. I was falling, falling…

"No you don't!"

Strong fingers curled around my wrist and yanked hard. A second later, I found myself in a tangle of limbs, Raven staring down at me, wild-eyed.

"Saints, you're a fucking menace. Just met him and you're already risking your life for this creature?" His throat worked and he closed his eyes for a long moment before opening them again. His face lit up into a weak facsimile of a grin as he added, "Did you mistake him for a McClaren or something?"

"Fuck you, Raven." I could make a joke at one of my clans' expense but he didn't have that right. Not after what he'd done, trying to force my will to bend to his. He'd have to rescue me a dozen more times before I'd forgive him, and I would *never* forget…

"Thank you, Your Majesty," a low voice called. Raven rolled away to stand and held out a hand to help me to my feet. I found Gabe standing there, staring at me with appreciation and something like awe.

"I was sure he was dead."

I waved him off, glancing toward the white hellhound. Then, I strode over, holding out a hand. "Good job, Kevin. You're a fine boy, aren't you?"

He assumed the same nervous, submissive posture he had in the kennels, but this time his tongue snaked up and licked my hand a few times.

"Let's keep moving," I said, noticing that the other dogs were growing restless.

We jogged behind them for another few minutes before I noticed a hint of something familiar.

"He's close," I said, taking a huge whiff of the air. I did smell him, but it was still faint, and hard to pinpoint. The dogs had led us this far, though, and it should only get easier if he was that close.

Anticipation prickled at my skin as we continued to run. This had all been a rollercoaster of emotions. We'd found our quarry and lost him in such a short period of time. Now that we'd found him again, I wasn't walking away empty-handed.

The dogs exploded into a frenzy, barking like mad, and I dropped into a full-on sprint. The dagger at my back warmed, and a light vibration rumbled through it like a hum. A figure came into view at the top of a small hill, and I let out an enraged growl as I sprinted toward him.

"You're not getting away this time, you weaselly bastard."

Raven passed me a moment later, his vampire speed

on full display, and Gabe was just behind me. Maverick was in good shape for a human, but there was no way he'd be able to evade us all. It was only a matter of time. Minutes at best.

Furious yelping split the sky as I crested the hill, and Magnus nearly bowled me right over, sprinting away from Mav and back toward the casino. What the hell? Had Maverick wounded him somehow?

Athena came tearing past next, ignoring Gabe's shouted commands for her to stop. Something had happened over that hill, and I needed to figure out what. I surged forward, searching frantically in all directions. The visibility was much better here, with far fewer trees, but there was still no sign of Maverick or Kevin, for that matter.

"I don't get it. It's like he just disappeared," Raven said, having slowed to match my pace as Kevin came into view. The dog's ears were drooped and his tail was tucked between his legs, but he circled the area, continuing to sniff the ground.

"Good boy. You can do it, Kevin. Pick up his scent for me, you sweet boy," I murmured, watching with bated breath. The rain was coming faster now, in sheets that poured down my face, obscuring my vision as thunder boomed loudly overhead.

I drew in a breath. Maverick had been here, that much was sure. But something else too. I scrunched up my face and kept on scenting the air, because I had no idea what it was—a bit of sulfur, a bit of ocean water, and something... more. What in the hell was it?

We stood there for another five minutes, maybe ten, as Kevin's circle grew wider and wider, to no avail. As he circled, the wind began to pick up, howling and whipping around us so hard that my feet were lifted from the ground not once, but twice. I crouched, clinging to the sod, keeping my body low.

"It's over for tonight. We need to go back," Gabe yelled from a few yards behind me. "Mav's in the wind, and the weather...we can't stay out in this!"

"He was right here. He's not a fucking magician, so he didn't just disappear!" I yelled, frustration lacing my body.

Raven dropped his hand to my shoulder, pulling me back toward the hill. "Gabe is right, Diana. Magic or no, he's gone. We'll have to figure out another way to find him, but it won't be today."

"Godsdamnit!" I yanked my shoulder free, but strode back the way we'd come, muttering a curse as the wind pushed and pulled at me.

We all but slid down the other side, and through a low spot, the wind eased for a moment.

"What happened with the other hounds?" Raven asked as he and Gabe fell into step beside me.

"I'm—I'm not sure," Gabe said. "I've never seen them behave that way before. Even Kevin seems nervous. Or afraid...Could Mav have done something to them with that gemstone?"

I shook my head. "I don't know. There was another scent beside Maverick's. Maybe whatever that was spooked them."

"Nothing that I know of spooks hell-hounds," Gabe said. "Nothing."

All I *did* know was that my clothes were soaked, I was chilled to the bone, and we'd lost Maverick.

Again.

Everything had been going so well the night before. My whole mission was almost complete in such a short time. And now? We were back to square one.

That's what I got for letting men make the decisions. From now on, I was taking the reins and holding on tight.

And gods have mercy on anyone who tried to stop me.

CHAPTER 11

Raven

"I don't know why we had to leave The Wild Queen," Myrr muttered under her breath for the tenth time in as many minutes. "It was warm, dry, and they had prime rib and crab legs on the buffet menu tonight. Very selfish of you, this," she said with a sniff of indignation in Diana's direction.

I almost felt bad for the crone because I saw it coming. After a miserable failure of an afternoon, by the time we'd gotten back to our suite, Diana had been fit to be tied.

"Pack your stuff up. We're leaving."

Nicholas had tried to convince Diana that giving the demons one more chance to help might be prudent, but she'd shut him down quickly.

"This is twice Gabriel has 'helped' us, and twice Mav

escaped. I don't believe in coincidences, and I am done trusting demons to do a woman's work."

She'd wheeled around and skewered me with a glare.

"And you! Don't even try to lord your vampire parlor tricks over me to get me to change course. You ever try to fuck with my mind again, you better make damned sure it kills me, or you'll regret it." She perched her hands on her hips, looking for all the world like the soaking wet, gorgeous, sexy queen she was as she glanced at each of us in turn. "Now, I'm taking a shower and leaving here in one hour. Pack. Your. Shit. Or, you can stay here and find your own way home. I don't care."

Nicholas and I had taken her words to heart and packed our shit.

Myrr, on the other hand, had dilly-dallied. Nicholas and I had to all but drag her kicking and screaming from the buffet line, where we'd found her packing a trio of plastic baggies full of braised beef and crab.

Now, an hour later, as our sad-sack little group of failed crusaders trudged to the nearest bed and breakfast on the island, Diana had clearly had her fill of even Myrr.

She slowed to a stop and bent low until she was eye to eye with the stooped old woman.

"You aren't even supposed to be here. You came of your own free will...against orders, and if you don't stop complaining, I will have you drawn and quartered, then toss your parts in the sea for chum. Is that understood?"

She didn't wait for a reply. She just turned and walked away, leaving us to watch her go. I wished I could say her intensity scared me, but the truth was, it only made me want her more. The pressure in my gums as my fangs threatened to break free was only rivaled by the pressure in my groin. Fuck this woman was going to be the death of me yet.

"Geez...Touchy much?" Myrr whispered. That didn't stop her from getting it into gear and hurrying after Diana, though.

By the time we stepped foot into the Rusty Scupper Inn, we were soaked through again and hunger was gnawing at my belly. I'd forgotten to feed before we'd taken the hell-hounds out and I was feeling it now.

A bell rang as we pushed through the doors, and then the man behind the reception desk looked up with a toothless smile.

"Good evening to yeh and welcome."

He was likely somewhere in his eighties, but the years had been kind to him, aside from his head that was bald as an egg. He summarily ignored the rest of us, his gaze locked on the Oracle.

"Oh, Ms. Myrr! You've come back, have yeh? When yeh went out and didna return last night, I was worried maybe one o' the bloodsuckers or demons got hold of yeh and drained yeh dry."

I cleared my throat and raised a brow at him. He

flushed, tipping his head in an apologetic nod. "Begging your pardon, sir."

Myrr shot him a broad wink. "I'd like to see them try, Phineas. No, me and my manservant had some business to take care of at the casino," she explained, tossing a wave in Nicholas' direction. "We're back now, though. Any chance you've got some of that shepherd's pie left?"

"We sure do. I can have the cook send up a batch with a nice crusty loaf of sourdough to sop in it. What say yeh to that?"

"You already have an entire carpetbag full of—ouch!" Nicholas broke off as Myrr stomped on his toes, hard.

"Sounds lovely. I'd appreciate it."

Diana stepped forward, nudging Myrr none-too-gently out of the way.

"I'll need two additional rooms as well, please. At least for one night, possibly longer."

Phineas' wiry brows caved on his forehead, clearly displeased by the interruption. "We're pretty well booked up, ma'am."

Nicholas spluttered. "Surely you have something, when we were here earlier, you said there was room..."

He bent his head low and rifled through a leather-bound book.

"I'm not seeing anything. Must have booked up."

Diana was obviously at her limit and there was a fair chance that she was going to leap over the desk and strangle this poor old man. Instead, I called his name softly and he lifted his head to meet my gaze.

"Offer us your best available rooms please, kind sir."

Phineas blinked and then shook his head as if to clear it.

"Uhhh, ah yes." He turned his attention back to the book. "Seems we do have...actually, no sorry, just the one room. The honeymoon suite, though, so there's plenty of space."

"We'll take it," Diana said, to my surprise.

She must really be at the end of her rope if she was agreeing to share the honeymoon suite with me, spacious or not.

Phineas toddled off and came back with a key and Diana accepted it with a saccharine smile.

"Two floors up, all the way at the end of the hall."

Myrr led the way across the lobby, hefting her own stuff because she refused to let Nicholas help carry her crab bag.

As we followed the pair to the rickety set of stairs, Diana muttered to me under her breath. "You didn't need to do that, you know. You can't be going around sticking your fingers in people's brains."

"Well, maybe if you weren't so intent on cock-blocking poor Phineas, I wouldn't have had to," I shot back.

"You are a foul, foul man."

When we reached the top of the steps, Nicholas pointed to the room directly across from the stairwell.

"This is us." He paused as Myrr produced a key and let herself into their room and Diana swept past us both to continue down the hall. He dropped his voice to a near-whisper. "Look, can we meet for dinner or something."

"I didn't plan to stay here for dinner. There are a couple places I used to know in the seedier part of town that I'd like to check out."

"There's a seedier part of town than this?" he asked in surprise.

"You have no idea."

"Be that as it may, I need some..." he glanced over his shoulder at the closed door and mouthed the last word, "Space. She never stops talking when it's just the two of us, which is most disturbing because she's usually also chewing. Let me come with you. Surely, I can be of some use other than playing nursemaid to that crazy old bird."

I'd planned on flying solo, but his particular skillset might be of some use here, in any case.

"Fine. If you agree to let me do the bulk of the talking."

"Can I have a pint and a hot meal while you're doing the talking?"

"You can."

"Then I'm in."

"Meet you in the lobby in half an hour."

He looked like he wanted to weep with relief and I tried not to chuckle as I made my way down the hall. I'd been having my own woman troubles but apparently, dealing with Myrr had been no picnic either.

I was still pondering how to deal with Diana as I approached the door to our room and it swung open. Her hair had started to dry into a mass of wild curls around her shoulders, and her icy eyes were filled with fire. If her temper had cooled any, it definitely didn't show. And, since I didn't want her cutting off my balls in the middle of the night, I figured I'd better try to make things right.

"Look, I know you're having a tough time right now between the heat thing and—"

Her eyes narrowed to slits, and she slammed the door in my face. "See if Myrr and Nick will let you bunk with them. Or sleep in the hall. I don't much care which."

If a person could lock a door as aggressively and loudly as possible, she did it in that moment.

"As if I couldn't get in if I wanted to," I murmured, rolling my eyes.

"Good night, Raven. If you value your miserable hide at all, don't bother me until morning."

I turned on my heel and made my way back down the hall. It was probably better this way. If she knew I was going out, she'd have insisted on joining me, and she wasn't in the headspace to make good choices. Besides, she probably wouldn't be a fan of my information gathering methods, and the last thing I needed was someone policing my every move.

Luckily, Nicholas and Myrr found my company less offensive, and had no problem letting me into their room to shower, change, and suck down a much-needed shared blood meal with the other vampire. The space was tight, though, with just enough room for two single beds and a tiny table and chair. I was going to have to find a place to bunk at some point, but I'd deal with that when we returned.

"Don't let anyone in, and don't leave the inn," Nicholas instructed Myrr for the third time. "I'll be back in a couple of hours. If you need anything between now and then, go to Diana's room down the hall and nowhere else. Agreed?"

Myrr never looked up from her over-filled bowl, swirling the contents with her spoon. "I've got shepherd's pie and a cozy spot to lay my head. What more could I need?"

With that, young Nicholas and I headed out into the night. The second we stepped outside, the cold hit us with a sharp stinging slap. The wind was gone, but that didn't mean it was an improvement.

"Bloody hell, the temperature seems to have dropped twenty degrees, we are well below freezing," Nicholas said with a shudder.

I shot a grim look to the sky. "And it smells like snow. Not good."

The more precipitation that came, the less chance we had of catching Maverick's trail again.

As Nicholas and I headed down the cobbled street, I found myself thinking on our quarry. He might still be human, but he definitely wasn't standard issue. Not anymore, if he ever was. He'd been touched by magic somehow, which made guessing his next move tricky.

Gabe had assumed Maverick would be unable to leave the island due to the high seas and weather, but in truth, without knowing exactly how *extra*-ordinary he was, we couldn't rule anything out.

So information was going to be our greatest asset at this point. And what better way to get it than by hobnobbing with the locals. I knew plenty of guys like Maverick. Brash. Cocky. He was the man I often pretended to be so people didn't look at me too closely. Whatever special abilities he possessed, there was no way he hadn't shown them off to win a drunken bet at a pub, or impress a woman into flipping her skirt for him.

Nicholas had his hands deep in his pockets, his shoulders hunched against the cold. "Where are we going?"

I didn't answer right away, I was busy taking in the streets, and damage, and trying to remember how to get to where I wanted. "Siobhan's Place. If it still exists."

And something told me that it would. It had been

around as long as I had albeit under different names, and was the cockroach of establishments, staying alive through feast or famine, locust infestations and pandemics. A few hurricanes certainly wouldn't have shut it down.

I hoped.

After we'd walked a couple miles, and I caught sight of the sign in the distance, relief flowed through me.

"This city is truly in ruins," Nicholas said as we skirted around a mountain of rats tearing into a carcass of unknown origin on the side of the street. "Makes the end seem much nearer than I'd ever imagined."

I could hear the concern in his voice and couldn't help but agree. Our quest was growing more urgent by the day. Maverick was one, small piece of the puzzle. If we couldn't even find him, then we were going to find ourselves in a fuck-ton of trouble, and fast.

I paused at the door and held an arm out to stop Nicholas. "Like I said, let me do the talking. I should know at least a couple people inside, and they don't take kindly to strangers."

He gave me a tight nod. "Got it."

We stepped into the pub and were instantly assaulted by the sour smell of ale and unwashed bodies. My boots made a snicking sound as we crossed the floor, and I didn't need a superpower to sense Nicholas' thoughts because I could hear him trying not to gag.

He spoke low, under his breath. "This place needs to

be fumigated. What the actual fuck is that smell? It reminds me of an old man I knew with gangrene."

Another gag.

A waft of ripe bodies had me gritting my teeth. "I think we can skip the meal part. I don't think even I could–"

"Well, my days! If it isn't Raven, Lord of Seattle! You sexy beast, you. Come give Sheevy a hug, won't you? Lordie be, you look good enough to eat."

A smile tugged at my lips as I turned to find Siobhan herself at the far end of the bar, tossing a rag over her shoulder as she headed my way.

As she stood on her toes and wrapped her arms around me, I had to admit, much like the pub, she hadn't changed a bit. A small bundle of tightly packed but lethal curves, she'd been thirty when I'd met—and bedded—her. At fifty, her sable hair had a streak of gray, but she was still a looker by any standard.

"You're a breath of fresh air, Siobhan," I said, giving her a squeeze before releasing her and stepping back. Her perfume was strong enough to overpower the other scents for a moment at least.

"And that's saying something," Nicholas said under his breath.

"Who's your friend, Rave?" she asked, smoothing a hand over her hair and eyeing Nicholas like he was a slice of cake.

"Nicholas of Southwind, meet Siobhan, the owner of this fine establishment."

Ever the gentleman, Nicholas bent in a half bow and offered her a wide smile.

"It's a pleasure."

"It could be, for sure, handsome," she said, folding her arms just right so that her breasts threatened to spill over the deep vee of her neckline. "In fact, I could probably get Lefty to watch the bar for half an hour and maybe the three of us could...have a tour of the upstairs?"

"A generous offer, madame," Nick said with a grin. "But my interests lie elsewhere."

"As do mine tonight, I'm afraid," I added with a wistful sigh for good measure. For reasons I didn't care to explore, my cock didn't even twitch at the thought of bedding Siobhan, but I needed to stay on her good side. "I'm looking for a man and was hoping you or someone you know might be able to help me find him."

She nodded, eyeing me shrewdly.

"This fella got a name?"

I watched her closely as I replied. "He's called Maverick." Her expression didn't change even a little bit, but that didn't mean shit.

Siobhan was a shark.

"And what would you be paying for information about this Maverick?"

"Depends. If it's actually something useful..."

"I've got a bag of gold in my pocket we can use for bribes," Nicholas chirped.

Siobhan must've picked up on my exasperation because she held my gaze with a cheeky grin even as she spoke to my companion.

"Well that's really nice to hear, Nicholas. I'll make sure to spread the word."

"Excellent," I muttered, more to myself than her. She'd already swept away, making a beeline for a trio of men playing what looked like a dice game in the far corner of the room.

I dropped a hand onto Nicholas' shoulder, just enough to direct him. "Come on. Let's get a pint and try not to look so conspicuous. Did you forget the whole 'no talking' thing or you just figured you'd add some spice to our evening by making sure we have to fight our way out of this place?"

Nicholas fell into step beside me and we bellied up to the bar. "Two pints," I said to Lefty, who was fairly easy to identify on account of him only having the one arm.

He grunted in reply and poured us a pair of foamy beers and slammed them onto the sticky barter.

"Twenty pounds."

"For two pints?" Nicholas demanded, frowning.

He eyed Nicholas' pristine black waistcoat and let out a snort. "You can afford it, fancy-man."

"I can, but I won't. It's the principle of the thing," he

said, his usual affable smile morphing into one I'd never seen before. One of a predator.

Interesting. It seemed our puppy was cutting his teeth.

Lefty must've sensed it too, because he shrugged. "Fine. Six pounds then."

Nicholas tugged out some coins and set them on the bar just as Siobhan returned to press between us.

"Caleb Mathews and his crew claim they can help. They said they know a guy who was on the crew of Maverick's ship. For a hundred pounds, they will hunt him down tonight and have him meet you in the alley behind the pub tomorrow at eleven sharp. Fifty now, and fifty when they bring him to the meetup."

"And how do we know that they won't just take the fifty and disappear in the wind?" Nicholas demanded, clearly feeling his new balls now and settling into them.

If he thought he had bigger balls than Siobhan, though, he was sorely mistaken. "You don't," she shot back. "So that'll be a hundred fifty now."

"You said fifty now," Nick protested.

"And a hundred for my finder's fee."

She held out an expectant hand and Nicholas grumbled as he pulled out his velvet bag of coins.

Siobhan took her money and then sailed off. "Pleasure doing business, boys. Let me know if you change your mind about that tour..."

We didn't. Instead, we finished our beers, and headed

back into the frosty night a little poorer but slightly hopeful that we'd scored a lead.

"Do you think this guy is going to show?"

"Possibly. They want that other fifty for sure. But it's just as likely that they lure us there in hopes of robbing you blind."

Nick winced. "Yeah, I shouldn't have mentioned anything about the gold. I was just nervous and out of my element. Won't happen again."

I believed him. It looked like our little man was growing up.

"We need to make sure we prepare for the worst tomorrow, just in case." I wasn't all that worried. It would take the human Caleb Mathews' crew and thirty more like them if they had a hope of taking us down.

In fact, I was far more apprehensive about what awaited me back at the Inn.

Because I'd rather take on a hundred men than one, pissed off she-wolf queen.

CHAPTER 12
Diana

Diana

"Stop being a baby and pull it together," I muttered, dipping my head low as I splashed my overheated face with cold water. I lifted my head and swiped the water away with a towel. "You're the one in control here," I said to my reflection. "Act like it."

My eyes glinted ice as my wolf raised her hackles, her voice ringing in my mind clear as a bell.

You are only in control because I allow it. Never forget that.

I let my lids drift shut as the clawing need tore through my body and nearly brought me low.

"Please," I whimpered, the sensation so keen it bordered on physical pain.

Why was I being punished this way? Hadn't I suffered enough of late?

I'd lost the only father I'd ever known, not to mention several beloved packmates in the battle prior, and the Territories were crumbling before my eyes. And now, despite utter exhaustion, my wolf was in full-on heat again. Could a queen get a fucking break for just one day?

I stepped out of the bathroom and began pacing the room in tiny circles, mainly because that was the only sized circles I could manage in the tight space. Honeymoon suite, my ass. Or maybe they called it that because you'd be forced to sleep nearly on top of one another if you tried to fit two people in this room? The bed was essentially two twin mattresses shoved together, and there was just enough space to squeeze a small nightstand on either side. At the foot of the bed lay a 5 by 7 rug that I was currently wearing a hole through, and there was a tiny bathroom with pedestal sink and small tub. I guess I should've been grateful I had that, but I couldn't help but wonder if Myrr had been right. Maybe I'd been hasty, hot-footing it from Gabe's place so quickly...

I hadn't exactly ingratiated myself to him when we'd left. But damn it, I felt like I was surrounded by fools, and I didn't suffer them lightly.

And on that note, where the fuck were Raven and

Nicholas? Surely, they should've been back by now. Myrr had told me they'd gone out to see what they could find out in town, and didn't want any company.

Strike that.

They didn't want *my* company.

Fair enough. I didn't want theirs either. But where the hell were they?

"Diana?" Raven's low voice called through the door a moment later.

Speak of the devil.

My heart leapt to my throat as I stopped pacing but didn't move toward the door. I was dying to know what had happened on their little field trip, but no way could he be in here right now. Not if I wanted to keep this robe on.

A low sigh sounded through the door.

"Just tell me now, are you going to let me in or not?"

If he doesn't, we can just go out there, straddle those lean hips and—

"Stop it!" I hissed under my breath.

This was ridiculous, and unseemly to boot. As soon as I got back to the Territory, I would have a sit-down with my science team. If they could protect vampires from the sun, surely, they could stop my moon-cycles? This was barbaric, for a woman to be a slave to her inner beast, against her very will.

I am your will, Diana. We are one. And we have needs, so open the door and fulfill them.

"Go stay with Myrr and Nicholas. Or better yet, get another place to stay down the road a bit. We can talk in the morning," I muttered, trying to sound stern instead of breathless and needy, and failing even to my own ears.

"You know I can't do that. I swore an oath to protect you. Either I can stay in the room with you because we are two adults and that's the most reasonable solution, or I will sleep on this doorstep."

Not ideal, since I could already scent him through the door, and worse, so could my wolf.

Down girl.

All of which made it a full no brainer not to let him in. Not even for a second...

I yanked the ratty comforter and one of the pillows off the bed and then opened the door.

"Do what you have to do." I tossed the lot at him and closed the door, cursing myself for opening it in the first place. Had he always looked so vibrant and sexy and delicious?

Why was he torturing me like this?

My only question is, why are we not torturing him back? Take what we need and send him on his way. A means to an end. and revenge, to boot. He's gone out of his way to make our lives difficult from the start. Surely we can make things...hard for him too?

It was pure evil. And part of me was ashamed to stoop to it. But if I didn't, I was truly unsure if I could complete the mission before me. How was I to lead my people...worse, the entire population of the Alpha Territories, from the clutches of extinction if I couldn't even think straight? I needed relief, and revenge was as good a reason as any. My wolf had offered me a solution my heart could live with, so I snatched it with both hands.

I would do this. I would allow Raven to appease the beast inside me, and get a little retribution for his insolence while I was at it. What could go wrong?

I prowled to the door, already trembling in anticipation.

When I opened it, he was standing there, as if he'd always known I would give in and was just waiting for me to catch up.

He cocked his head, the fire in his eyes almost enough to finish the job and nearly burn me alive. "You going to let me in, Frostbite?"

"That depends." I wet my lips, and stood strong, still blocking his entrance. There needed to be ground rules before he crossed the threshold, because once he was inside, I wasn't sure I'd have the strength to deny him anything at all. "Are you prepared to give me what I need, and ask for nothing in return?"

"As always, I'm yours to command, my Queen."

The words sent a shudder through me and I gripped the doorjamb to stay upright as my wolf tossed her head back and howled.

"Come on, then."

I backed up and he stepped inside.

When I closed the door, I felt a little twinge in my gut, as if I'd just heard the sound of my own death knell. My brain knew this was a bad idea, but my body and my wolf did not give a fuck.

"Rules," I snapped, folding my arms around my belly so he couldn't see me trembling. "Hands and mouth only. Keep your dick in your pants. Don't even think about biting me."

But that didn't mean I wouldn't think about it.

In fact, it was suddenly all I could focus on. What would it feel like...the sting of those fangs I could see threatening to spill over his lips, even now, sliding into the tender flesh of my neck. Him sucking, long and slow, drinking from me while he drove his cock in...and out.

A moan bubbled from my mouth and his eyes went dark, the turquoise deepening to a midnight blue.

"I tease you because it gives me joy to get a rise out of you, but that doesn't change the fact that I want you like I've wanted no one else. So whatever the rules, I will obey as long as I get to touch you."

Raven stood by the sole window; his silhouette framed by the light of the half-moon. The stark need on his face paired with the sincerity in his voice was nearly my undoing. The roguish charm and easy smile had been stripped away, leaving nothing but naked want in its wake. It was almost more than I could bear, and I very nearly sent him away, sensing my impending ruin.

But I didn't.

I couldn't. Because suddenly my wolf took the wheel.

My fingers dropped to untie my robe of their own accord. With a shimmy of my shoulders, it slid away, catching for just a moment on the very tips of my breasts before pooling on the floor at my feet.

"Jesus, Diana. You're killing me. Ever since I saw you in the bathtub on the boat, I've thought of nothing else," he said, his voice tight and gritty. "Keeping those breasts covered is a war crime."

He closed the distance between us in two slow, deliberate steps, until we were toe to toe. Then, he reached out to trace my jawline, sending shivers down my spine.

"Put your mouth on me, Raven," I hissed, sinking my fingers into his dark, silky curls. "Please."

The heat that had started out as a fire had suddenly roared into an inferno as just the smell of him sent my wolf's heat into overdrive.

"Lick me, suck me until I scream," I begged in a voice that was barely my own, tugging him close as my pussy pulsed in time with my heartbeat.

"Yes, my Queen," he muttered back, lowering his head, his lips suspended above mine as he traced one finger down my spine, sending a delicious shudder through my body.

"Your skin is like fucking silk," he whispered, his forehead resting against mine as we both fought for breath.

We hadn't even kissed yet. And we wouldn't tonight. Because even as I fisted his hair and yanked him closer, he let out a growl and dropped to his knees before me, ever so reminiscent of his teasing days before.

But all I could do was watch, frozen with anticipation, as he growled my name and pressed his mouth to the part of me that ached for him most.

"Ah, fuck!"

When his blazing tongue flicked out to lap at my throbbing clit, long and slow, I proved his prophecy right as I screamed his name.

"Raven!"

The release crashed over me in waves, wrecking me as surely as the tides on a stormy sea. I arched my back, clutching him close, sealing his mouth to my aching pussy, as pleasure rolled through me in delicious waves. The second the crescendo slowed and eased, another started.

"Fuck, I—Oh, gods."

It was almost too much, the clawing need that rose hotter and faster than before as he worked that tiny bundle of nerves with his tongue in a tight circle even as his fingers slid between my thighs.

Unable to stand, I leaned back, hitting the wall hard, but he never let go. He just growled his pleasure, and moved with me, supporting my weight with one hand as he plunged two fingers of his free hand into my waiting channel.

I shook my head wildly, trying not to give in to the urge to howl as his fingers drove in and out of me, hard and sure, even as he sucked.

"Raven, please. I can't—Ah!"

Light exploded behind my lids as I came again, a puppet under his command.

"You taste like cinnamon and rain," he muttered, pulling away for a scant second just to look up at me. "I could never get enough. One more, little wolf?" he asked, his nostrils flaring as my grip tightened in his hair. "I'll take that as a direct command."

And then he was back again, that unholy mouth driving me to hell and then heaven all over again.

By the time it was over, I was bathed in sweat and drooped over him like a broken doll. Even my wolf was quiet in the corner, licking her lips in satisfaction. It took me a second to realize that he'd lifted me off the ground. My shoulders were currently wedged against the wall, my legs wrapped around Raven's neck, his hands using my ass to hold me up.

"Oh, I'm sorry, I—"

"It's me who is sorry for any man who has never gotten to taste a woman in heat. You are..."

He licked his shining lips and shook his head slowly. "A miracle."

Something like pain flashed over his face as he slowly, deliberately, lifted my legs away from him and set me on my feet. Then he stood, tall, strong, and hard as a rock. I could feel the massive length of his cock against my thigh, which had my wolf perking her ears.

Down, girl.

"Do you...are you okay?" I asked, my revenge plot suddenly feeling petty. Still, in the moment, as much as part of me wanted to experience more of this man, the rest of me knew it was a recipe for disaster. He needed to go before I wanted to never let him...

Maybe he felt the same.

Or maybe he'd had enough of me, because he traced one finger along the slope of my breast and then turned away.

"Good night, Frostbite. I hope you and your wolf get some sleep."

CHAPTER 13
Raven

I would have to forget what happened between us the night before. There was no other choice as far as I could see it. For so many reasons, it had been a terrible idea.

If for nothing other than the fact that while Diana had found a release in my mouth and hands, I had gone away aching as never before. But more because it had been a life altering experience that I wasn't sure I would ever come back from. Even now her scent filled my head, her taste consumed me. If just taking my own pleasure would have been enough to release the tension, I could have done that right here in the bed that smelled of Diana's pussy.

I groaned and sat up, running a hand through my hair. A glance at the bathroom door showed me that it was very much still locked, and likely would remain that way.

Probably it was for the best. I wasn't sure that I could contain myself around her right then, and I doubted she'd appreciate me slavering over her when she'd already found relief.

"Fuck," I muttered.

It wasn't like it was far past dawn—at least by what I could see of the light outside. And it wasn't like I was about to get any more sleep.

A hard bang on the door turned my head and then Myrr yanked the door open. "Aha!"

I frowned. "Aha what?"

"Damn, I thought for sure you two had finally done the bump and grind last night. No matter, there is a breakfast waiting for us, and I am insisting that you come with me." She didn't shut the door.

Which meant I had to stand with her watching.

She let out a cackle. "Left you blue-balling it, did she?"

I schooled my face. "Breakfast, isn't that what you wanted?"

"Well, that and a few other things." Myrr turned. But left the door open. I followed her, pulling on my shirt as we went. Not that I had to worry about getting my pants on, those had never come off.

Down the rickety steps and into the main dining area we went, all the while my thoughts on Diana, the taste and feel of her under me. Damn it.

She'd ruined me.

The realization hit me like a brick between the eyes.

I flinched and stumbled sideways. "What the fuck was that about?"

Myrr stared up at me, a shoe in her hand. She slid it back on, surprisingly balanced despite her advanced age. "Get your head out of the gutter, and back in the game! I'd prefer to have this breakfast conference with Diana, but she's irritated me. Telling me she's going to chop me up and throw me out for chum! We'll see about that!"

She plunked herself down at the trestle table and spooned food onto a plate.

Scrunching up my face, I sat and a moment later Nicholas joined us, a mark on the side of his head.

"Did she hit you with her shoe, too?"

He shook his head. "No, a book. Smashed it right on my head instead of just waking me like a normal person."

Myrr sniffed. "Something is coming for us...possibly just a bad case of food poisoning, but still I am motivated by my guides to make sure I speak the words."

I sighed and rolled my head side to side. "Okay. Something bad...Like the end of the world, maybe? We're all very aware."

"Smart ass." Myrr flicked a spoonful of eggs my way, but missed entirely. "No, something else. I think it has to do with why Maverick is missing. Probably it's the dragon, that's the more likely issue with one of us dying."

My eyebrows shot up. “Back it up, woman. A dragon? Who said anything about a dragon?”

“Well, you know them as Hunters, but did you never wonder how the vampires made the Hunters? Created them from the First Dragon. A hoarding, miserable old bastard who's been alive since long before we started recording time. Who happens to like shiny, powerful items. All dragons do. As does this one.”

Nicholas sucked in a sharp breath. “But that...can’t be. There are none, certainly none in the Human realm.”

“These are strange and perilous times, my boy. Thinking in absolutes is a relic of the past.”

She wasn’t wrong there.

“But at least we’d have heard if a dragon had shown up on the lands around here. There would be terrible destruction. The animals would have lost their minds.”

My own mind shot back to how Gabe’s hell-hounds had behaved when we’d lost Maverick’s scent. How they’d run from the spot as if their tails were on fire and their asses were catching.

“Well, don’t listen to me then!” Myrr snapped her fork and knife downward and I almost thought I saw a glimmer of tears gather. “I’m just the Oracle, after all. What would I know about the future, hmm?”

I realized that Diana’s threat to Myrr had been taken far more seriously than she realized. We’d all gotten so used to Myrr acting like nothing bothered her, it seemed we'd forgotten that she still did see the future from time to time. That she was useful, even if she was a gluttonous pain in the ass.

And now I was feeling bad for the old crone, even though she'd hit me with a shoe. "Look...Diana didn't mean what she said. You have to know that it's just the stress and she's in heat—"

Myrr poked at me with her fork. "Which is exactly what you should have taken care of last night! But you didn't, did you? Your job is to protect us all, and that includes her, does it not?"

"It does," I kept my voice calm, with some difficulty. "But—"

"I know she's being a rude bitch, so it's probably hard to work up the will for it and all." Myrr stuffed more eggs into her mouth and spoke around them. "I've dealt with the wolves for a long time. I know how trying they can be. Regardless, you need to take care of that, because it's becoming a real issue."

If only working up the will was the problem...

"Back to the dragon, Myrr," I said, trying to get her back on topic. "What did you see?"

"The crimson stone is a shiny, shiny thing, with a fair bit of its own magic. And we brought the second stone—or at least pieces, very close to it. They would have sung to each other. Mates if you will. And that song? Lit up the world."

Nicholas leaned forward. "You mean the stones are alive?"

She let out a snort. "Everything's alive, you nincompoop!"

Nick opened his mouth to pop off, already miffed about the blow to the head, so I put my hand between them.

"Stop. Just...let's stay focused. Myrr, you mean that by getting close to Maverick and aligning the stones, we somehow set off a signal?"

"Yep."

And then she said nothing more. Just ate her breakfast. I shot a look at Nicholas and then motioned for him to follow me.

"We will leave you to your meal, Oracle. Thank you."

She didn't even look at us as we left the room.

Nicholas waited until we were outside the bed and breakfast, the cold so deep his breath frosted the air. "You think she was really hurt by what Diana said?"

"You think that a dragon showed up and stole our mark?" I tossed a question back at him.

We both shrugged, and that was about the whole of it. Without another word between us, we headed back toward Siobhan's place. We needed to keep our wits about us, and worrying about a dragon that may or may not be an issue would only muddy the waters.

One problem at a time.

"We're going to be very early," Nicholas said. "Is that on purpose?"

Learning, he was learning. "We'll go to the pub. Suss things out, see what we can see."

Which is how we ended up playing an early morning game of dice. Nicholas was surprisingly good at it, and kept a steady win rate going. I took note that with each new player he made sure to shake their hand, wincing a little each time.

Touching on their memories. Seeing if there was any info we needed.

As the time to meet the men who would help us find Maverick drew nearer, one of them—the leader, Caleb, no less—joined our table. "Well boys, didn't think you'd be here this early."

Nicholas held out his hand. "Good to meet you, in person as it were."

"I don't shake bloodsucker's hands." Caleb spit toward Nicholas, the gob landing between his feet. "But I'll take your money here too."

I moved and was next to Caleb before he could sit down, my hand at the back of his neck as I drove his face to the table. "You will shake his hand and be polite, or I'll relieve you of your head right now."

Caleb tried to squirm, but there was no escaping. With a grunt, he agreed. "Fine."

I let him go and he sat up, his eyes locking on me—idiot.

I raised a brow. "Let me guess, I'll pay for that?"

Nicholas shook the man's hand—briefly. So fast that I almost wondered if he'd even made contact.

"Raven!" Nicholas stood, shoving his chair back as he scrambled toward the door. "It's an ambush! They contacted local Vanators. They don't know where Maverick is."

Even as he spoke, the door to the pub crashed open, and a Molotov cocktail flew in. Before it landed, I shot forward, grabbed it in mid-air and threw it back outside, to a chorus of screams.

"Siobhan. You owe me, and I mean to collect!" I shouted as I bolted for the stairs that led up to the second floor. "Nick, come on!"

Nicholas bolted after me, and we were at the top floor and climbing before the Vanators were even through the door—I was sure of it.

"How are we getting out of this?" Nicholas yelled as I yanked open a window and leaned out. The walls were covered in thick wisteria trunks, weaving their way around the building, all but holding the crumbling structure together.

Vanators circled around said building, guns in hand. And me without even my swords. Just a single damn dagger that I really didn't want to lose while I stood in the full sun.

Fucking Gabe and his fucking no weapons rule. I was going to shove it up his ass the next time I saw him. "The roof. Now."

I all but tossed Nicholas out the window, making him climb to the roof. I followed him, a shot from below shattering the plaster to the left of my head. A shard sliced across my chin, but I ignored the sharp pain and climbed the wisteria, throwing myself over the edge.

"We're trapped!" Nicholas said. "There's no other building to even leap to!"

"I know," I said, making my way over to the far edge of the building, and peered over. "We're going to split up. I'll draw them to me. Once I have them engaged, you leap down the other side of the building—"

Nicholas snorted. "Think you're superman, do you?"

I shot a look at him. "What?"

"I saw how many they had coming, Raven. Six Vanators. Six of the humans who are getting paid for finding us. That's twelve. You think you can take twelve?"

I shrugged. "They are all human, Nick. And you didn't let me finish. I'll engage them, and you come around from the other side. Take them from behind." I gave him a slow smile and a wink. "I'd think you'd be good at that."

Nicholas gaped at me. "Did you seriously make a joke when we're about to get slaughtered?"

"Yes. What better time to lighten the mood? Now get ready—and don't lose your dagger. You lose that and poof. Crispy Nicholas." I ran to the side closest to the water and leapt over. As I fell, I caught a bullet in my right forearm—just a clip, but goddess of the night did it burn a path.

The human who'd shot at me was not one of the Vanators, but one of Caleb's men. I grabbed him and snapped his neck, then dropped him.

They swarmed me, the steady pop of someone's gun ripping through the air. I grabbed a body and yanked it in front of me as it was peppered with bullets.

"You're wasting the silver!" someone yelled.

"I'm a vampire," I laughed as I took a short sword from one of the men, and gutted him with it, dancing out of the way of another shot from the gun. "You think silver would work on me?"

Caleb's men were dispatched in a matter of two minutes, perhaps even less.

"I think that's a record, even for me." I looked around at the bodies on the ground. None of them stirred.

None of them were Vanators. Which meant...fuck.

I took off around the building. The scene was like a really shitty movie, one that you knew the ending, and you had to stop it no matter what.

Three Vanators held Nicholas on his knees, his arms spread wide as a fourth Vanator raised a shining sword over his head.

The other two Vanators came at me, one with a double headed axe, the edge pitted and broken yet still wicked. The other had a long staff with curved blades on each side. I could defend myself, or save Nicholas.

"You protect her!" I yelled as I threw my newly acquired sword, end over end, burying it into the Vanator's chest that stood behind Nicholas.

I managed to dodge the axe as it swung my way, but the long reach of the pole was another thing.

The blade caught me in the thigh, digging deep into the muscle. With a snarl I grabbed the pole and yanked it away from the Vanator. Rage and bloodlust roared through me as I swung the pole, decapitating the first Vanator, following through to the one holding the axe, driving the tip deep into his belly, wrenching a scream from him.

"Raven!" Nicholas yelled for me but I was already moving, ignoring my wounds, leaping from where I was to the Vanator closest to Nicholas, yanking the man's arms backward as I buried my fangs into his neck, and ripped the carotid free of its confines.

Blood sprayed as I threw the body to the side, already locking onto the next Vanator, fully expecting him to run.

He engaged me, moving at a speed that was...more

than human. I didn't slow, just grabbed at the blade as it came toward me, clasping it between the flats of my hands and twisting hard to the left, yanking it out of the Vanator's hands.

He should have run.

But he kept on fighting, and that alone gave me pause.

"Nick, you okay?" I growled the question, the blood lust making my voice thick. Dark.

"I'm okay...but...they are getting back up, Raven."

They weren't dying like humans either. They weren't behaving like humans. So what the fuck were they? I licked my lips with a shake of my head. "They taste human."

Only no, now that I was letting myself taste the blood all over me, that wasn't quite right. Human...But also not. Something more or less, I wasn't sure which.

What was this fresh hell?

"You will all die," the Vanator in front of me said, his voice calm as if he was speaking of the weather. "The bitch wolf. The Oracle. All of you."

There was no moment of thought, no moment of should I or shouldn't I. Because mention of Diana's death sent something in me over the dark edge I tried so carefully to walk.

I was on the Vanator, his throat in my hands as I ripped it free of his body. His eyes were wide, but he stared up at me.

Very much still alive.

Grabbing the top of his head in one hand, shoulder in the other, I removed the offending body part. "That should do it." I threw the head to the side and glanced at Nicholas who was wide-eyed.

"Raven. You're wounded."

I waved a hand at my thigh, and the blade in my gut that I hadn't realized was there until just now. "It will heal."

Only...that's not what it felt like. Not at all. The places that the weapons had been buried into me, the last from my final kill, they burned...as if they contained a piece of the sun itself. What the fuck?

There was only one person who might know what the fuck was going on—seeing as he was the master of this island.

The world around me faded as I crumpled to the ground, I whispered the only words I could manage.

"Get me to Gabe. Now."

CHAPTER 14
Diana

I waited in the bathroom until I was sure that Raven was gone from the room before I so much as opened my eyes. My body—and more than that, my wolf—was only partially satiated by what he had offered me the night before. But damn, had it been good...

Everything in me tightened from my nipples to my core, just from the memory of his touch. I scrambled to reach the water and flicked the cold on, letting it pour down over me. How in the world steam didn't roll from my body, I didn't know.

But it did help. A little at least.

Shivering, I stepped out of the tub and let my body continue to shiver, forcing it to think of something other than the heat I was so deeply enmeshed in. I yanked a brush through my hair, the pain another sharp discomfort to help me settle my wolf. We had a job to do, and we had to move our asses.

Nodding to myself in the mirror, I braided my hair and pulled on my clothes, binding my breasts as usual. Partly out of habit, but also to ensure that Raven didn't think just because he'd owned my body last night it meant he owned *me*.

Once more in my everyday clothes, no more of this dressing in fancy human attire that only attracted more attention than I needed, I went to the door.

My hand hovered over the knob, and I took one more, steadying breath.

Don't think about those hands…

That mouth—

"Pull it together, Di," I whispered and forced myself to leave the room, making my way downstairs.

I paused as the sound of raised voices caught my ear.

"Well, don't listen to me then!" Myrr snapped, a thump following her words, like she'd hit the table maybe. "I'm just the Oracle, what would I know about the future?"

I winced, hearing the tremor in her voice. She was upset, and no doubt it was my fault. Now I would have to deal with that mess, and face Raven, all in one fell swoop. But when I entered the dining hall, Myrr was alone, staring at her half-eaten plate.

"Oracle." I tipped my head in her direction, taking the

bull by the proverbial horns. "I'm glad you're here. I...need to apologize for my words, and my behavior yesterday."

She grunted and stirred her food around. "You are the Queen, and under a stra—"

"It does not matter what I am," I cut in. "Nor is it fair to blame bad behavior on my current predicament. You are the Oracle, and while I do not always understand you, or your methods, or your reasoning...I do respect you."

Her eyes lifted slowly. "Overheard me bitching to the boys, did you?"

I dipped my head. "A little. Enough to prick my conscience."

Myrr shook her head. "There is much fog around us, girl. And it has agitated me almost as much as wanting to bang-arang with Raven has agitated you."

I clenched my hands into my thighs, choosing to focus on only one piece of her concerning observation. "Why... do you think there is fog in the future?"

"Uncertainty." She rolled her shoulders. "Changes to the powers that rule our world. New players like this Maverick. Like the dragon."

I blinked. "Say again?"

"Dragon."

My stomach knotted, and I shook my head. "Myrr, I know that the Hunters were created but—"

She sighed. "They *are* real. Where did you think

vampires of old got the initial genetics from? They stole blood, created new creatures, imbued them with all the mind fuckery that they have, and voila! A new type of dragon. But call it a Hunter to be clever."

I would have laughed if not for the seriousness of what she was saying. "So this Dragon, what has it got to do with what's going on here and now?"

Myrr spoke rapid fire. "Dragons like gems, and the gems spoke to one another, resonating and creating a song that the dragon heard. The dragon came, found Maverick and scooped him up. But this dragon is not like the Hunters. This one is old. This one will not attack, but instead will only protect what is his, and so you need to find..." her eyes closed, "Something."

My mind raced and I almost stood up to pace the room in sheer frustration, but Myrr's hand shot across the table to grab my wrist.

"Sit. Eat something. It will help you think. You know hunger only makes your wolf restless and irritable."

Damn it. To be reminded of basic care was an embarrassment that I did not need. I reached across the table and grabbed a plate, loading it with eggs, farmers sausage, toast and a fresh made fruit jam.

I stuffed my mouth and ate in a hurry, my mind already working over the problem. And a dragon, that was a serious problem. If it was true...

"You still question me?" The Oracle said, reading my

face or my mind, which was a terrifying thought I didn't even want to entertain. "You think I don't know everyone thinks me crazy? Well what would happen to you if all you saw were the people you'd watched over for an all-too long lifetime dying, and you were the only one who could see the path that no one wants to follow! And here...in this place...the fog is heavier. The magic more dangerous. I wish I'd never come."

I found myself reaching across the table for her hand, a sudden rush of sympathy coursing through me. "Why did you?"

"Because. It is where *my* path took me."

She froze, as if suddenly turned to stone. Her milky eyes widened and her mouth dropped open as a voice that was not her spilled out. A voice I'd heard before. The same as the dark entity that had tried to end Sienna.

"Queen to queen. I would speak to you."

My mouth dried but I forced out a reply. "You think yourself a queen?"

Laughter, halting and stuttering spilled from Myrr's lips. "I am a queen. You may call me Lilis. Queen to queen, know your death is coming."

Her threat filled the air, Myrr gasped and blinked over at me as she shoved in a mouthful of eggs like nothing had happened.

"So what will you do now with all this, wolf queen?"

I blinked back at her. "With–"

"The dragon! The fog! All of it!"

Myrr's eyes were locked on mine, clear and hard like a slice of crystalline from the waters of the North Lake. Sharp, as if the silly old woman who toddled around speaking of little but food had never existed. I wasn't sure she even knew she'd been spoken through.

Had the silly old woman been an act all this time?

"I will believe you," I said quietly, tightening my hand over hers. "And I will tell no one of your playacting as if you haven't a care except for what you're having for lunch."

She snorted. "Playacting? Surely not. Who wouldn't love a good buffet?"

But it was too late. I was already onto her. I'd underestimated her, and wouldn't make that mistake again. Now I needed to focus on how to proceed from here. And, apparently, hunting down a dragon was the next step in finding Maverick. That was good. Gave me something to do besides worry and wait for Raven and Nicholas to return.

The dark entity...Lilis...that was another matter. All I could do was handle her when the time came, and for now I would focus on the task at hand.

"If there was a dragon on this island, who would know of it better than Gabe?"

It was "his" island, after all. He'd made sure to mention it often enough. It meant I would have to play nice after leaving the casino in a fury when we'd lost Maverick a second time, but I wasn't above eating a little crow to get what I wanted.

I waved for Myrr to join me, but she shook her head.

"Nope. Not my path. Gotta stay here for now. Probably will wait here until you come back with the gem."

I blinked down at her. "You see us with the gem?"

"That or roasted by the dragon. That's the problem, super foggy." She shrugged and began to shovel food into her mouth again, humming a little tune that told me she'd said all she needed to say.

"Thank you, Oracle." I tipped my head in her direction, but she ignored me.

Funny, how someone letting you in could allow you to forgive them the things that drove you crazy about them.

I ran back up to my room on a spur of the moment thought. Flipping open my backpack, I pulled out the knife sheath that housed the blade Maverick had stolen from the demons. Tucking the whole thing against my lower back, under my belt, I felt better. I mean, at least I knew I could take care of any demon that might decide to cause me grief.

Hurrying now, I let myself out of the little bed and breakfast and jogged back toward Gabe's casino. Not that I wasn't in a hurry, but the run helped burn off some of the excess energy that had been piling up since we'd stepped foot on this fucking island.

The entrance to The Wild Queen Casino was locked. That didn't stop me. I banged a fist on the door, continually, until a ruffled looking demon opened the door and peered out.

I stared at him. "About time. I need to speak with Gabe. Or I suppose Raphael will do."

The demon did a slow blink and a yawn. "Pretty fucking early to be demanding those two. They're both still in bed."

"Take me to them. Now." I put the command in my voice as I would for a lesser wolf, one that was misbehaving.

He cleared his throat and let me in, quickly leading me through the silent casino, and down the stairs to the lower levels.

"What is your name?" I asked as we walked.

"Huh? Oh, my name. Right. I guess...you can call me Paul."

I shook my head. "Have you not had a name before?"

"Just got here from the Territories." He shrugged and then seemed to realize what he'd said.

"I won't tell anyone." Though the timing was interesting. "You know anything about that big storm that rolled across the ocean a few days ago?" I asked. "Looked demon driven to me."

Paul went pale and shook his head. "Yeah. So anyway, here's the boss's quarters. Good luck."

And then he was gone, all but running back the way we'd come. Fine by me, but I did find it interesting that he was terrified of the territory run by demons. I knocked on the door.

"Gabe? Do you know anything about a dragon living on this island?"

The door jerked open and a very naked, very aroused demon stood in front of me, wings spread out behind him. "What the actual fuck are you doing here, wolf?"

Perhaps another time the image and the sound of his voice might have made my knees weak, being in heat as I was. But all it did was piss me off. My wolf all but climbed up my throat, and I had to force myself to stay calm.

"Your new man, Paul, brought me. To be fair, I didn't know you'd be busy fucking someone."

He blinked and shook his head. "Gods above and below, you are a pain in the ass." He slammed the door in my face and a moment later he re-appeared, with pants on at least. "I thought you were done with us?"

"Yes, well, I'm...undone with you now."

He raised one brow.

"And I apologize for leaving in a huff. I'm not myself right now, and the fate of the entire world relies on me finding Maverick. It's made me a little touchy. I know you were trying to help, and I overreacted when we failed." I shot him an imploring half-smile. "Truce? We do have a common goal, after all."

He shrugged. "Truce."

"Excellent. So back to the point...do you know anything about a dragon on Isla Naranja? And maybe how to find it?"

Those three little questions were all it took for Gabe to lead me to a well-stocked library. Not well organized, but well stocked.

"Myrr, I assume?" Gabe asked as he handed me another book, on Hunters as all the others had been.

"Yes. She thinks the crimson stone that Maverick took reacted to the mate stone that we carry and created like a... song for the dragon to follow."

Gabe leaned over the table set up in the middle of the room. "I don't know much about dragons and do not know of one on the island. They were definitely real at one point. More serpent than the winged Hunters you know in the Territories."

I flipped through a book of monsters that had everything but a dragon...almost like...I turned the book sideways and ran a finger down the inside edge.

"Pages have been ripped out. Any particular reason?"

Gabe motioned for me to hand him the book. He did the same as me, flipping the book and running a finger down the interior of the spine. "The question isn't just who...but how. These books, I've had them in my collection for a very long time–not very many people come in here."

“Could it be another demon?”

“Could be, but why?” He sighed and slid into a chair.

The knife sheath at my back rubbed a little, and I found myself pulling it out and laying it on the table between us. “While I’m here...what can you tell me about this?”

Gabe leaned forward. “Is it a special weapon?”

“You tell me.”

He flipped off the strap holding the blade in and pulled it out, his eyes widening as it came free. Glowing lightly, a soft blue, it lit up the space just under it.

“How in all the hells, of all the territories did you come to have this?” He breathed the question out, and I wasn’t sure if it was awe or fear that held tight to him.

“I took it from Maverick, who took it from his demon captors. You know it?”

He gave a slow nod as he rolled the handle, inspecting the blade. “It’s a sacrificial tool, used by the priests of Darykana a thousand years ago. Held now–or supposed to be held–by Morock. It is reputed to have powers over... not only demons, but the Fallen as well. Malach has the sister blade to this one.”

Morock, cousin to Malach, and the demon’s dark king. The connections between the Fallen angels, and the demons was tighter than I knew. I wasn’t sure they weren’t all the same.

"I've not had any dealing with Morock. He responds to none of my letters."

"He wouldn't." Gabe said. "That's not his style. He will only contact you if you want something. Classic demon."

He put the blade back into the sheath and slid it back across the table to me. "Keep this hidden. The fact that I did not know it was missing means that Morock is keeping things very, very close to the chest."

I frowned. "You would give a weapon of that magnitude back to me, without a fight?"

Gabe leaned back in his chair. "I do not want power, Diana. I want safety for my people, for my friends and those I consider family. Me taking that weapon would be declaring war on not only Morock, but Malach as well—I am related to both of them." He tapped the table lightly with two fingers, his eyes thoughtful. "And declaring war on them both? I might as well put my head on the chopping block and pull the guillotine blade down on myself."

I stared at him, thinking through all the symbolism on the doors, throughout the casino. "Both?"

He grunted. "Yes. I am related to both those pricks. Lucky me."

Abyss, the black cat from the kennels leapt onto his lap and started pestering him, giving me an excuse to leave the conversation of the blade. I took the sheath and tucked it once more against my back, flipping my shirt over it.

"Does she know she's not a hell-hound?" I asked as I turned through the pages of another relevant book—this one missing sections as well. I handed it silently to him.

"No. She was a scrawny kitten when I found her ten years ago, nearly dead so I let one of my top hounds raise her. Head bitch taught the cat to be head bitch. Now she runs the kennel." Gabe shook his head. "Fucking prick whoever it was who wrecked my books."

I found myself staring at him. "You are not what I would have expected in a demon, Gabriel. A man fond of his animals, and protective of his books."

He shrugged his broad shoulders. "We can't all be the charmer that Raven is. But to be clear. I let him win in the ring." He grinned and I laughed, the sound echoing in the big room. He joined me but the laughter was overshadowed by shouting from above.

"Boss! We got bad injuries!"

Gabe took off, and I was right behind him. Before we even found them, I knew who it was.

"Raven's hurt."

"Fuck," Gabe snapped. "Get the blood supply!"

"We're out!" Raph yelled. "I went to get it. It's all gone!"

We skidded to a stop inside the back room, where the poker game had been played. Raven was on his back, his leg tied and Nicholas above him, holding pressure to his stomach.

"Diana, we can't get the bleeding to stop! They used some sort of anticoagulant on the weapons! It smells like bloodworm to me. They...they did something with bloodworms to make this!" The panic in his voice was real. Bloodworms were one of only a few things that could kill a vampire, and I had no doubt Nicholas was telling the truth, but right then we needed calm.

"Vanators?"

"Yes," Raven managed. "They aren't...they aren't human. They don't die unless you take their heads. I'd lay money at least one of them was from the ship."

I made myself approach him, and I say made because my wolf...she was melting down.

Mine mine mine mine mine mine.

The chant was insistent and demanding. I did all I could to block my wolf out. To hold her at bay with every ounce of my strength.

"He needs stronger blood than human anyway," Nicholas said. "To hold this off long enough to figure out how to counteract it. I'd offer, but mine won't work," Nicholas said.

I felt their eyes on me, but I was already moving.

I pulled the dagger from under my shirt and pierced through the veins on my wrist, shoving the now open wound across Raven's mouth.

"Don't say I never gave you anything back."

His eyes shot to mine, only I looked away. I would not

fall under his spell, and that's all this was. An attraction because of my heat cycle, because of Raven's charm and vampire powers.

He groaned as he sucked on my wrist and for just a moment I wondered what it would be like to let him drink from my neck. There was no pain in my wrist—if anything, a warmth flushed up my arm, striking its way through my core, and lower yet.

Whatever dormancy my heat had been in, tore away under the onslaught of his mouth at my wrist.

Trembling, I struggled to keep my mouth shut, but the low moan was working its way up my throat.

"Fuck, not this again," Raphael muttered from somewhere in the room, his voice seeming distant.

"Everyone out!" Gabe yelled. "Before this turns into a fuck fest. You too." There was movement, the sound of bodies scrambling, Nicholas yelped and then the room was clear except for me and Raven, the big doors shut tight.

He pulled himself up to a sitting position, his shirt sliding open, my eyes drawn to the flex of his muscles. The wound in his belly was slowly closing, but he did not take his mouth from my wrist.

His tongue circled around and around the cut, before finally pulling his mouth free. "Diana. Look at me. I swear I will not spell you. I just need to make sure you are okay. That I did not take too much..."

I did look at him then, anger snapping clean through the rising arousal. "Am I okay? You're the idiot who got run through like a pig on slaughter day!"

I jerked away from him and stormed out of the room, leaving him on the table alone. Because I was not just running from him. I was running from *me*.

Because I hadn't wanted to just fuck him in that moment. I'd wanted to hold him, to breathe him in and make sure he was okay. Unhurt.

I'd been worried....that I'd lost him.

No. No. I wouldn't let my heart get torn out of my chest again. Not by Maverick, and sure as shit not by Raven.

I couldn't do it. I wouldn't. That's what I told myself as I ran from the casino, and out into the open air of the island.

CHAPTER 15

Raven

A wild storm raged inside my body as Diana's blood ran through me, closing the wounds that I knew were meant to kill me. I had to keep my eyes closed as the magic of her very essence sunk into my blood and bones.

She'd been the one I'd drunk from the stock of blood, before we'd left the Territories. I was sure of it. Only this, straight from her body...it was like seeing a piece of her soul, of seeing a piece of her as she ran from me.

"Raven."

Gabe's voice pulled me out of the fog of nearly dying, and of coming back to life. "What is it?"

"You alive?"

I grunted and slid a hand over my neatly knit wounds. "Seems as if."

Gabe let himself the rest of the way into the room, his nose wrinkling a little. "She took off."

I nodded and turned my head a little to the south. Shit, I could pick up her direction? That was...handy. "She hasn't gone far." I slid from the poker table and glanced back at the blood. "Sorry about the mess."

Gabe made a soft clicking sound with his tongue. "It is what it is. The Vanators. Tell me about them while we wait on your Queen."

I opened my mouth to say she was not my Queen. Gabe held up his hand. "Spare me the argument. Semantics and truth. We both know that she is something more to you."

I grit my teeth. "The Vanators...they did not die as they should have. Wounds that opened them up, gutted them, snapped their bones...they kept on going."

Gabe crossed his arms and put his knuckles under his chin. "And you killed them how?"

"I took their heads. Nicholas finished them off I think." I couldn't quite remember. "All of that is one thing, but for them to find a way to use an anticoagulant, that could be problematic."

Gabe gave a slow nod and paced the room. "True. Why did Diana's blood heal you then?"

I snorted. "Why didn't you want to let me try demon blood? I've drank it before."

Gabe had his back to me as he spoke. "Things are

changing, Raven. I don't suggest you drink demon blood ever again, not if you wish to live."

Another time I would have snorted, blown his words off. Only they felt like he was truly trying to warn me. "Something your dear brother Malach is up to?"

"Possibly. I just know that...we've lost a few friends we used to share with." Gabe finally turned back to me. "You were very lucky Diana was here. But again, it does not explain why her blood healed you so quickly and—"

"Leave it be, Gabe," I strode for the door.

I did not know that many people outside the Werewolf Territory truly understood what had been done to her. What she'd allowed to happen so that she'd survive. My gut instinct, my guess, was that the combination of werewolf and vampire genetics had been enough to act as a...type of super blood. Super food.

I shook my head. "What was she doing here anyway?"

Gabe frowned at me, his eyes thoughtful. "Research. About a dragon here, on this side of the water."

Which meant that Myrr had told Diana her theory about Maverick being snagged by a hoarding dragon, and Diana had gone to work looking for it. "Any luck?"

"Everything in my library with even a passing mention to a dragon has been...removed." Gabe growled. "My books have been tampered with, and fairly recently, if I were to guess."

That drew my own frown. "How could anyone know

that a dragon would arrive here, and that we would need information on it?"

We walked together out of the room. "Go get some fresh clothes on, I'll meet you back at the library." Gabe gave me a push in the direction of his own rooms. "We're about the same size."

I could have done just that, but my feet drew me out the front doors, down to the southern side of the town, not far from where we started tracking with the hell-hounds.

Diana stood on the edge of a cliff, overlooking the sea. The wind whipped around her, dragging her long dark hair out behind her.

"Why can I sense you in my head?" she asked as I approached.

"When blood is shared, at times a bond can form." I made sure to stand with space between us. "It has not happened to me in...a very long time."

"How long?"

"Not long. Days and it will fade." *I hoped.*

"Can you read my mind?" Her question was soft and full of fear.

"No. Nor can you read mine. We can find each other, I don't know what the distance would be, but it will work to our benefit on this trip." I wanted badly to reach out and touch her, to just take her hand. To feel her skin against my own.

To tell her the connection wouldn't last, that it would be fine. The blood bond would fade as long as she didn't give me any more of her blood. I swallowed hard, the horror of losing this connection with her hitting me right between the eyes.

But I didn't want it either. That much was true at least.

I did the only thing I could. I changed the direction of our conversation to safer footing. "Did you find anything about the dragon?"

She folded her arms over her chest. "No. There is a bookstore in town. I walked past it on my way to Gabe's. I thought we could try there."

Footsteps turned us both around. Nicholas approached us, carefully. "Are you really okay?"

I gave him a bow from the waist, no mockery in the gesture. "You have saved my life, Nicholas. Thank you."

He shrugged and a quick blush touched his cheeks. "You saved mine first. It's why they got the drop on you."

Diana's eyes darted between us, but I did not look fully her way. "What do you mean?"

"He gave up his weapon, to save me," Nicholas said. "Wounded and dying, he still saved me."

I snorted and waved a hand at him. "I did not think you the one for spinning a yarn, Nicholas. We took them together and that is that. Now, Diana, you said there was a bookstore?"

Her eyes narrowed. "Yes. A bookstore."

Which is how the three of us found our way to the very old and closing up for the day bookstore.

A Tale Too Many.

That was the name of the bookstore.

"Wait!" Diana called out, leading the way. "Please, we have need of a book."

The owner turned, his bald head mostly hidden under a flattened cap. He looked at us over dark gold spectacles. "We all have need of a book from time to time. But I am closing—"

"It is a matter of life and death, sir," Nicholas said quietly.

The owner sighed. "What is this book you need? I will tell you if I have it."

Diana looked at me and I shrugged. I had no idea what the book would be called. "Something on dragons. Not lore...but truth."

The owner looked at me and squinted. "Dragons in truth? Everything I have is a fairytale. A story."

That was what I'd been worried about—if Gabe's library didn't hold the information, there was no way a small store run by a human—

"You should head to the old church on the hill. St. Barnabus, on the northwest side of town. The clergy have a section of the church dedicated to St. George, the Dragonslayer," the owner said. "Lore is that he was buried here.

I would suppose that if one wanted truth around a mythical dragon that you believe to be true, that would be your best bet."

Diana thanked him and led the way once more. I was content to follow her, to watch her muscles working, her legs eating up the distance. She was a wolf trapped, I could see it in her now, more than ever before. She needed to run. To be wild and free.

No doubt the blood bond was freaking her the fuck out for that reason alone.

We stopped at the bed and breakfast so that I could change clothes and drink down another vial of stocked blood. While I did that, Diana checked in on her wolves quickly, but all was quiet on our commandeered vessel.

The human blood was bland compared to Diana's—water to a fine wine.

I sighed and made myself finish off the bottle, tipping it back.

"Find it yet?"

Myrr's question had me choking on the last mouthful. "How the hell did you sneak up on me, old woman?"

She grinned. "Did you find the dragon yet?"

"No."

"Pity." She looked actually disappointed. "I see you survived the ambush? I knew you would."

My eyebrows shot up. "Did you want to warn me next time?"

"Nah. You didn't need a warning. You just need her. Some things need to unfold in their own time."

And with that she thumped her way down the hall, the sound of the bedroom door slamming behind her.

Nicholas met me in the hall. "Diana said that she didn't get through all of Gabe's books. I'm thinking... maybe I should go back. Keep looking there while you two head to the church."

I gave him a slow nod. "Run it by Diana, but yes, sounds good."

Nicholas stared hard at me. "You want me to...run it by her? Why not just let me go and do it?"

I patted him on the shoulder. "You want to piss her off again? I don't. Her wolf is volatile at best right now. We need to help her."

Where was this coming from? Not that I didn't want to help Diana. But I'd spent the better part of the trip poking the wolf, so to speak, and now...what had changed?

"Fucking blood bond," I grumbled and wiped a hand over my face. "It makes me...soft where she is concerned and will continue to do so until it has run its course."

"You bonded her?" Nicholas all but hissed the words. "What the fuck were you thinking, man?"

"I wasn't! I don't know what happened. It certainly wasn't intentional; I can promise you that." Which was the truth.

"A blood bond usually requires at least two feed—"

I glared at him, and he clamped his mouth shut. "Right, I'll run it by her."

He was gone and I took another minute. He was right, a blood bond like this required at least two feedings. I'd drunk that first bottle when I'd still been in the Keep, back in the Territories, not knowing it was Diana's blood.

This second feeding had locked things into place. Diana was moving toward me, I could feel her approach before I heard or smelled her.

I turned as she stepped into the doorway. "I've sent Nicholas back to Gabe," she said. "He wanted to run it by me first."

I nodded, but kept my mouth shut.

"Nothing to say?"

I let a smile play about my lips as my eyes drifted, taking her in. "Well, we could discuss staying here, seeing if your wolf is still...hungry, but I doubt that you'd be receptive, knowing that each time we touch during this period of the blood bond, actually ties us more closely together."

Her face paled. "You...you're kidding me."

I shook my head. "No. So I will be doing my level best not to touch you. I did not come here to find myself bound to any woman. Not even you, Frostbite." I swept past her, out into the hall and down the stairs. "We should hurry, before the church closes its gates for the night."

I felt her at my back, felt her presence just under my skin. The last thing I wanted on this trip—besides dying—was any sort of an attachment. Take a tumble with the werewolf queen? Absolutely. She was a jewel hidden in the forest that I would truly enjoy exploring given the chance.

But bind myself for the rest of my extraordinarily long life to a single woman? No thank you. That was not my style.

That's the lie I told myself, even as I panicked at the thought of not having her under my skin, of somehow losing this connection so tentatively formed.

I was so very well and thoroughly screwed.

CHAPTER 16
Diana

Raven did exactly as he'd said he would. Not once on the walk to the church did he so much as try to touch me. Moon goddess above, he barely looked at me.

"This direction," I said, turning to the north, where the hill sat and the church perched on the top of it.

Raven did not speak, not even to answer me.

I blew out a breath, my wolf itching under my skin. This was the kind of night to go for a run, to rip my clothes off and shift to four legs and run until I collapsed. The weather was quiet, almost a summer's night with the warmth on the air currents.

"What is bothering you?" Raven asked as we drew closer to the church.

"You said that you can't look inside my head," I said, "So how do you know something is bothering me?"

He laughed at me and shook his head. "You are easy to read, Diana. The heavy sighs, the longing looks toward the forest, the obvious distraction of your wolf. Even your scent changes when she comes to the surface."

I shrugged. "My wolf wants to run. I want to run."

"Away from me."

"Amongst other things," I said.

It was true, I did want to run from him, but...maybe not for the reasoning he had in mind. I wanted to run because being close to him made me angry, and confused, and adding a blood bond to those emotions was not helping. Even if I couldn't feel the bond, I could sense him on the periphery of my mind.

Like a compass, I could point to him if you'd covered my nose and my eyes.

"Are you sure it will wear off?" I asked.

"Yes. Like I said, a few days." Long pause. "A week at most."

A week?

Seven fucking days of avoiding him when we were working together to find Maverick? Fantastic.

The church gate loomed ahead of us, gargoyles perched atop the edge of the wall surrounding the courtyard. The wings reminded me of Gabe's and Raphael's.

"Ladies and queens first." Raven motioned for me to lead the way.

I sniffed in his general direction, rolling my eyes. He was still going to act the fool, even now.

I strode through the gates, along the cobblestoned path that led straight to the main doors of the church. There were tombstones on either side of the path, like an honor guard of the dead. No flowers, no markers that anyone ever visited. Just stone slabs and the dead.

The door to the church opened as I lifted my hand to knock.

An old priest, if his dark robes were any indication, opened the door. "I'm so sorry, but we are locking up for the evening."

"We just need a few minutes of your time." I tipped my head in his direction. "It is a matter of utmost urgency."

The priest shook his head. "I am sorry, you will need to come back tomorrow." He began to shut the door.

Raven slid forward and put not just his foot in the door, but half his body. "Sorry won't work." With a shove he opened the door fully and stepped through. Bending at the waist he bowed to me. As if now was the time to show manners.

Fool.

The priest was spluttering, yelping for help.

"We need to know if you have any books on dragons," I said. "I know it is an odd request but—"

"Father Mauricio, if they need to get into the library, I'm happy to help," a high-pitched voice rang out. "A flock needs a shepherd, after all."

Mauricio sighed and ground his teeth, not very priest-like if you asked me, but then again, we didn't have priests in the Werewolf Territory. "Jeremiah. Go back to your meditation. We don't need to entertain strangers' whims—"

Jeremiah skidded into view, his robes disheveled, his hair wild and his brown eyes matching. "It's just...I've seen a dragon myself," he blurted. "I know it sounds crazy, but about six months ago, the seas were high, and I swore I saw one rolling in the waves..."

I held a hand to Jeremiah and he took it, his fingers cold. But I immediately felt the pulse of magic around him. "You can see things that the other humans cannot, hmmm?"

His eyes widened. "You...who are you?"

Father Mauricio spluttered, trying to step between us. "What do you mean, *other humans*? As if you are not? Please, don't fill the young man's head with nonsense."

Raven held up both hands, in a surrender gesture, but I saw him turn fully on Mauricio. "We are not human, but we are here because only you can help us. And help us, you will."

Father Mauricio softened under Raven's gaze. As much as I hated the idea of him using his powers on me... stealing my will, it was a tool that we needed right now.

Jeremiah looked from Raven to me and back. "What are you?"

I gave his hand a gentle squeeze, drawing his eyes to me. "Is there a place we can talk? Somewhere quiet?"

Jeremiah shivered. "Yes, we can use the upper library. It's where...it's where I spied the dragon in the sea."

He turned and, as we walked away, Father Maurico mumbled something about needing to go lie down, just as he slumped against the wall and slid to the floor. Raven stepped over his sprawled legs.

"What did you do to him?" Jeremiah whispered. "Will he be alright?"

"He'll be fine. Drinking too much of the Communion wine again, I suspect," Raven drawled the words as he followed just behind me. I could practically feel the warmth of his breath ghosting over the back of my neck.

I tried to shake it off, to push those thoughts away, but my damn wolf...she wanted me to push my ass back into the man behind me and grind against the hardness we both knew was there.

"Here." Jeremiah motioned to a mere slit in the wall that turned out to be a winding set of stairs that curled up a solid four floors. When we reached the top, there was indeed a small library, with windows on all sides.

"Unusual, I know," Jeremiah dry washed his hands. "The glass is tempered with a substance that keeps the UV from the sun damaging any of the tomes. And this way, under natural light we can see things better."

Raven stepped up to the window that faced the ocean. "Excellent view."

"What are you?" Jeremiah asked again, his voice low and shaking. "Not demons, I hope?"

I smiled. "Neither of us are demons, though Raven will act the part of one at times."

Raven snorted but continued only to stare out the window.

The young priest stared hardest at me, looking over my clothes, and my face. "You are from the Territories, aren't you?"

Though I was surprised he could figure that out, I kept my reaction quiet. "Yes, and we are seeking the dragon that you spotted. He took...something and we need to get it back."

Jeremiah fisted his hands upward, shook a moment and then turned away, unable to contain his excitement. He drew a short breath and then spoke, the words spilling out of him. "Here. I have a few books on dragons. The others believe that everything in here is false. That these are just stories. But since the Territories appeared, I wonder how they can believe that still? I just don't understand." He flipped through a book, the pages whispering under his hands.

"Because it is easier to be blind than to allow your eyes to see the truth," Raven said, finally turning around. "Easier to live in the dark, than to let the sun illuminate."

Jeremiah gave a slow nod. "That dragon I saw, it did not have wings. It was more like this—" he tapped the page he had open. I moved over to look at the image.

The dragon on the page was dark gray and green, and had a massive set of rough looking horns, like a bull, that curled out from its head. The underbelly looked like scales of a slightly different color, a lighter hue of the grays and greens across the scales of its back. And Jeremiah was right. No wings.

Raven took the book and held it up. "Lovely. We have an image now, but we don't know where to find it, or how to defeat it."

Jeremiah paled. "You would kill it?"

I sighed, wanting to club Raven for his blunt words. "I'd prefer not to. It is a creature of magic, even if it is a monstrous one, and possibly the last of its kind. Even so, we must find it and do it quickly. Many lives are depending on our success."

Like...all of them.

The young priest turned and pulled down a notebook from the top shelf. "This is...this is a journal. I believe it was written by St. George himself. Before he was a saint anyway."

He laid the small journal on the table. Buttery soft leather and the smell...I wrinkled my nose. It smelled of sulfur and sea water. Very similar to the scent we'd encountered on the hill, where Maverick had been taken.

"But I can't decipher it. The code, or maybe language it's written in...I can't find anything like it."

I reached for it without thinking, my fingers brushing the leather. Heat and darkness encompassed my mind and I yelped, pulling my hand back, as if I'd been burned. "Raven, see if you can open it."

He stepped close to me, almost touching as he used one finger to flip the book open. "Ah, I see the issue."

"Can you read it?" Jeremiah breathed. "Is that what you're saying?"

"Some of it," Raven said, his voice distant. "It's very, very old. The writing is a mixture of two languages. One I recognize, the other at the back looks more like symbols, like a code."

"What languages?" Jeremiah almost yelped. "Please, I've been trying to break his code for—"

Raven scooped up the journal and held it carefully in one hand. "It will ruin your image of St. George if I tell you."

Jeremiah did a slow blink. "What do you mean? Was he a terrible person?"

Raven laughed softly. "Depends on your idea of what makes someone terrible. A blood drinker? A shifter? A fae? What makes them terrible? Not human?"

Again, Jeremiah did a slow blink. "You're saying that St. George was...not human."

"You think a human could come up with a weapon and the skill set to defeat a dragon?" Raven flipped through the pages, then handed it over to me. "The spell on it is broken now. It was just an initial bite to make you recoil."

Which it had. I flushed and took the book, flipping it open.

The language of the Fallen.

Demons. St. George had been a *demon*? Of course, it was more than ironic that he'd then been made a saint.

I had some knowledge of the demons' language, and I skimmed it quickly, looking for key words as Jeremiah spluttered and tried to get Raven to tell him more about the book's language of origin.

The journal was tough to read, the words in a scrawling hand. There was something about the sea, and a journey. Some lines were repeated over and over. A book of spells and not a journal at all, possibly?

At the very back, after a dozen or more blank pages, was one final sheet. This one was written in a shaky hand, unlike the others. This time, I could suss out none of the words. It was a strange collection of dashes, stops and starts that looked like alien symbols.

"Sometimes I wish I could just go out there, wake him up and ask him what this all means," Jeremiah said softly.

My heart beat faster as I wheeled on him.

"Wait. George is buried here?" I found myself not wanting to give him his saint title now that I knew he'd been a demon, but he'd signed the dang thing.

"Well, yes. That's the folklore within the church, at least," Jeremiah said with a frown. "I assumed you knew, although we do try to keep it a secret. We don't know which grave, and there is no way that the bishop would allow us to dig it up even if we did...hey, where are you going?"

I was running, and I knew that Raven would follow. "George is here, and he had the weapon buried with him, Raven!"

"You think you can find it?" He nearly collided with me as I slowed, recoiling as if I were the item covered in demon darkness.

I clutched at the journal. "We have to."

Outside, true dark had fallen. I handed the journal back to Raven. "Hold this. I need to be able to scent without the book interfering."

Raven did not ask if I was going to shift, or just how I was going to do this. St. George had been gone a long, long time. But if the journal had held the strong scent of a dragon, then why not George himself? Especially if he had a weapon that had killed a dragon. There would be blood left on it, no matter how long ago it was. At least, that was what I was hoping for.

Jeremiah followed us out. "You can't dig up anyone. This is consecrated ground. I'll be banished!"

"Death is worse than banishment," Raven said, his voice low and flat. "And that's what you'll face if we don't find this grave."

He gasped. "Is that a threat?"

"No, death is what we all face if Raven and I don't find this weapon," I slowed my steps as I moved through the graves, breathing deeply. An hour ticked by, but I could pick up nothing. Damn. I rubbed a hand over my face. I'd been so sure that I would be able to pick up on the scent. Maybe in my werewolf form, but I couldn't trust my wolf, not with everything that had been going on.

A howl in the distance spun me around and Raven and I locked eyes.

"Kevin!" we both said at the same time.

"I'll go." Raven handed me the journal back but I shook it off.

"No. Kevin doesn't like you."

"Point taken, I'll wait with the young one here, see if I can figure out anything else from the journal."

Our eyes met again, and the heat between us flared.

The blood bond tugged on me, and I swayed toward him, wanting nothing more than to have him draw me into his arms and bury his fangs into my neck.

"Fuck," I whispered, closed my eyes and backed away until I stumbled over a grave, breaking eye contact.

I kept moving, until I was well out of range, and running down the hill toward Gabe's place. I let my legs and body go, allowing the movement and the burning in my lungs to push away all the thoughts of anything else.

Luck seemed to favor me as I reached the Wild Queen Casino. Kevin and one other hell-hound sat on guard at the front door. "Kevin! Can you come?" I realized I had no idea what his commands were or how much he understood. "I need your help...scenting a demon, and that dragon again."

His eyes crossed more than usual and he huffed in response, stepping toward me. There were no words between us, but I could sense his willingness to help.

"This way." I turned and ran back toward the church, with Kevin keeping up easily.

We reached the church courtyard, the whole trip there and back taking me less than ten minutes. I was sweating and out of breath, but I felt better at least. Less anxious.

Raven stepped out of the shadows as Jeremiah popped out of the main doors, holding up a lantern. "I got the light you requested, but—holy mother of god, what is that?"

I placed a hand on the massive hound's shoulder. "This is Kevin, he's going to help us sniff out the grave." I motioned for Raven to give the hell-hound the journal to sniff, then I let Kevin loose in the graveyard.

His nose to the ground, he worked his way across every grave, thoroughly.

"You think he can really find it?" Raven asked. Kevin gave a low growl of irritation. I smiled.

"I know he can."

The hell-hound gave a pleased sounding chuff, and then paused, his body stiffening and the hair along his massive back standing on end.

Bending, I touched the soil. "It's been disturbed."

"What?" Jeremiah demanded. "By whom? This can't be..."

I ran my hands over it, feeling a tingle of magic. "Someone covered it up, but it has been disturbed for certain." I glanced at Raven, making sure not to catch his gaze fully. He approached and crouched beside me.

"Who would be looking for Georgie boy, too?" He ran a hand over the soil.

"That's the question of the day, isn't it?" I asked as I stood. "We're going to need shovels—"

Kevin let out a low, rumbling growl and stepped forward. With his giant paws tipped with three-inch claws, he began to claw at the dirt, flinging hunks of earth behind him.

Raven and I stepped back, clear of the flying dirt. Beside me, Jeremiah trembled.

"I'm sure this isn't seemly, and it's definitely not legal."

“You won’t get in trouble,” I said, trying to keep my tone soothing despite wanting to cuff the man upside the head for ramping the stress level up even more. “We’ll cover it all back up. No one will even know we were here. I promise."

Kevin kept digging, and Jeremiah kept shaking.

"I just think it would be better if maybe you came back during the daytime hours," he managed through chattering teeth, gathering the courage to sidle between me and the grave, reaching a hand toward Kevin's collar ever so slowly. "Mayhap with a warrant next time, or some sort of legal documentation—"

"Enough!" Raven snapped, clearly as over the melodrama as I was. "Be silent or I will silence you. Is that understood?"

Kevin's digging ceased as he let out a sudden yelp and stumbled like he'd been clubbed upside the head. And as for poor Jeremiah, we never did find out whether he understood Raven's directive or not, because his eyes went wide as he pitched forward. If I hadn't lunged to catch him, he'd have landed flat on his face. Not that my quick hands helped him any, due to the massive scythe buried between his shoulder blades.

I laid the priest onto the ground but didn't spare him

another glance. My gaze was locked on the shape rising from the hole in the ground.

"Raven..."

"I see it, Frostbite. Do me a favor and take a slow step back."

He stole in front of me, partially blocking my view as someone–some*thing*–crawled from the grave. A creature of darkness, a demon in its unholy form, wings and all faced us full on. Only "faced us" wasn't quite right. Because it had very little face left. No eyes, no lips, just a skull barely covered by crepey skin.

"What the fuck is it?"

The creature took one step toward us.

Kevin whimpered and whined, belly pressed firmly to the ground, as the creature spoke, his words in the high demons' tongue.

"I warned you not to disturb me again. Give me one reason not to kill you both where you stand."

CHAPTER 17
Raven

The threat toward Diana while I was in the fresh throws of our bond made me want to tear the fucker's throat out, but there was no point. I could scent not a drop of blood running through the creature's veins. No, this particular entity was of the undead variety. Which meant a torn jugular wouldn't work, more's the pity. And making eye contact to mind-fuck the thing was out of the question, what with it having no eyes. Until I figured out what it was capable of, and how to "kill" it, I would have to rely on my only other notable skill.

Charm.

"We didn't mean to disturb you, Sir George. We are just two desperate souls who've found ourselves in a bind that only you can help us with. We came to beg your counsel, and then the dog got away from us and started digging of his own accord—"

Kevin lifted his head at that, lips quivering in a low growl at the slander, but I couldn't be worried about the hound's tender feelings right now. I had to talk our way out of this mess and into George's good favor.

The creature wheezed out a laugh and then bent to yank its scythe from Father Jeremiah's back with a sticky snick as the wheeze developed into a deep, dry cough. "Being underground makes a body parched, that's for certain."

I could sense Diana standing up behind me and I held a hand up to stay her.

"Would you like me to get you some water?" I had no earthly idea how he would drink it, but it only seemed polite to offer.

"Flames, the bluer the better, are the only thing that could quench my thirst."

"I'll see what I can do...Actually, maybe we can trade favors. We need your help, as I mentioned."

"So you're not here to take a piece out of me?" he asked, empty eye sockets widening slightly. "I thought you'd come to cut me up like the others."

It was only then that I noticed that his bones were covered in what looked to be a hundred cuts, like he'd been chipped away, bit by bit.

His expression darkened as he glanced down. "Oh

my." He nudged at the fallen priest with his foot, as if expecting him to move. "That's unfortunate, then. Do you think he'll be alright?"

Diana and I shared a bewildered glance.

"I'm going to say no?" Diana replied, shaking her head grimly. "And while it is unfortunate, if you thought he was here to harm you, it's not really your fault, I guess. More like self-defense." She paused and cleared her throat. "You mentioned others had disturbed you. What others, George?"

He frowned. "We'll get to that soon enough. You've piqued my curiosity. If you aren't here to gain access to my magic, why are you here?"

"We need help finding a dragon," Diana said. "One took our friend, and we need a way to get him back. The fate of the world as we know it depends on it. Perhaps if we were armed with some kind of weapon, we could—"

George lurched forward suddenly, a shudder making his bones clack as he brandished his now bloodied scythe. Kevin jolted upright, and a flurry of barks split the air as he stared at something directly behind me without daring to advance. I whirled to see Father Mauricio approaching, his wrinkled hand holding a blade to our own Nicholas' pale throat. And the priest looked...weird. Wrong. Not at all like the annoying old man we'd met a short while before.

What was this fresh hell?

"I tried to hold my cards close to the chest, but I cannot allow this to continue any longer," Father Mauricio hissed, his eyes filled with something like madness.

I froze, brain whirring at a mile a minute as I tried to fit this insane sequence of events into a single, coherent picture.

"I'm sorry," Nicholas whispered. "Myrr saw trouble coming, so I came to help, and I—" He slammed his elbow into the older man's stomach mid-sentence, allowing the blade to slash part of his throat as he tore free.

The priest's face bulged, dark veins appearing at his temples, and his voice took on an otherworldly hollowness as he looked skyward. "By Lilis's grace, I command thee: rise, my army, *rise*!"

The moisture seemed to drain from the air in an instant as dozens of thin lines of black energy streaked into the ground from the priest's outstretched hands. His fingers writhed, moving and twisting at unnatural angles in a sickening imitation of a puppeteer. A moment later, dirt and grass exploded into the air as a skeleton still dressed in tattered clothes sprang from the ground to block Nicholas' path.

The rumbling of the ground beneath my feet told me that old Bones wasn't alone.

A sound wooshed through the air, and I spun, blocking the first blow from the now-possessed George's scythe with a half heartbeat to spare. My blade snaked forward in a blur, catching the dragonslayer in the chest, but he hardly seemed to notice. Bones clattered all around me, and I rolled out of George's scythe attack only to smack directly into a risen skeleton who'd been pulling free of the ground. Two more appeared at my sides, this time with a little more meat on them, and I decapitated one as I pulled back, assessing.

The priest's unholy incantations echoed through the night air, and at least a dozen corpses had already risen from their graves, with others climbing up before my eyes. Diana appeared at my side, several zombies hot on her trail, and her hand shot sideways, open and reaching.

My second sword was flying toward it before I'd even registered a thought, and I felt her catch it even as I turned to block an axe swing from a skeleton on the other side. His bones clattered to the ground as my blade caught him in the ribs, and each movement seemed to flow from the last as I leapt to Diana's side, deflecting a blow from George's scythe that'd been aimed at her neck.

And she had seen it coming, I realized, somehow knowing it as surely as if it was me myself who had seen it. Flesh squelched against my sword as I caught the next corpse with a stab to the cheek. Its head popped off like a bottle cap as I withdrew, rushing to slash at a pair of arms reaching from the ground to grab at Diana's legs. Kevin was right behind her, tearing the femur from another attacker, growling menacingly at the others.

Nicholas was surrounded as well and seemed to be holding his attackers at bay for the moment, but it was clear that we could not allow this to be a battle of attrition. For each corpse we cut down, two more seemed to rise. Nicholas' position was even more difficult to hold than our own.

George swung again and I charged forward, leaping cleanly over the strike and jamming my blade into his kneecap. He staggered, dropping the scythe as he reached to grab me, but I rammed my weight into his chest, sweeping his injured leg out from under him with my own. We slammed into the ground in a heap just as Father Jeremiah's risen corpse fell dead for the second time, just inches to my right. Diana's sword—my second sword—jutted from his chest.

I rolled to the side before George could attack again, shoving my blade further into his leg before pulling it free. I pulled out of his reach, watching him flail helplessly in my direction for a moment before striding away.

"Mauricio. We have to stop this madness where it starts," I grunted to Diana, though I knew that communication was unnecessary. Our blood bond had given us a far deeper connection than I'd realized. We cut our way through the sea of zombies as one, even more in sync than the two Vanators that'd given me such a hard time on the ship.

The priest grew louder still, controlling dozens of corpses like a team of marionettes, but we reached him before long. Nicholas had managed to escape his attackers, but hadn't retreated entirely. He fought skillfully, engaging enough to keep their attention but not enough to risk being surrounded. If I'd had time, I'd have been impressed.

Father Mauricio cursed as we approached, backpedaling quickly with his puppeteer's hands conducting wildly. I bared my fangs at him as Diana and I cut through a half dozen freshly-revived corpses. He could stall us a little longer, but we were closing in on him. The end was near.

His rumbling, hollow voice trembled just slightly as he beseeched the moon once again, "We must cleanse the world of evil before we can begin anew! In the name of the Dark Mother, I smite thee interlopers who dare interfere with our sacred plan!"

I dove into Diana on pure instinct as the beam of solid purple lightning took shape, scorching through the air where we'd been standing a moment earlier. The grass below withered and died, and I suppressed a gag as the scent of rot and decay filled the air. We shoved ourselves to our feet in unison and charged forward, keeping pace as we closed in on the dark priest.

Sweat poured down his face now, and his robe had parted to reveal a shockingly muscular chest. He couldn't have been a day under eighty, and all of my senses told me that he was human.

What did that mean?

My concerns only deepened when I caught sight of the tattoo on his left pectoral muscle. There were four of the swirling spirals with the spiked edges that marked him clear as day. The same as I'd seen on the neck of the Vanator. Motherfuckers were everywhere it seemed.

"Alive," I barked simply, knowing Diana would already have decided the same.

Energy gathered in Mauricio's fingers once again as he cried out to the sky in a last attempt to defeat us, but my blade found him before he could release it, shearing through his wrist with the sickening sound of metal against bone. His hand flopped to the ground in perfect unison with the other, cut by Diana.

He fell back, screaming curses and prayers to the one he worshipped, but to no effect. His hands were necessary to his magic.

"Gods be," Nicholas hissed, striding up from behind us. "That was terrifying."

"Carry him inside," Diana barked, gesturing to me. Her eyes met mine, and the horrified expression there was not lost on me. "We'll interrogate him just as soon as we stop him from bleeding out," she added, turning her head before we could lock gazes for long.

I sucked in a breath, striding over to grab the struggling priest. The fight had made it apparent that our bond was even stronger than we'd known. It had been useful, sure, but it was going to be a grueling couple of days that I would be happy to see the end of. The connection was almost as unsettling as this night had been.

I hefted the old man, ignoring his arms and the blood pouring from him, as he struggled against my grip. The scent of blood pricked at my nose, and I forced down the urge to feed. Whatever was in his blood, I didn't want any part of it.

"The Vanators shouldn't have access to this type of magic," I muttered as we strode toward the church. "How did they even know where to find it?"

"Vanators?" Nicholas asked, wiping at the blood on his already healing neck.

"Fucker has four of the spiked spirals. I would say he outranks any of the ones we captured. The marks on them faded. These look permanent."

"Captured?" Mauricio demanded as if he himself were not captured. "Those damned fools. Did they—"

He shut up as I tossed him roughly to the church's floor, and I strode quickly toward the bell that hung at the back, eyeing the rope. "We'll tie his wounds off with this, and then get some answers," I said, turning to Nicholas. "You're up. Before he bleeds out completely."

"I can...?" Nicholas asked, turning to Diana.

Her lip curled in disgust, but she nodded curtly. "We need to know everything, and we're in a hurry. He'll never choose to give us the answers, so we'll take them."

I tore the rope free of the church bell that hung nearby and turned around. The priest's eyes had rolled toward the ceiling. Thank the gods, no dark energy seemed to be gathering this time as he prayed.

"Oh, Dark Mother, I beg of you; look past my failure and bless me with your fiery embrace. I wish not to betray you."

Thunder cracked overhead, and I staggered back from a horrible vertigo as he leapt to his feet in a blur. A chill ran down my spine as a deep and primal terror surged through me. For just a moment, there was a presence, otherworldly and impossibly dark, in the room with us. Whatever it was, it was watching us. Like an apex predator stalking its prey. I could see every step the priest took. I wanted desperately to stop him, but, for the second or two that it lasted, my body simply wouldn't respond to any commands. I was frozen.

"The Dark Mother blesses me!" he called as he stumbled toward a large bowl of holy water, his final words echoing through the church as he dunked his head directly into it.

He writhed and twisted as he straightened, his face melting like wax into a horror of a man, more terrible than anything I'd seen in all my years. Then, he fell to the ground, dead. I spun, glancing at Diana and Nicholas who were still frozen in shock. Then, I glanced at the door, where a tiny silhouette had appeared.

"Well fuck a duck!" Myrr called as she strode into the church, crunching on an apple. "I didn't see *that* coming!"

CHAPTER 18
Diana

"We really need to work on your ability to follow directions," I murmured as we made our way back through the church out to the little graveyard. I was kinder about it this time, mindful of Myrr's feelings, but it needed saying, no matter how gently. The woman was going to get herself killed. She'd lived a long life and if that's what she wanted to do, she'd earned the right. But we needed her. Not just our little crew, the whole world.

"Can you just try to be a little more..."

"Obedient?" Myrr chirped, shrugging one, lopsided shoulder as she brushed past me. "I can try, but something happens inside me, even when I have the best intentions. It's like a little voice."

"And what does it say?" Nicholas asked.

"Mostly it says, 'these people ain't the boss of you, Myrr.' But," she turned to scowl at Nicholas, "Right now it's saying, 'tell that handsome young whippersnapper to mind his own fucking business. The adults are talking.'"

Either Nicholas had grown accustomed to the Oracle's insults, or he was too traumatized by recent events to care, because he didn't even flinch.

Myrr shoved the door open and stepped outside into the cemetery before letting out a low whistle.

"You guys did a real job on this place, huh? Can't imagine what service tomorrow is going to be like. Awkward, is my guess..."

I stepped out into the warm night air and winced at the scene laid out before us. She wasn't wrong. It was almost as gross out here as it had been inside. Not to mention it looked like someone had bulldozed the place. Bones and leathery body parts were strewn about the grass, gravestones upturned or smashed. In fact, if it wasn't for the groaning figure draped over the body of Father Jeremiah, gods rest his soul, it might've passed for a staged scene. Something to scare children on trick or treat eve or whatever it was humans called the odd little tradition where they dressed up as the very creatures they despised and vilified.

I scurried over to George, Kevin hot on my heels.

"Well that was wholly unpleasant," he muttered, clearly back to his normal self, normal for him at least. He used his bony arms in an attempt to sit up. "I've had my person molested by dozens of Vanators over the past few months, but being under the control of a necromancer was even worse, if you can imagine."

I couldn't even bring myself to glance at Raven, because I could imagine. We'd shared a blood bond for less than 24 hours, and I was already way past uncomfortable. Even while we'd fought, when all my energy and attention should've been on the task at hand, the connection had been constant. I was never *not* aware of Raven. Where he was, what he was doing, even how he was feeling to some degree. And I hated every second of it.

"At least we have some idea of what's been going on now. The dark entity, Dark Mother as Mauricio called her, wants to cleanse the world and is using the Vanators as her army. But how long has this been going on? Who else is a part of this plan?" Raven raked a hand over his face in frustration. "Fuck...it'd be a lot easier to get a handle on things if our prisoners would stop offing themselves."

"Lilis," I said. "The entity we face is named Lilis."

Everyone looked at me, but it was Myrr who asked. "How in the world could you know that?"

I gave her a nod. "She spoke through you, briefly. Long enough to give me her name. 'Queen to queen', as she said."

"And?" Raven prodded, as if he knew there was more

to that short conversation. I didn't see the point in keeping it from him.

I shrugged. "And she told me that she would see me dead."

"How about we defy her on that part, Frostbite?" Raven drawled.

That *would* be great. I was about to say so when a sudden snarl halted my reply.

"What the fuck, Diana?"

I turned to see Gabriel standing in the doorframe, his expression one of banked fury.

"I've tried to be nice to you because you're the Queen and I want to remain on good terms, but diplomatic relations do not extend to you coming to my island, destroying our churches, and murdering priests. I'm no fan of the Christians, but if you know anything of history, you'll know that they're a formidable enemy. Even worse than all that, though..."

He moved toward me and Raven stepped between us.

"You're going to want to back up there, my friend," Raven murmured, his fangs extending even as he spoke.

Gabe cocked his head like he was considering his next move, but then held up both hands.

"But, *worse* than all that, though," Gabe continued from where he stood, craning his neck to glare at me over Raven's broad shoulder, "You took my fucking dog without even asking? Unacceptable, Diana."

I gnawed at my lower lip, irritated with myself for feeling bad, but feeling bad nonetheless.

"Look, we didn't really have a lot of time, and I was desperate. See, Saint George was buried here," I jerked a thumb at the man himself, "and he is the key to getting through that dragon and finding Mav. We wouldn't have found George at all without Kevin. So he's kind of a hero."

The hound stepped close to nuzzle my neck and I gave his floppy ears a scratch.

"Still, I'd like to formally apologize..."

"Wow, this is new," Raven said, shooting me a look of disbelief.

"But also note once again, for the record, that I really had no choice."

"So, translation, 'sorry, not sorry'?" Gabe said with a short laugh.

"I'm the one who's sorry for interrupting here, but, as entertaining as this is, can we get on with it?" George interjected with a groan. "It's been a bit of a day, and I'm afraid I'm exhausted..."

Gabe let out a sigh and then nodded to Raven, who stepped back to let him pass.

"Saint George, eh?" Gabe asked, popping a squat in front of the grave beside me. "More like Satan George, am I right? I can smell the demon all over him. I can't wait to hear the story behind this one."

We quickly filled him in on everything, including the Vanators recent activities, what we'd learned about Lady Lilis, and Father Mauricio's words about their sacred plan to cleanse the world of evil. We also explained to George about the falling of the Veil and the current state of affairs in the world.

"Getting Maverick and the stone back is imperative if we want to avoid Armageddon," I finished with a grim shake of my head.

"And you, George," Gabe asked, "This isn't some trick? You truly have some way for them to find and defeat this dragon to get Maverick back. Assuming of course, that it hasn't eaten him yet."

George managed to shake his head weakly.

"She won't. She eats fish exclusively."

"She? Wait...are we talking about the very same dragon?" Raven demanded, hulking over us now like a gargoyle. A super sexy gargoyle...

Stop it and focus.

"But...you're Saint George," Nicholas said, incredulous, "The Saint George. Surely this isn't the dragon you were said to have slayed?"

"That's what they called me, yes. But I was more of a dragon whisperer of sorts. Once I realized that the creature was fairly harmless, I didn't have the heart to kill her. So I subdued her powers and kept mum. She still lives in a cave right here on the island, as far as I know." He turned his sockets on me, and I grimaced as a worm wove through the left one. "If you help me and promise not to kill her unless you've no other choice in self-defense, I will tell you where to find her and give you the tools to get your friend back."

"Not my friend," I corrected, "And help you, how?"

"These Vanators...they won't stop. I am a demon but I've also been dragon-touched, and have other powers that make me a bit of an anomaly. They've somehow figured out that if they grind my bones into a powder and consume it, they can absorb my strength. They're insatiable. One leaves, more come. They will continue to pick me apart like carrion, disturbing my slumber, week after week, until there's nothing but the tiniest morsel left. I've suffered in the in-between for centuries, certain I deserved it, but I've paid for my sins. Now I just want to reach the demon's eternal flame. You can give that to me." He turned to Gabe. "Or he can, at least."

Gabe stayed silent as I considered George's request, trying to think of a downside. No matter how I turned it, though, I couldn't see one. Worst case, he lied to us, and we were no worse off than before. And still, while Gabe had proved useful, demons were a cunning lot...

"Where did you say the dragon was now?"

George hesitated.

"We can't go in there like gangbusters without whatever you have hidden away, so telling us could hardly hurt."

He sighed. "Promise me you won't hurt her. That is the only way I will tell you."

There was no choice at this point. "We will do our level best, not to harm her."

George sighed heavily again. "I will take that. She is beneath Mount Aphrodite, on the other side of the island."

"Aphrodite is a live volcano," Gabe murmured. "A good hiding spot for a dragon if you don't want anyone to smell the sulfur and you like it hot. Lots of easy access to the sea as well."

And still...

I locked eyes with Raven and he nodded.

"Agree. Better safe than sorry."

I nearly let out a snarl at this most recent melding of the minds, but held back as I turned my attention toward Nicholas.

"Can you touch him to be sure we aren't falling for yet another trap as Raven did behind the pub yesterday?"

The little jab made me feel slightly better because I wasn't above being petty on occasion.

"I can," Nicholas said, making his way forward with hesitant steps.

I could hardly blame him. Getting all close and personal with what was essentially a zombie was probably not on his bucket list, but we all had to make sacrifices here.

Nicholas laid a hand on George's bony shoulder. For a long moment, he stood motionless, a puzzled expression etched on his face.

"I'm not getting anything. Maybe because he's technically dead—Oh!"

Watching Nicholas was like watching a movie unfold. His face gave everything, and whatever he was seeing, it was a doozy. By the time he spoke, my pulse was pounding so loud, I could hear it in my head.

"H-he tells the truth," Nicholas muttered, his throat thick with tears as he yanked his hand away and stumbled backward. "The dragon lives beneath the volcano, and he knows how to subdue her. Do as he asks."

My stomach roiled at the violation I'd asked Nicholas to commit, but even more so for the demon, George.

"I apologize for that. He won't tell a soul what he saw unless absolutely necessary. Nicholas, heard?" I called over my shoulder.

"Heard," he replied, his voice still raspy with emotion.

"I care not now that peace is close at hand," George said. "As for what you need, you have it already. You just didn't know how to read it. Take the journal to the volcano. Once you get there and locate Saldraenaen, the dragon, tear out the last sheet and fold it into the shape of a star. You'll know exactly what to do from there."

“Surely, you can do better than that,” I urged, knowing he was suffering, but loath to go away unprepared.

“Yet, just as surely, I’ve done more than enough?” he countered. “End it,” he pleaded, looking past me toward Gabe. Gabe glanced my way and I nodded reluctantly.

“I can do that," Gabe said.

The rest of us stepped back to give him room as he knelt in front of George. I wondered briefly whether we should leave and give them privacy, but then the Dragon Whisperer spoke.

"Please stay, all of you. I find myself not wanting to be alone in my last moments."

We all murmured our agreement and stood in place, waiting.

Gabe bowed his head and began to chant in the language of his people. I didn't know the meaning of much, but there was no mistaking the solemn reverence for the task. He was putting one of his own into the grave, and it mattered to him.

Another point in the demon's favor.

As his words grew faster, and more impassioned, the ground began to shake. Great, black wingtips exploded from the back of George’s shirt, unfurling into a glorious pair of wings spanning a dozen feet from tip to tip.

"Whoa," Myrr whispered, bumping me as she leaned in closer. "Cool."

Gabe seemed not to hear her as he pressed his thumb to the center of George's forehead and closed his eyes.

A crimson light began to glow from Gabe's heart, and then spread, flowing up to his shoulder, and down his arm, like a current of lava. When it shot from the tip of his thumb, it instantly ignited George's skull, enveloping it in flames.

"Thank you, my brother," he hissed, his mouth curved into a gruesome smile. "Thank you."

A second later, the rest of him caught and sparks shot high in the night sky as the fire consumed him. The flames went from red to ice blue, and within seconds, George was no more. All that remained was a pile of ash.

“I feel sort of bad for the guy,” Myrr said. “He’s been stuck here for a really long time, in limbo. Rather nice to see a happy ending.”

I wasn’t sure I’d call burning to death after being dug up and hacked to bits for weeks on end a ‘happy ending’, but I was trying to kick the whole bubble bursting habit.

I looked to Myrr and Nicholas, who was still very obviously shaken by whatever he’d seen of George’s past. I could hardly blame him. Even just watching this ageless ritual between the demons had my throat aching with unshed tears. There was no time to coddle myself or anyone else, though.

“We need to get out of here before the Vanators show up and realize George’s All You Can Eat Buffet is closed and figure out who's to blame. The two of you," I pointed at Nicholas and Myrr, "will stay behind. If we don't come back within three days, you can safely assume we likely aren't going to. You'll need to go back to the Territories and tell my brothers so they can figure out their next moves. Is that understood?"

"They should come back to The Wild Queen with me. They'll be safest there," Gabe said. "Vanators are much less likely to make a move with my hounds and all the guards in place."

I knew he was right, and given what he'd done to help so far, it seemed like I had little choice but to trust him.

"Alright."

"I didn't want to mention what with all that was going down, but you should know...Mount Aphrodite has been rumbling lately. Deep belly rumbles like I've never heard before. With the strange goings on with the weather and all, I'm not sure how safe it will be."

"Safe?" I said with a snort. "That ship sailed when we did. We have no choice, Gabe. And if the volcano is threatening to blow soon, we best go tonight."

I turned to Raven and he nodded. "Ready when you are, Frostbite."

That stupid fucking nickname was the bane of my existence. I made a mental note to put a stop to it ASAP on our travels. We'd be alone for hours, if not days, so at least it would give us something to talk about besides this thrum in my veins calling his name...

I turned on my heel, said goodbye to Myrr and Nicholas, and made for the church gate.

"Yeah, don't worry about this mess. Your buddy Gabe will take care of it. You guys just go right ahead," Gabe was muttering.

It took a second for me to realize that Kevin was trotting next to me. I chuckled and stroked his soft fur, my hardened heart giving a squeeze.

"Oh, no boy. Thank you so much for your help, but you need to stay here with your master."

"I'm not his master," Gabe called, pausing to pick up a skeleton arm and toss it into a pile of other bones. "I never really was."

I blinked at him, the words not computing as his lips curved into a sad little smile.

"He may seem sweet and passive, but hell-hounds, including Kevin, have no master. They have wards. And, for whatever reason, once you selflessly chose to save him, you became his."

CHAPTER 19
Raven

"You know, Frostbite," I drawled as we pushed through another dense section of jungle, "if I didn't know better, I'd say it's almost as if you are craving more time with me. Alone."

If there was one sure fire way to get her to lead—it was to piss her off.

Diana snorted, careful to take the branch from me so it didn't swing back and smack her in the face, but also careful not to touch me. "What makes you say that?"

"Choosing not to take Gabe's offer to use one of the vehicles to get us to the base of the volcano quicker. We'd be at the dragon's little hideaway by now. All this time together...I think maybe you want it."

Her growl made my pulse thrum a little faster, settling

in my groin and making me hard. Damned if that growl didn't make me want to pounce on her.

"That's not why I turned him down, you arrogant prick. We can't spook the dragon, she might take off with Maverick, or kill him, or goddess help us, what if she swallowed him and the gem whole? What then, mister you-can't-get-enough-of me? You going to climb down the dragon's gullet and retrieve the gem? Or wait till it takes a shit and dig through the piles?"

I laughed at her over my shoulder, causing Kevin to shoot a cross-eyed glare at me as he let out a low rumble. "All of that? You came up with all that instead of just admitting you like to watch me walk in front of you? Creative."

"Fine." She snapped a branch off and jabbed me in the ass with the pointed end. "I'll lead then. Get out of my way."

Feeling victorious, I gave her a mocking bow as she strode past me. I didn't like her bringing up the rear—for all the shit we were still in the dark about—and there was a lot of it—I knew one thing for sure. There was danger coming in from all directions, and I wanted Diana where I could see her. Kevin paced along beside her, the big white hell-hound scenting the air as we went along. Much as he didn't like me, I knew he'd protect Diana with his life, much the same as I would. It was all that mattered.

The tension in me eased, even as the weather around us began to shift again, the night sky deepening with sudden cloud cover.

Diana spoke over her shoulder, her irritation already seeming to fade as she grew thoughtful. "Raven...that dark mother, Lilis, that the priest Mauricio spoke about. It's the same entity that tried to kill Sienna and haunted her dreams...and she knows we are here."

Lightning lit up the night sky, high above the jungle tree tops, a distant rumble of thunder announcing the storm that approached.

"Seems like it," I said as we started to slide down a gentle slope, the ground soft under us as the heavy rain loosened the soil. "We know that the Vanators are taking strides to become stronger, harder to kill and using magic they shouldn't know how to use. We know that a necromancer was working with them—again, something that shouldn't be, and yet is. And there was a...presence in the graveyard that felt..." I didn't want to say familiar, because that would mean admitting that yes indeed, whatever dark presence was out to end the world had taken note of our attempts to stop her.

I sighed, hating the implications. We hadn't even identified the second key yet, and already we were fucked. Our entire quest—not just this one to retrieve Maverick, but the end goal...to find all the keys—would be fraught with danger. The changing weather, the shifting tides, all that had been bad enough. Now, instead of just Mother Nature wanting us dead, we had this evil bitch Lilis after us too. But after all that had happened, there was no point in fooling myself any longer.

"Now that she knows we're actively trying to put the Veil back in place, I think she decided to widen the scope of her attacks and make herself known."

As if my words were the trigger, the air grew colder, and the slope beneath us suddenly dropped, a mudslide triggered by an unseen force. There was no warning, just the land disappearing beneath us. Laughter in the air that belonged to neither of us.

"Raven!" Diana screamed as she was sucked down the now not so gentle slope, tumbled over and over. I bolted after her, barely keeping my own balance, not only because of the heaving ground, but because of what I was seeing.

It was as if an unseen entity attacked Diana, her body jerking, thrown into the air by...nothing. And yet it was happening. Kevin snarled and lunged, but there was nothing he could grab hold of.

"Hang on, Frostbite." I charged down the slope and dove after Diana, grabbing her and rolling her body under my own, acting as a shield between her and her attacker. The first blow was to the middle of my back, and I grimaced, air whooshing out of me.

Diana blinked up at me, her face covered in mud, lashes wet and eyes wide. “What the fuck is that?”

“I think we called her out too many times,” I let out a grunt as another blow landed.

I tucked her tight to my body to wait out the onslaught, but Diana had other ideas.

“Let me go!”

“No! Hold still, Diana!”

Her eyes locked on mine as I absorbed blow after blow, mind on the end game. Lilis was not all powerful. If she could’ve killed us directly, she’d have done it by now. So I hung on tight.

“Raven, you have to let me go, the bond will deepen!” Diana squirmed under me.

“She’s not done yet,” I grunted as I took a shot to my ribs that made them groan. Why she wanted at Diana specifically…that was a question that dug at me. I knew that my Frostbite was a queen, even without the crown. Because every blow was meant to pull me from Diana. To leave her defenseless. Diana wasn’t Sienna. She wasn’t a key.

So why, then? Just because we were searching? Did this Lilis realize what a threat Diana was? That had to be it.

One more, massive shot battered my ribs, like an anvil being shot from a cannon. It nearly tore Diana from my arms and had me gasping for breath.

"Diana!" I breathed her name. "I can't hold on for much longer!"

She gasped. "The blade, at my low back!"

I didn't see how a blade was going to help at this point, but I shoved my hand under her and pulled a leather sheath out. I held tight to it and Diana yanked the blade free, and held it up like a torch.

A bluish light emanated from the blade, lighting up the darkness that had surrounded us. There was a pulse of magic, and the blade hummed with a vibration even I could feel.

A screech lit the air, and the blows stopped, but I waited a moment longer.

Wincing, I pushed off Diana, struggling to my feet.

"What is that?"

Diana stood and took the leather sheath back from me, extinguishing the light off the blade. "Maverick brought it out of the demon lands when he escaped."

"Right...but..."

"Not here." She shook her head. "Maybe later. Gabe told me to keep it quiet. I'm just glad I had it on me."

She'd talked to Gabe about the weapon? I didn't like the spurt of jealousy that burned off some of the ache.

I pulled my shit together. "Fine. We'll talk about the knife another time. But I think we have to assume *she* can hear us at points. Bringing her up seems to almost call to her." Another time I would have made a quip about female emotions, but my ribs already felt like they'd been pulverized. I had no desire for another ass-kicking so soon.

Diana wiped the mud off her face. "Why did you do that—"

"I am here to protect you, Diana. No matter the cost. In the scheme of things, my life is not important. Yours is. The fate of the world is riding on you." I motioned for her to lead on. I glanced at the big hell-hound. "Thanks for nothing, Kev."

He huffed in my general direction and brushed past me to get to Diana. At least he had his priorities straight. But Diana still stared at me as if I'd sprouted a second head.

"We should get going, Frostbite." The use of the nickname I'd given her, that she clearly disliked, snapped her out of whatever stupor the encounter had caused and she started walking.

I settled into following her again through the deep jungle. The vines, trees and bushes only got bigger as we went on, the rain heavier. But that wasn't what stopped us. A crack of lightning snapped down at our feet, blasting the small patch of ground between us. We were all blown backward, in three different directions. Kevin let out a low growl, but Diana didn't so much as squawk.

Apparently, Lilis was not done trying to scare us off this path—which only confirmed that it was indeed, the right one.

Fucking hell.

"Diana, we need to find a place to wait this storm out."

Punctuating my words, another bolt of lightning snapped down to my left, the heat and light scorching me. I stumbled sideways, felt a pair of hands on my elbow and then she was dragging me along.

"Kevin, find us some shelter!" she yelled over the next ear-splitting boom of thunder.

I blinked to clear my vision, but as I tried to focus, there was nothing but a sea of white. I'd been looking almost directly at the place where the flash of lighting had struck.

Shit.

"I can't see!" I yelled, tightening my hold on her hand.

"Just don't let go!" she yelled back. "Don't let go."

Our fingers locked and I let her pull me along. I kept my eyes closed, but even so the bright flashes of light hit around us, so close, so very close that one wrong misstep and we would both be toast.

"What happens to one, would happen to both. That is the way of a bond between vampire and their fated blood mate."

The words were that of my mother, and I had not heard her voice in my head for a hundred years.

Not the time, Ma, not the damn time.

And yet with my eyes closed and my hand clutched

by Diana, there was nothing for me to do but replay the words of the woman who'd been my mother, protector, and friend until her death. Words I'd forgotten until now.

The waves crashed over the sides of the boat as we sailed away from the Territories. Away from the mess I'd made.

"I know you saved her," Ma said, her arm around my shoulders. "But...did you know that it was Edmund you faced off against? You tried to kill the Crown Prince. If Evangeline hadn't interceded and blocked the guards view of you, you'd be dead now. Executed."

I hunched narrow shoulders against the question. "Yes... I knew."

"Then why do it? I'm not saying you shouldn't have, but there is a time and a place to put lives on the line—"

"Because I had to!" I blurted out, my young voice cracking under the weight of my actions. We were on the run. A serving maid and her son, thrust away from all we'd known because I'd nearly killed the Crown Prince. "I had to," I whispered. I couldn't find any other words, I didn't understand myself what had overtaken me that day on the beach.

"Here!" Diana tugged hard on my hand, dragging me to the left. "In here."

I put a hand out to guide my way and dared to open my eyes.

Kevin had found us a cave, about ten feet deep, four

feet across, and just high enough for me to stand. "My sight is back."

"Good. Then you can help me start a fire."

I turned to see her shivering, a bruise blooming across her right cheek, a slash from a branch above that same eyebrow. Wide frosty eyes stared up at me, tugging at something I did not want to look at inside of me.

Frosted eyes stared up at me from under the water between the waves.

I walked past her to the back of the cave, shaking my head, banishing the strange thoughts. "There is some tinder here." I focused on getting the fire going. Outside, the lightning crashed and boomed, the rain came down sideways hard enough to drive us to the back of the cave.

I got a fire going quickly, driving back some of the dark and cold of the storm.

Kevin curled up next to Diana and she leaned into him like he was a giant pillow. I sighed and sat with my back to the wall and closed my eyes.

Silence fell—or as silent as it could be with the electrical storm raging outside our cave.

"Thank you," Diana said softly. "Are you okay?"

"Fine," I swallowed hard. "You should rest, I'll keep watch."

We hadn't packed for a long journey; Gabe had said it would be at best five hours there and back. But we hadn't counted on getting waylaid.

Diana's breathing deepened and I sat there, staring out into the darkness of the jungle, the past crowding around me. Forcing me to pay attention. Forcing me to look at what I'd been running from my whole fucking life.

"My son, you are not in trouble." Ma stroked a hand over my head, settling it on my shoulder. "You have always had the heart of a protector; from the moment you were born."

I shivered and leaned into her, letting my mother take the burden of guilt from me. Because I knew we'd had to leave because of what I'd done. Our lives would not be easy from here on out. "What if he dies?"

"Oh, I'm sure they will make sure he lives. He's the Crown Prince, after all. They won't want to let it out though that a servant boy beat him to a pulp. They will want him to look strong, fierce. A proper future king." Her hand made small circles between my shoulder blades, soothing my fears. "Tell me everything, Slo—Raven." She swallowed hard.

They'd had to change my name. Because if anyone came looking, they would be looking for a boy named Sloan. Not Raven. They'd cut my hair short, and my mother had a tattoo pressed into the left side of my chest. A mark of the mainland vampire lord that we were going to. A huge twisted tree with the root system spreading outward. To try and hide who I truly was—just in case anyone should remember who had attacked Edmund. She bore the same mark now, her own hair cut and the color changed.

I looked up at her. "She was so little. He was holding her under the water."

She nodded at me to go on. Licking my lips, I told the tale. "I saw her eyes, Ma. Frosty, like the first snow in winter. I just knew...I couldn't leave her to him."

My mother stared down into my face. "I understand that, but I need you to tell me why Raven. Why this girl? Why this moment? Because you could have just stopped him. We both know that. But you didn't just stop him. You attacked him like you were possessed by something else. The guards struggled to pull you off him, even once he'd stopped fighting. Your fangs had dropped, and...I was there, Raven. You lost control. If it was not for Evangeline intervening, you would have been sentenced to execution. She says that Edmund did not see you, and the guards have had their memories of you wiped. Everything we do now is a precaution."

I was shaking, the knowledge that I had ruined our lives heavy on me. "I know."

"Why then did you do it?"

I couldn't tell her. And yet I had a feeling she already knew the truth. A truth that, at thirteen, I couldn't understand.

"I had to protect her," I whispered. "I...had to."

My mother cupped my face, keeping me from looking away. "There will come a day, Raven, when you will have to face it head on. Until then, the memory will bury itself. But your soul recognized something you couldn't in that moment."

Fear laced my thoughts. Was I mad? A monster? I'd seen what was left of Edmund, and was shocked that the other boy would live. "What did it recognize?"

Her smile was soft and sad. "You found her, and the moment your soul understood who she was, there was nothing that could ever change it. From this day forward, there can be no other for you."

I jerked out of the memory, as if I'd been dreaming. At some point, I'd slumped to the floor, a warmth on my left, the smell of Diana sinking into me. The truth sinking into me.

I should have jerked away, should have run from this woman who'd found me in her sleep even now. From across the cave she'd made her way to me. Her body tight to mine. The bond between us hummed and danced, crackling through me like the storm outside.

A part of me flipped the fuck out and I struggled to breathe. Because this could not be happening. Not here. Not now. Certainly not with Diana. And yet the longer I sat there *feeling* Diana, as if she were the part of me that had been missing my whole life...fuck me. I couldn't deny it.

My whole body shook, not from the cold, but from the understanding that crashed over me—a truth that deep down I'd known. There would be no other for me now. This was what my mother had been trying to tell me —that once I realized, once I understood what—and who Diana was to me—that was it for me. The finality of it sank into my bones, and with one last miserable attempt to deny it. "This is not happening." I whispered to myself.

But those words did nothing to stop the feelings, or the desire to protect her. I could fight it, but what good would that do me? Not a damn lick of good.

So I did the only thing I could. I let it come, let the bond wash over me and embraced it.

Then, and only then, I reached for my Frostbite and drew her closer...let the bond between us deepen. Resistance was futile.

I would do what I had to do to keep her. Lucky for me, memories of my mother were not done with me yet.

"But, Mother... What if she doesn't choose me back?"

My mother's eyes closed. "Then what is left of your life will seem hollow. You will have to prove yourself to her, for if she is your match, she will be as fierce and strong as you to the core of her. And just as stubborn."

Fierce possession rolled through me. "I will fight for her if I must."

"I know you will, my son. I know you will."

Kevin curled up tight to Diana's other side, his eyes finding mine in the dark, almost as if he could read my thoughts. He gave a soft huff and I nodded.

"She can't know it, or she will resist out of sheer stubbornness, but I will. I will fight for her, my friend. And this is a battle I will win."

Because there was no other choice. I had finally accepted the truth.

A life without Diana by my side was no life at all.

CHAPTER 20

Diana

If I was being brutally honest, safe was not something I'd felt in a very, very long time. The memories I had of my life in the Vampire kingdom were shadowed with fear, and pain. My life in the werewolf keep had been dangerous from the beginning because of what I was. And because of what I became. And while I'd always known my father would fight for me, there had always been a threat waiting for me around every corner—safety had never been something I'd known.

So how, here deep in the jungle, being chased by Lilis, an enigmatic, evil bitch, while we were hunting a dragon of all things...could I feel safe?

My hand splayed across a broad chest, fingers curling as I woke from the deepest slumber I'd had in...forever.

Blinking, I realized that I'd made my way across the cave to wrap my body around Raven.

Goddess above, this blood bond was going to last forever if we did not get some space between us. It had even created an illusion of safety of all things! With him, a man who'd been clear from the start that he did not want this bond either.

And yet...I found myself looking at his face, really looking at his face as he slept, taking each piece of him to my mind, memorizing him.

Dark lashes against pale cheeks, one fang hanging out as he gave a soft snarl in his sleep. It shouldn't have been adorable, it really shouldn't have but...the urge to reach up and touch his cheek, to turn his face to me was so very strong.

I didn't like how the blood bond made me feel—like I belonged with him, like he would be the man to stand by me through all the darkness and hard parts of my life. When I knew there was no such thing in this world. Men were fickle, they were liars and they would take as they pleased with no concern to a woman's heart. I shoved myself away from him, overcome by a sudden onslaught of emotions I didn't like—weakness and pain were not something I needed right now. Ever, really, but especially right now. Yet they crowded around me, clamoring for my attention.

Raven gave a grunt and was on his feet. "What is it?"

I had my back to him as I struggled to get control of my emotions that had nothing to do with a heat, nothing to do with anything but the broken pieces of my past—of my heart, if I was being honest. I shook my head. "I thought I heard something, is all."

Raven made his way outside, leaving me alone in the cave which was just fine. I drew in a long slow breath, forcing my heart to slow. This was ridiculous. It *had* to be the blood bond. I fought to get angry, to let the rage of being tied to Raven burn away the fears and loss of the past coming back to haunt me.

Kevin butted his head under my hand, lifting it so I had no choice but to pet the top of his head. "Thanks."

He gave a deep huff, then followed Raven out of the cave. I frowned after the hell-hound. He'd made it clear he didn't like Raven, yet now he followed him. What was that about?

I scrubbed a hand over my face and took a step toward the cave opening, then another and another. With each step, I pushed my fears and emotions further away until I could look at Raven and just see a vampire who was as forced to be near me as I was to be near him.

Mutual dislike.

Mutual desire to be away from one another and to break the blood bond as soon as possible.

“We should get moving,” Raven had his back to me. “While the weather is quiet. We can’t be far from the volcano now.”

Kevin sat next to him, staring out in the same direction that Raven did. “Do you see something?”

“I think the top of the mountain.” He pointed as I drew close to him. “There, as the wind blows and the trees sway, you can see the very crest of it.”

I leaned closer, trying to see and he drew away as if I smelled bad. In fact, the thought was so clear that I lifted an arm and checked. “Do I smell?”

“No. I just am aware that the blood bond deepened last night when you latched onto me, and I am also aware that you will want to blame me for that, as if I magicked you closer to me in your sleep.” He glanced at me, then away so fast that I almost missed the fear in his eyes. Almost.

I opened my mouth to speak, but he beat me to it.

“I know we both wish the blood bond to ease as quickly as possible,” he said. “Let’s go. Kevin, why don’t you lead with that nose of yours?”

“He won’t listen—”

But I’ll be damned if Kevin didn’t trot out ahead of us to do Raven’s bidding.

“What did you do to him?” I demanded, squinting suspiciously.

“Nothing. We came to an agreement. We are both

protecting you. Now get in the middle of the line." Raven pointed and there was no teasing, no careful flirting. Just all business.

"You seem...different today," I said.

"Clarity of purpose is not something I've ever felt, until this last night," Raven said as he fell in behind me.

I thought he'd explain what he meant, but he clammed up after that, leaving me to my own thoughts that fought to spiral out of control. Desire. Pain. Loneliness. Grief. Loss. Need.

I focused on Raven, pushing my own emotions aside as best I could.

I could sense him behind me as I had in the graveyard when we'd found the undead. I could feel the ache in his lower back, the twinge across his ribs. "You're still hurt, from yesterday."

He grunted. "I'm healing. It would be faster if I had... but it does not matter. I'll be fine. I heal faster even than you."

I wanted to roll my eyes at him. "You think so? You believe I retain nothing of my vampire blood or abilities?"

Where the hell had that come from? Never in my life had I ever tried to convince someone that I had any vampire blood in me.

"Do you?" he asked the question quietly, as if he didn't quite want to.

I shrugged, hating that I'd started this line of discussion. I pushed through a thick set of ferns, still drenched with rainwater. "Nicholas seems to think so. And while I made the change to werewolf many years ago…I still feel the sun at times, and it makes me flinch. As if it knows I am not…all wolf."

He was quiet for a few minutes. "What do you remember, about the day that Edmund tried to kill you at the beach?"

I stopped and looked at him. "Why?"

He shrugged and looked past me, his brow furrowing. "It is what started you on the path to become a werewolf, and I wonder about the servant that saved you. What happened to him."

"It was a woman," I said, "or so I was told. She was given a great deal of money and sent out of the Territories, with her son. To be kept quiet that Edmund had ever tried such a thing. Even then they protected him." A mistake that we all knew nearly cost the Territories their tentative peace.

Raven's eyes darkened. "Is that so?"

"I have no memory of that day, Raven, I was a toddler," I found myself wanting to smooth away whatever caused his face to darken. "So I tell you only what I myself know, which is very little. What Evangeline was able to tell me when I was old enough."

He gave a slow nod. "Of course, Evangeline would have told you that."

"Why do you want to know?"

We were walking again, him just to the right of me, now that the path widened a little. The urge to reach out and take his hand was strong, and as soon as I thought it, he stepped a little further away.

It was smart, good. The right thing to do.

But damned if it didn't cut at a part of me, I didn't like to admit hurt when he rejected me.

Rejection was a bitch, no matter who handed it out.

"I remember a different story, one we heard in Seattle," he said. "One where another boy saw what Edmund was doing, and pulled him off you."

I smiled at the thought of a young lordling fighting for my life, when I'd been so little and helpless. "He would be a hero then, wouldn't he? I wish that was the true story."

Raven laughed. "Well, the rest of the story I heard was that the boy beat Edmund so badly, he nearly killed him. Had to be dragged off by guards and was summarily executed for the damage caused to the Crown Prince."

My throat closed. "That can't be...true."

"You think not? Edmund was the heir apparent," Raven said. "There are many, many people who have been killed, or had their lives destroyed because of him and his actions. You know that firsthand."

My eyes welled with unexpected tears. "But to kill a boy, one that saved me? Surely that..." I wanted to say that it surely would not be the case, but I knew better. We both did.

He sighed. "How would it be, Frostbite, to have a boy that was obviously stronger, and more dangerous than the Crown Prince? One that was not afraid to stand up to him. It would not do at all. Best to be rid of a boy like that."

An unexpected tear slid down my cheek, because I could almost see it now, a young vampire lord, leaping to my defense. Rescuing me from my own brother.

And losing his life because of one act of compassion. Because he chose not to look the other way.

I wiped the tear away. "If that is a true story, then I grieve for that boy."

Raven grunted as if I'd punched him in the belly. "Perhaps he was meant to be your one and only."

I gasped and turned on him, every fear I'd had about finding a mate bubbling up. My father's words. My inability to connect with anyone.

Find a mate.

Make an heir.

But there had never been anyone that had drawn me to them, except...Maverick. I would not count Raven, the blood bond had obviously been in play from the beginning, when he'd drank from the keep's stores.

"You are a bastard," I growled. "How dare you say that?"

He bowed at the waist. "As always, I am your bastard to command."

I wanted to slap him, to make him take the words back, but Kevin interrupted us with a deep woof.

We both turned and it was only then I realized how close I stood to him, my body seeking his out even when I was furious with him.

The path opened before us, and the base of the mountain—check that, volcano—was less than a mile away by my quick estimation.

"We'll be there in thirty minutes," I said. "Less if we pick up the pace."

Kevin trotted out in front of us, and I followed him at a jog.

As much as I heard Raven's footfalls behind me, I felt him at my back. The urge to fuck him senseless still lay under my skin, but his words had struck at something in me. A need to know if his story was true.

And so much pain if it was.

Was there a boy that had saved me all those years ago? Had that boy been killed? My heart cracked at the thought and the years of loneliness that had eaten at me...what if they were because that boy had been the one? The one that matched me in every way. The sob that worked up my throat was painful to swallow back down.

I had to focus on the here and now, and yet that was part of the problem. Because Maverick was ahead of us and he'd called to me—maybe he'd run, and he'd stolen something of mine, but he'd still called to me.

And that part of me that wanted a mate in truth had never given up hope that he was out there. Whoever he was.

Kevin slowed ahead of me, lowering his body to the ground, a whine deep in his throat.

"Down," Raven snapped, tackling me to the ground and rolling us under the cover of a stand of huge ferns. He stared down the path, and I followed his gaze.

At the base of the volcano, the dragon crawled out of a hole that I'd not seen. It sniffed the air, tongue flicking out and around as it paused at the entrance. The scales were the deep green and gray of the picture from Jeremiah's book. But the belly was lighter in color, almost white, and smooth like a fish.

Apparently satisfied with what it found, it made its way around the base of the rumbling volcano, and slid into the water, gone with barely a splash.

"Get off me!" I jabbed my elbow into Raven's chest, driving him off. "We have to hurry."

I bolted forward, Raven and Kevin right with me as we raced toward the opening. The gods were looking on us favorably to give us an opening of this magnitude. I was not about to spit a gift horse in the eye.

We reached the entrance and stared down into a hole

that seemed to go straight down. But I could see water, could hear gentle waves inside.

"A cenote," Raven said. "Makes sense for a water dragon."

"Cenotes usually are a part of a cave system, right?" I asked, mostly because I was nervous. Cave diving was not something I'd ever done, and the water could kill me as surely as it could kill any other creature.

"Yes. But we might not have to dive..." Before I could tell him to let go, he took hold of my hand and yanked me to his chest. "Hang on, Frostbite."

I yelped as he leapt for the hole in the ground, dropping us into the darkness. I wasn't afraid of water exactly; I enjoyed a swim here and there. But I didn't much like heights either. It was a shitty combination.

We fell and I clung to him until we hit the water together, crashing through the crystal-clear pool and plunging deep.

Raven didn't let me go, not right away. He held me there, with him, under the water, his eyes finding mine. As if he were searching for something. My hair floated around us, the light filtering in through the opening above sent sunbeams down in shafts, brilliant bars of light.

He finally released me and we kicked to the surface, the moment broken.

Kevin bobbed to the surface beside me and paddled closer, my loyal companion.

"Hello? Is someone there?"

That voice echoed out through the cave, making it hard to pinpoint. Even so, it struck a chord in me. I'd know his voice anywhere.

"Maverick?" I called out, hoping I hadn't lost my mind.

"Yes, it's me. I'm here! Shit, get me out before she comes back!"

I couldn't believe he was really here. The thought was distant, far behind the need to get Maverick and get the hell out.

"Seems we found him," Raven drawled, and it was like watching a mask settle into place. For a few minutes, I think I saw the real Raven. Or as real as he would allow anyone to see.

"We're coming. Keep calling out!" I said as we reached the edge of the cenote.

Following the sound of Maverick's voice was no easy thing. Trying to find his scent was not a lot better. It was as if he'd been dragged through every cave to mask his true location. That or his scent was blowing through the cave system.

Minutes ticked by as we moved as fast as we could. There were shafts of light here and there, breaking up the total darkness I'd expected.

The ground rumbled and the mountain above us let out a belch that had me reaching for the sidewalls. A wave of heat rolled toward us; the air heavy with toxic fumes from the lava that was bubbling above us.

Raven coughed. "If we don't find him quickly, the fumes alone will kill him."

Panic clawed at me, and I picked up the pace. "Mav?"

Raven stiffened at the nickname.

"Here. This way, I think." Raven turned to the right and then we were out into another huge cenote. The pool was larger than the first, but the openings above it were not big enough for a dragon. Across the miniature, underground lake was a massive rib cage, the stripped bones of some ancient mammal, the size of a truck. And inside of said rib bones?

A man I hadn't seen for nearly sixty years. I expected him to be old, to be frail and on death's bed, as any human would be. What I saw though, made no sense. His hair was still long, braided here and there. His light brown facial hair had grown in the few days that he'd been captured. More than that though, he was still young. Almost as young as I remembered him. My heart was pounding, and as much as I hated it, that same draw I'd felt all those years ago?

It was still there. Demanding I save him, demanding I help him.

"Maverick?"

"Diana?" He gripped the bars of his bony prison and stared across the cenote at me. "It...it can't be. I must have died and finally found my way back to you. The gods have given me my only wish...to look into your beautiful eyes one last time."

Raven snarled and stepped between us. "Yes. I agree. One last time, motherfucker."

CHAPTER 21
Raven

We were able to get around the cenote on foot, and I made sure I was between Diana and Maverick when we reached the thief. Perhaps I deliberately blocked her view.

"Raven, stop that," Diana growled, trying to shove me out of the way. But I wouldn't be moved. I was rooted there, like the tree etched into my chest. A quaking-with-fury tree, locked in a battle of wills with this Maverick character.

"It's just the bond making you...us feel this way," Diana murmured, tugging my arm more gently now, switching gears, using honey instead of vinegar. "We need to get Mav out of here. That's what we came to do. Not kill him."

Mav. Her easy use of the affectionate nickname made me want to break shit.

Mostly, *Mav*'s face.

"Like, now. Before the dragon scents us and we're in serious danger."

I still didn't budge.

"Okay, before *I'm* in serious danger," she pressed.

That did the trick and I backed away slowly. Not much, just a foot or so, but enough for her to speak to Maverick face to face.

"Are you injured?" she demanded, looking the thief up and down. He wasn't bleeding anywhere, or I'd have smelled it, but now that the red haze of fury obscuring my vision had cleared some, I could see that the guy was definitely looking rough around the edges. "Can you walk out of here on your own, or will we need to carry you?"

"I'm alright. Just hungry and exhausted," he said, reaching for Diana's hand before shooting a glance my way and thinking better of it.

Not as dumb as he looked, then. Good for him. He might live through this after all.

"She's off hunting for fish. She's usually gone another hour or so, but as soon as she gets back, she'll come here straightaway to bring me some as well, not that I can stomach it raw. Can you use your blades to cut through the bone?"

"Why not just lift it up?" I snapped.

"Not possible. It must weigh a thousand pounds—"

Maverick broke off and leapt back, releasing his hold on the bone cage as I took hold of two ribs and hefted it off the ground.

"Nobody ever taught you to lift with your legs there, Swindler?"

He gaped at me as I jerked my head impatiently. "Well don't just fucking stand there, crawl on out."

He scrambled forward and shimmied through the space I'd made. It was only the fate of the world combined with Diana's warning glare that kept me from letting it drop on him halfway through. Once he was clear, I lowered the carcass to the sandy cave floor with a thud.

"This way," I said, prepared to head back out the same way we'd come.

Diana shook her head and held up a hand. "Wait." She turned to Maverick. "The gemstone you stole from my father. Do you have it on you?"

"I did. It hung from a chain around my neck, but the dragon took it. I actually think that's why she took me. She likes shiny things, she made that clear—she can speak to your mind, it's...draining. She has a whole trove of treasures that she sleeps beside." He paused for a long moment, and stared at Diana, searching her face. "Look, about the gem, I know it was wrong to steal it, and I'm so sorry. I was a different person back then—"

"Can it, Romeo," I snarled, slashing a hand through

the air. "Stick to the here and now. Which way to the shiny stuff?"

Maverick snapped his mouth shut and motioned toward a tunnel to our right. "Follow me."

I let Diana fall into line behind him, Kevin took the spot after her, and I brought up the rear, senses engaged and on high alert for the dragon to return.

A short ways into our walk, the tunnel took a sharp turn and a moment later, light spilled in as we stepped into an open cavern. In the corner, a pile of leaves and brush made up what looked to be a bed large enough to fit a yacht. Diana and Kevin skidded to a stop as one.

"How...how big is this thing?" she hissed. “From the hill, I didn’t think she was as big as our Hunters.”

"Really fucking big," Maverick replied gravely. "She doesn't seem to be aggressive except when I try to escape, but I don't think she realizes her strength either. If she turned and hit you with that tail—" he sliced his finger from one side of his neck to the other. "You're not waking up from that."

"Maybe you're not, Meatbag, but I'm pretty sure Diana and I would be fine."

Maverick turned and shot me an assessing look, a cocky smile playing at his lips. "I thought it was Swindler...or Romeo, was it? I'm all for nicknames, Bloodsucker. But let's pick one and stick with it, yeah?"

I was on him before he finished his next blink, fangs

exposed and six inches from his face as I stared down at him.

"You know the saying 'don't poke the bear'?" I asked, my tone barely above a whisper.

His Adam's apple bobbed as he swallowed hard. "I'm familiar with it, yes."

"Well imagine if this particular bear was immortal, and could tear your arm off and beat you to death with your own fist, then drink you dry and leave you nothing but an empty husk."

"I'll admit, it doesn't sound pleasant..."

To his credit, he didn't shrink away, but he wasn't looking quite as cocky, either, his face on the pale side.

Progress.

"Act accordingly," I replied, releasing him and stepping back.

"Um, if the two of you are done measuring dicks, we'd better get searching..." Diana drawled, pointing to something behind us.

I turned to see, and let out a muffled curse when I caught sight of a literal mountain of stuff. And stuff was the perfect description. Yes, there were gemstones, big and small. Gold coins, silver necklaces, copper chalices, anything you could think of. But there was also just as much trash mixed in. Mounds of sea glass in every color, wads of tin foil, broken mirror shards. This creature was nothing more than a massive magpie, for gods' sake.

"I don't know how we're going to even find it before she gets back..." Maverick said just as the dagger at my hip suddenly began to shake and rattle. A second later, it shot across the room on its own and buried itself in the top of the pile, followed by Diana's, so that the bejeweled ends stuck out and were visible.

"Well that's handy," he observed with a nod, seemingly unfazed by the turn of events. He had clearly been up close and personal with otherworldly magic before, which explained why he didn't look a day over thirty despite his age.

I sprinted over and scaled the first ten feet of Mount Shiny Shit until I was perched right beside the hilt of the dagger. It took a minute or so of pawing around, but soon enough, I came up with the gemstone in hand.

"Got it."

"Perfect. Let's get the hell out of here before—"

An unholy screech echoed through the cavern, and my stomach clenched. Could we catch just a single fucking break?

I pocketed the jewel and chain and my dagger, then leapt back down to the ground just in time to see the dragon barreling in, full speed. For a second, I was rendered motionless in sheer awe of her size. She was like a double-decker bus, and fierce as anything I'd ever seen—as fierce as any Hunter we'd encountered, even without the wings. Covered with spikes from her head, down her spine all the way to her tail, she sported a pair of horns that made her look like some sort of demon dinosaur from hell.

Kevin clearly agreed because while he didn't leave his post by Diana's side, he dropped to the ground and showed his belly in surrender.

The creature skidded to a sudden stop in the middle of the space, great chest heaving, smoke pouring from her nostrils.

I locked eyes with Diana, who held up a hand as I reached for my sword.

She was right. If we could handle this without bloodshed, it would be best. Not to mention our promise to George. Judging by the raw, wild fury in the animal's emerald green eyes, though, that was looking unlikely.

"Hello," Diana called, her tone gentle but loud enough to be heard over the breath sawing in and out of the panicked animal's lungs.

The dragon whipped her head toward Diana and lifted her head to scent the air, her great nostrils flaring. Her eyes narrowed as she closed the distance between them in two great strides.

Fuck it. That was too close. I drew my blade and was about to pounce when Diana called to me.

"Hold!"

I lost sight of her a second later as the dragon's massive body blocked my view.

"I don't like it," I shouted, creeping closer.

"She's just smelling me," Diana called. She sounded nervous, and rightfully so, but not terrified. "She's...interested in my bag. I had the journal in there for a time. Maybe that's what she smells? Her old friend George the Dragonslayer? It's alright, girl," Diana cooed, her tone low and soothing now. "No one is here to hurt you. We just want our friend—we just want Maverick back."

The dragon lifted its head and froze for a long moment, again, sniffing the air. A second later, she wheeled around, her gaze locked on me now.

Decision time. She was already advancing. I either had to lower my weapon and let her get close enough to smell me or start swinging.

"I don't think she will hurt you if you don't attack," Maverick called as the gigantic beast closed in.

"Oh yeah? Well your opinion means about as much to me as a pile of dragon shit, so save your breath. I'll take it from here, Einstein."

She had her glittering eyes locked on me, taking in my every move. But as furious as she looked when she'd first come charging in, now she looked more bewildered than anything. Going with my gut, I slowly lowered my sword, muttering a prayer under my breath. When she leaned in, craning her neck until her nose was pressed against my chest, and I could smell the sulfur pouring off her, I was second-guessing myself.

"You alright, Raven?"

I didn't trust myself to shout a reply. I just held as still as I could to wait out this inspection. She inhaled deeply, and then let out a screech that made the previous seem like a whisper. My ears rang, the stone walls trembled and some stalactites broke off and peppered the cave floor.

"It's definitely the journal," I confirmed, moving like molasses as I reached for it. She watched me like a hawk, eyes narrowed in suspicion. "I'm not going to hurt you. I'm just getting it from my pocket."

I produced it, holding it out for her to see. One second I was there, in the cave with Diana, Kevin, Maverick and this dragon. The next, I was swept into a vortex of love and pain and grief. The world spun, and I couldn't see or hear or smell. I could only feel. Not my own emotions, but the emotions of the beast before me. Diana's gasp told me she felt it too.

This had to be the mindspeak that Maverick mentioned.

Saldraenaen was her name, as George had said. I knew it was her in my bones, like a memory. And Saldraenaen was heartbroken. The ache was so true, so deep, that I was blinded by tears as I opened the journal and searched for the page I needed.

"You...you need to read the journal like George said," Diana called through broken sobs.

I knew it, but I wasn't quite sure how I'd manage it

through the knot in my throat. I let my sword clatter to the ground and tore out the final page of the book, folding it into a star with shaking hands. The impossible to read symbols married together with their counterparts, and with a burst of red sparks, unfolded into a full sheet of paper. Only now, what had been gibberish became words.

A poem?

No. Not a poem at all.

A song. The last George the Dragonslayer ever wrote. I opened my mouth, and the words poured from my soul...

"One love, one man, one life so blessed,
To rest my head upon Helga's breast
My stars, my moon,
My sun, my sky,
Until another caught my eye,
I fell hard and fast for this new maid,
Mind as sharp as a fae-made blade,
Eyes like emeralds, heart so true
My weathered soul felt born anew
But Helga would not set me free,
As her fury raged like Poseidon's Sea
There would be no rest for me and Sal
If I chose her to be my forever gal
And so I did what needed done,

I married Helga, played the loyal one,
But my soul was never whole again,
As I mourned my Sal to the very end
Life moved on, though it all seemed hollow
Fame and fortune was hard to swallow
Reverence bought with a dragon's scale,
Patron Saint of betrayal."

Sal the dragon roared and stumbled backward, hitting the ground, her keening wails filling my head to the point of pain. But it was nothing compared to the pain in my heart. I dropped to my knees, the note floating to the floor as I tried to get some control over my rioting emotions.

Images flowed through my mind, and I knew I was seeing the dragon's heart, spliced open by George's song.

She thought he'd left her because he didn't love her. That it was all a lie, and he'd stolen her precious scale to sell for fame and fortune. After centuries of mourning, she learned this very day that everything he'd done was to protect her from his jealous former lover, who would've had her killed if he'd stayed. He'd offered up the scale as proof that the dragon was dead.

In that moment, as Sal's heart wrenching cries filled the cavern, I couldn't help but wonder if death would've been a kindness.

I closed my eyes, wracked with an agony so unbearable, I wondered if I'd survive it. And then suddenly, it was over.

I sucked a mouthful of air into my burning lungs, and realized I'd been holding my breath.

"What happened? Where did she go?" I said, searching the cavern and realizing with a start that Sal was gone. A loud splash sounded in the distance, and Diana looked up, her gaze trapping mine.

"She...she went to the place she considers her true home. The sea."

The silence between us was absolute. Even Kevin and Maverick seemed shellshocked. What was there to say? We'd witnessed grief in its purest sense from what was surely the fiercest creature to ever set foot on this earth, and each of us as a man was left changed.

Humbled.

And a little broken for old Sal.

A deep rumble rolled through the cavern, and suddenly, the mountain let out a belch.

For a second, we all stood motionless, and then all hell broke loose as Kevin began to howl and a sound like water bubbling over a pot echoed through the space.

"Son of a bitch," Maverick muttered. "She's going to blow!"

Of course she was.

CHAPTER 22

Diana

It took a long moment for my brain to shift gears. I was still lost in the story of George and Sal, entrenched in her grief as if it were my own, lulled into a trance by Raven's beautiful, mournful voice.

But it seemed like the hits would keep coming. Now, we had a much more immediate problem on our hands...

"Fuck," I cursed, stumbling to find my footing as the ground began to rumble beneath us.

"Hell of a time for this to happen," Maverick said, swiping the tears from his face as Kevin began to bark and whine.

"That way," Raven shouted, jabbing his finger toward the passage just behind me.

Light was just visible in the distance, and I dashed toward it for a moment before glancing at Mav.

Raven reached over as if to carry him, but Mav pulled away with shocking speed, coming close to keeping up with me as he sprinted toward the exit. The man had more secrets up his sleeve than even I had realized, but it was hardly the time to consider it. I matched pace with him, and we charged toward the exit as three, Kevin right ahead of us.

The rumbling grew stronger with each passing second, and the urge to transform into my wolf grew in tandem. Would we really have time to escape before the whole thing blew? It seemed almost impossible. We'd come so far, gotten so close. We had the gem in our hands. Could it possibly end like this?

"Coincidence, or Lilis at it again?" Raven called.

It hardly mattered now, but that *was* a very real possibility. The timing was just a little too perfect, funky weather or no. Inexplicably cold air washed over my face as we swung around the corner, and the cavern opened up, revealing a steep incline headed toward the ground below. It was still midday, but you'd never know it by the look of the dark sky above. If Lilis was capable of something of this magnitude, she was about the last entity I wanted as my enemy. And yet, here we were.

Smoke pricked at my nostrils, and I spared a quick glance behind to see it rising from the peak above. Judging by that, and the rumbling that grew louder by the second, we wouldn't have long. I slowed just slightly as we reached the edge, letting momentum carry me down the slope, as much a controlled fall as it was a run.

Raven skipped from rock to rock with vampiric agility, slowing down every few steps to allow us to keep pace. Maverick, to his credit, was right on my heels. We continued in this way until we were only a few dozen feet from the bottom. I sucked in a gulp of smoky air, exhaustion beginning to set in.

Boom.

The ground roared beneath me, throwing me face first down the hill. My arms shot up defensively, and I let out a growl as they smacked into the ground. Gravity pulled me forward, and I rolled, jagged rocks jamming into my shoulder as I tried in vain to right myself. I gasped as something hard caught me in the stomach, but relief washed over me as the world came back to a standstill. I found myself staring up into Raven's eyes, his arm still around my waist where he'd caught me.

"You good to keep moving, Frostbite?" Raven asked, eyes meeting mine. "I can carry you if you—"

The skin on my stomach seemed to burn beneath his touch, and I swatted him away. "I'm fine."

This fucking bond would be the death of me. I would be much more careful in the future about sharing blood with anyone. And the very idea of sharing blood with anyone except Raven made my stomach churn, and I had to shove the thought away.

"No time for flirting, kids, we gotta go," Mav called, jabbing his finger back as he sped past us.

Lava burst out from the volcano behind us and was now speeding our way at an alarming rate. I broke back into a sprint, ignoring the pain that streaked through my ribs and left thigh with every step.

But the race didn't stop when we reached the bottom. Thick, acrid smoke hung over the air in dark clouds, blocking out the limited amount of light that'd been visible earlier. Soot dropped on us like black snow, coating the rain-soaked grass in a sludgy paste. And through all of it, we ran. Ran until my legs forgot the pain and just went numb. It felt like hours, but it was probably only minutes before something told me to slow down and look over my shoulder.

I let out a triumphant roar as I turned back toward the volcano. The hot magma had begun to cool in the now-frigid air, no longer gaining on us with each step. I slowed to a halt, letting out a ragged breath as I dropped to the ground, staring at what we'd just escaped. Kevin nuzzled into my side, and I wrapped my arm around him.

Streaks of hot magma lit up the otherwise-dark landscape like orange paint. Orange magma still rolled into the ocean on the side of the volcano, but the water would speed up the cooling process. On land, much of it was beginning to darken and solidify. Sal's treasure had very likely been melted in the explosion, but I found myself hoping that the dragon herself had escaped unscathed.

The rest of our journey back to The Wild Queen on foot passed in silence as we were all lost in our own thoughts. Mine were as chaotic as this day had been.

I wondered if we'd seen the worst of Lilis, or if she was just getting started?

I thought about Maverick, and what he'd said to me when we'd first found him. If he wasn't the man he used to be, who was he? Did I even care?

Most of all though, I thought of Sal the dragon, and the loss she'd suffered that had haunted her for centuries.

I cursed, wiping a glob of sooty rain from my brow as we made our way through the front entrance of the casino and then toward our former suite, where Nicholas and Myrr had been hunkering down. Raven pulled open the door a few minutes later to find Gabe standing there, arms folded. He'd been keeping guard, judging by his stance, but his eyes widened as he saw us.

"What the hell happened out there? You look like hammered shit. All of you." Nicholas and Myrr flanked him, mimicking his shocked expression.

"Did someone set you on fire and then put you out again?" Myrr demanded.

I shook my head, "I'll explain everything after I get a shower. The temperature dropped at least thirty degrees and I'm filthy and chilled to the bone. For now, meet Maverick. Mav, this is Myrr and Nicholas."

Gabe inclined his head in a curt greeting. "Glad to have you back, Mav."

"Why don't you and Raven take Mav up to his room and pack his stuff? We'll want to move him into our suite for tonight so we can keep an eye on him."

Gabe nodded, his attention now turning to Kevin. The massive, cross-eyed hell-hound *was* mine now, but he strode amicably up to the man, accepting some light scratches between his ears.

"I won't be long," I said, glancing over to Myrr and Nicholas before heading into the bathroom. I threw my clothes in a pile and turned the shower on, looking forward to hosing off the disgusting soot and grime, even if it wouldn't get the lingering smell of smoke from my nose. But more than that, I'd needed a moment alone. George and Sal's tragic love story had shaken me to my core. I sank to the floor as I entered the shower, letting the hot water mix with my muddy tears as I let it all out.

All the pain and sadness since my father died. The weight of his loss felt impossible for me to bear. I'd been just barely managing to keep it together and stay whole. I couldn't deal with something like that again. I *wouldn't* deal with something like that again. Especially by choice with a mate. I'd seen what the loss of that could do to a person—twice now. Both with Sal and with Evangeline, and I wanted no part of it.

Fuck that kind of love.

Once this bond with Raven faded, I would never, ever get close enough to risk it again. I needed to get this job done as quickly as possible, and then make sure our paths never crossed again.

My people needed a *leader*, now more than ever. I'd be a fool to jeopardize their future, and my own, for some stupid crush that was the result of sharing blood. My resolve grew as I rose to my feet.

Maybe in another life, things could've been different. But not this one. I had to keep Raven at a distance, despite how much I wanted him. No. *Because* of how much I wanted him. He would only become a weakness to me, and a queen couldn't have a weakness like that.

I stayed under the spray until the water ran cold, and I urged my heart to go even colder as I stepped out. The decision was made, all that was left was to implement it. I dried off quickly, then pulled on a fluffy white robe from the bathroom closet.

I almost bowled right over Kevin as I pulled the door open. He nuzzled my hand as if he could sense my grief despite my best efforts to hide it. I cursed inwardly, letting out a sigh as I stroked his ear.

"It's okay, buddy. I'll be alright."

Myrr was chomping noisily on a lamb chop when I re-entered the living room. I shot a glance toward an exasperated-looking Nicholas, who perked up when he caught sight of me.

"So what happened out there?"

The words came out robotically, as if I'd burned up the day's ration of strong emotion during my shower. I filled them in on what happened in the dragon's lair, glossing over the devastation of George's last song and doing my best to stick to the facts. No reason to have their dreams haunted by the whole thing the way Raven, Maverick, and I would be from now on.

"And the gem? You still have it?" Myrr asked, setting her now-empty plate aside and holding out a hand.

"Do you feel anything from it?" I asked as I dug through my filthy cross body bag and handed her the gem that Raven had given me on the journey back. "Maybe it'll give us some idea of what we're supposed to do with it."

She let out a loud belch as she eyed it, picking at her teeth with her pinky nail. "Weird. Something tells me this isn't the jewel we need."

Irritation spiked through me, and I let out a tired breath. Of-fucking-course. Nothing could ever just go according to plan.

"What do you mean?"

"Well, we needed to find Mav for a jewel, but this isn't the one we need."

"What the hell do you mean?" Raven called from

behind us, stepping into the room with Gabe and Maverick. He whirled on Mav, "What do you know?"

They were clean now, apparently having showered in Mav's room. "Nothing. She's crazy," he said flatly.

"Don't toy with us, Mav. Is there another gem out there somewhere?" I asked, too tired and emotionally spent to be truly enraged. "Did you hide it or something?"

He shook his head, "I—No. I don't know. I thought that was the one. Look, I've stolen a lot of gems in my lifetime..."

It wasn't obvious, but there was something strange about his expression. He likely wasn't lying overtly, but he did know more than he was letting on. He looked... nervous.

I nodded slowly, stepping over to the cabinet. "Why don't you sit down and have a bourbon?"

I motioned with my head as he sat, reluctantly holding Raven's gaze for a beat until I saw the comprehension in his eyes. The two vampires were on our guest in an instant. Nicholas gripped his arm, firmly enough that he couldn't pull away, and Raven's hands rested on his shoulders, keeping him glued to the chair.

"What the fuck? Stop—" Mav said, struggling against their grip. The futility of that quickly became obvious. He was strong for a human, but vampires were in a whole different league.

His memories began to play out like a movie, painting

themselves on the air above his hand like some kind of strange, wispy hologram. Strangely positioned stones peppered the ground in front of him, as numerous as the orphans that stood amongst them.

"Stonehenge," Raven muttered, mimicking my own thoughts.

The tallest of the girls was standing, and I recognized her as Sienna almost immediately. Her hair hadn't yet turned from bright blonde to the flaming red it was now, but the brash confidence in her posture and her fine features were still the same, along with her unusual amber eyes. It looked to be a fairly peaceful and normal day, but that all changed in an instant when a dark figure flickered past the children, reappearing in the dead center of the stones.

Fire bloomed as a loud crack split the air, and a thousand shards of what appeared to be crystal surged through the air toward where Maverick had been standing. "That's —," Myrr began.

"The Veil," I finished. Hellfire and damnation. Maverick had witnessed the cracking of the Veil between the Alpha Territories and the human world. My nails dug into my palm as I continued to watch, realizing the importance of what we were seeing. That dark figure—who was it? Lilis? Somehow I didn't think so. It looked...masculine.

Maverick began to move immediately, running away, but his eyes locked onto a little girl who'd been thrown a dozen feet by the blast. Her shirt was caked in blood, and she wasn't moving. He cursed and made a beeline toward her, tossing her roughly over his shoulder before continuing to move.

Nicholas pulled back and let out a shuddering breath. "Just a second."

"She died," Maverick bit out, looking disoriented as he turned to face me. "That's all you need to know about it."

Bits and pieces of memories, staticky and hazy, reappeared as Nick touched his shoulder once again. Of Maverick feeding the frail girl by a crackling fire in a cottage. Of her growing older, and some happy times between them. But through all of it, she was never hale and hearty.

Nick looked paler with every passing second, and had begun to tremble slightly, but Maverick looked even worse. I strode over, laying my hand on Nicholas' arm. "That's enough for now."

"The rest of those memories stay with me," Maverick said firmly, holding strong despite his obvious exhaustion.

"Release him," I instructed Raven. He did, but Maverick didn't stand. Instead, he just slumped down on the desk, sucking in a ragged breath.

"I'm sorry. We have no choice in this Mav. Give us the whole truth today, or we take it from you tomorrow when Nicholas has regained his strength. You can't resist him forever, and we need to know the whole story."

He paused for a long moment, and I was just opening my mouth to say more when he began to speak.

"Her name was Opal."

The story he told was long and painful, on a night already rife with long and painful tales. Once he'd rescued her, he had taken care of Opal like she was his own daughter and had intended to continue raising her as such. The girl had been sickly as a young child, and whatever that crystal lodged inside her chest was, it had only made her sicker.

She had a twin sister named Jade, who she was separated from as a young child when their parents died in a house fire. Opal had been sent to the orphanage, and Jade had been adopted by a young family. Opal never forgot her sister, and never stopped loving her. When it was clear she wasn't long for this world, Opal had made it her dying wish that Mav would help her find her twin so she could see her one last time.

After months of searching, he finally succeeded just a week before Opal's death. She'd been the sickest she'd ever been, but the last week of her life had been her most joyful.

He gestured for Nicholas and closed his eyes.

"Go on, then. This is the important bit."

The vampire laid a hand on Maverick's arm. The images again blazed to life in the air like a hologram. Opal was lying in bed, a far-healthier mirror image sitting beside her, holding her hand.

As the girl let out her last, rattling breath, a shard of crystal shot from her chest and plunged into her unsuspecting sister's.

Maverick yanked his arm away, pressing his fingers to his temples.

"That's it. That's the whole truth."

"Ahh, yes!" Myrr shot to her feet, but her voice was uncharacteristically solemn. "*That's* the gem we needed from him. Jade is the second key. The gemstone that Maverick stole...was just part of our path to finding her. Can you bring her to us?"

"That's going to be a tough one," Mav answered with a grim frown.

"Why is that?" I demanded, my blood pressure already on the rise.

"Because she took off not long after her sister died, and I have no idea where she went."

Well fuck a duck indeed.

CHAPTER 23
Raven

I stood at the back of the boat as far as I could get from Diana, watching the proceedings. Hating everything about it.

Maverick and Diana sat side by side on the upper deck, going over maps and possible places that Jade could have gone. Planning the next leg of our journey.

Only that meant Maverick would be with us and it was taking everything in me not to throw him over the side of the boat. And wondering why Diana had not. If he'd broken her heart, why the fuck was she being so kind to him?

"It's the shits, isn't it?" Nicholas said softly from my right. "I mean, we thought we were done. Ready to go home and now we are here...it's like we're starting from the very beginning again. Except without any idea of where we need to go. No magic werewolf tech to give us a lead this time."

I took a quick look at Nicholas to make sure that he wasn't touching me, because his words reflected my own thoughts. No matter that what he could do was very useful, the idea of him touching me had me feeling a little squirmy even now. Which was why I managed a grunt and nothing more, hoping that he would take the hint and fuck off. Right then I needed to be alone with my thoughts, as dark as they were.

"They work well together," Nicholas mused, crossing his arms and ignoring my less than subtle hint. "I mean... I'll be honest, I am surprised that she's not more pissed with him, breaking her heart and stealing her father's gem. She doesn't seem the type to forgive that easily. It's not like she's let you off the hook easily."

It took everything in me not to grab Nicholas and strangle him dead on the spot. But the truth was, none of this was his fault. He was just saying out loud what I could see with my own eyes.

Diana...was soft toward Maverick. Sure, he was wounded, exhausted from his trial, and they had a history together. A period of time that, fuck, who knew how deep their connection had gone? On top of all that she was a woman who knew how to take care of others—she was a queen after all. But this behavior was softer than she'd been with anyone. Even with Myrr she'd been sharp to the point of hurting the Oracle's feelings. She felt something more for Maverick than just friendship or forgiveness.

At that moment, he leaned in toward her, his hip bumping up against hers. The railing under my hand creaked and groaned as I tightened my hold on it. I forced myself to look away. Forced myself to hold my breath and count.

"Did she recall Hamish and the others? Shouldn't they be back by now?" I bit the questions out, trying desperately to steer the conversation to safer waters. Trying to get my thoughts away from Diana and Maverick.

"Yes, they took off to the forest for a bit, hunting up some fresh meat for the journey home. Diana figured they should be back by morning. Hopefully with some food. We'll need the extra rations to get us wherever we're headed to next. How long do you think we will be gone for? Do you think this girl Jade is going to be easy to find?" The tides rocked the boat and I steeled myself not to lash out at him as the motion pulled him closer.

It wasn't his fault he had the abilities that he had, but it also wasn't in my best interest to let him anywhere near the murderous thoughts that were wreaking havoc inside my head. Mostly around relieving Maverick of the head on his shoulders, and draining him of every drop of blood in his body.

"What do you want, Nick? You want to make chit

chat, small talk? I do not." I made myself drawl the words, putting my devil-may-care mask firmly in place.

He shrugged and his shoulder brushed against mine.

I stepped back so fast that he startled. "You don't fucking touch me, Nicholas. Ever."

His eyes widened. "Shit, I would never, I mean, if I did it would be an accident—" He swallowed hard and I turned from him, striding away as fast as I could without sprinting. Feeling like a heel for treating him that way. He'd done nothing to deserve my ire, and I knew why I was touchy as fuck.

Diana laughed softly from the front of the boat, an answering rumble from Maverick that turned into a chuckle.

I felt myself snap and knew I couldn't stay here a second longer.

"Raven, where are you going? As soon as the crew is here we're leaving, with or without you!" Diana yelled after me as I leapt from the boat and landed lightly on the dock. I didn't look back—I wasn't sure what was left of my control could manage to keep myself together if she was touching Maverick. If I had any hope of ever convincing Diana she was meant to be with me, I had to leave before I did something unforgivable.

I let my legs take me where they would.

Something in the air tugged at me. And if I'd been paying attention, I would have ignored it because it was magic as sure as anything. But as it was, with all the raging inside my head I didn't take note of the magic that whispered at me to go a certain way, and before long I'd eaten up the distance between me and the Wild Queen Casino. The bouncer at the door didn't so much as flinch as I bowled on by him, heading straight for the stairs that led down to the ring. I wanted to beat the shit out of someone, or something. I needed an outlet and this was my best chance at one.

Maybe Gabe would let me take another round or two, or ten, with him. Maybe he'd let me take on him and a few of his friends. A beating would give me something to be truly miserable about. Maybe Diana would fawn over me then.

"Fat fucking chance," I growled to myself. The woman had no mercy in her where I was concerned.

But it appeared that a big showdown with the demons was not going to be my outlet.

Raph stood at the huge wet bar that was set up for spectators at the fights, like a bartender, right down to cleaning a glass. "Looks like you could use a drink, Raven."

"You can spike it?" I snarled as I dropped onto a bar stool. "With something, anything but human blood."

Raph's eyebrows shot up. "I've got something kicking around here. Be right back."

He turned and disappeared into a back room leaving me alone, which gave me more time to think.

To feel.

Distantly I knew that at least some of this emotion that was coming through had to do with the dragon. Sal's way of communicating had left an indelible impression on me, and even now her grief at the loss of her true love, her loss of George was eating me from the fucking inside out.

But her loss made my own that much more palpable.

What would I do if I couldn't convince Diana that we were meant to be? I groaned and clutched at the back of my head.

With my hands wrapped over the back of my head, I lowered my forehead to the bar.

How the fuck had Dominic handled it once he'd realized that Sienna was his mate?

Of course, I hadn't been around the whole time. Only near the end, when she'd finally given in. I'd seen how protective he was—but he'd always been a moody bastard so that wasn't really anything new.

The clink of a glass on the wooden bar drew my head up. Raph poured from a large bottle. The liquid was a deep crimson but it shimmered with bright white lights. "Normally wouldn't break this out for anyone without Gabe's permission, but...you look like shit. Thought you could use a hit of the good stuff."

I frowned as I reached for the glass. "What is it?"

His eyebrows shot up. "You don't know? Hell, I'm not going to tell you. Take a drink. Tell me what you think."

Swirling the glass, I breathed in the scent first, letting the process distract me. Floral notes, springtime, fresh water, magic...before I thought better of it. I tipped the glass back in a single shot. Alcohol, yes, but more than that it was laced heavily with blood that I'd never personally tasted. Though I'd heard rumors of what it could do for a vampire. And just how fast it would cause me to fall over.

The liquid was fire and ice, electricity and the calm of a babbling brook all at once. A whoosh of power flushed through me, and I struggled not to bolt upright. "Fae blood? Where did you get it from?"

Raph winked and poured me another glass. "That whole room is full of strange and fantastical items given to Gabe to cover gambling debts. You should see the collection of goodies he has. Pretty amazing."

"At this rate, I'll be drunk in two drinks," I mumbled even as I felt the liquid calming every part of me. Dulling every sensation. Weird, but I liked it. I tipped the second drink back, almost missing my face, a line of liquid dribbling down my chin.

When Raph poured me a third drink, I knew I shouldn't take it. But I wasn't in control anymore.

"Drink it," Raph said. "You're going to need it for what comes next."

I did as I was told, only thinking to question him after the glass was empty and ask... "Why?" Okay, I think I asked that, but I wasn't fully sure.

"I told him to feed it to you, you'll thank me later," Gabe said from somewhere close by, far away, it was all the same.

Maybe I would have spun around, but my reflexes were shit. I stayed where I was, barely able to stay in my seat, barely able to keep my head up. "Why? You gonna kill me? Diana would like that."

Slurring as bad as I was, I was shocked he could understand me at all.

"Nope." Gabe laughed. "You know that demons can see the bonds between others? It's how we are able to use a weakness such as love to our advantage. You, my friend, are well and truly fucked if you think Diana is for you. The only bond tying her to you as far as I can see is that blood bond."

I blew a raspberry at him. "What you gonna do about it?"

"Because you are my friend, I am going to cut you free." Gabe gave me a sad smile. "I know what it is to be tied to a woman who will never love you. And let me be clear, Diana will never love you."

His words were sharp as wooden stakes to my heart. "Not true. She could."

"It is true. She hates the very fact that she was born a vampire. She certainly will never give her heart to one, and you know it. Which is why I set the need in you to come back to me. So I could do you the favor that no one would do for me. I will set you free."

He poured a fourth drink and pushed it toward me. "One of the properties of fae blood is that it will burn through any bonds that are of the superficial variety. That blood bond you have set in place—accident or not—will be gone by the time you wake up."

I didn't grab at the glass. Because even this drunk, even this far gone, I knew I didn't want to lose her. "Won't work."

"Why?"

I drew in a deep breath and tried to find the right words. "Because."

They waited, and I dug around in the depths of my head for what I wanted to say. "She's mine. Since I was thirteen. Almost killed Edmund when he hurt her."

"Oh fuck," Raph groaned. "She is his *mate*? Is that what he's saying? That at thirteen he...fuck, he almost killed Edmund then?"

Gabe grabbed my face and tried to get me to look him in the eye, but I couldn't keep them open.

"Shit. I thought it was just the bond, you idiot!" Gabe

bellowed. "The worst thing you can do is chase her, Raven. Or try to get her to see Maverick as a bad guy..."

"I know," I mumbled. "But you...you shouldn't be giving me advice on romance." I chuckled. "I know why you're really here and not there."

Not *there* meaning the Territories. Why Gabe had run from the Territories.

Darkness seemed to fill the room. "You sure you want to be bringing that up?" Raph whispered.

I waved a hand in the air. "If anyone should know what it feels like to have their heart ripped out of their chest, it's old Gabe here. How's that wound? Healed yet? Still tender?"

The darkness around me increased, like the pressure from being too deep under water. But I really didn't care. Maybe he'd kill me and this pain in my heart, in the part of me that recognized what Gabe was saying as truth...it would be gone. Diana did not love me. And if I took a single misstep, she never would.

I didn't realize I was saying any of that out loud until the pressure and darkness eased and Gabe sighed.

"Your death would do you no good. And all it would leave is Diana to face whatever darkness this world is coming to on her own. If you love her, you wouldn't want that. No matter how she feels about you."

I managed to lift my head—barely. "No. I don't want her hurt. My job...my job is to protect her. Even if she hates me. I will always…" No I would not say I loved her. "Always protect her."

Gabe drummed his fingers on the top of the bar. "Fine. Lucifer's left nut, I can't believe I'm going to help you. Don't chase her, man. Whatever you do, let the wolf queen figure it out and come to you on her own. Got it?"

I shrugged.

"No. Do you got it?"

"Yeah, sure." I gave him both my thumbs in the air as I laid my face on the cool, wooden bar top. "How long for this to wear off?"

"Another hour or so. It'll go in a flash, as fast as it came on…" Gabe paused. "But I think I can help you, or at least make sure that there is something between you and that wild queen of yours. Raph, grab him and set him up on the table over there, with another drink—just a regular beer. I'm going to get Lucy."

Raph let out a bellow of a laugh. "Oh my gods, you're going to yank that wolf's tail, aren't you? Just make sure you get Lucy clear of her before she reacts. I like her, and I don't want to be cleaning her guts off the walls."

I tried to ask what they meant, but I could barely think, never mind speak. At least the pain and loss that Sal had left with me was gone, and even the pain of losing Diana to Maverick was somewhat dulled. Somewhat.

I closed my eyes and let my head roll back. "Not bad." I mumbled, not even sure what I was referring to.

Voices around me kept disturbing me from getting a nice deep sleep.

"Hurry up. Diana is on her way," Gabe's voice seemed so far away. Something warm settled on my lap. Smelled like...smelled like a cat?

"Nice kitty." I mumbled, flopping my hand over it's back. Soft, velvet, warm...giggling? I'd never had a cat giggle before but then maybe I was just that drunk.

"How you going to keep her from killing him?" Raph asked quietly.

"I'm not," Gabe said. "Either she'll still feel a spark or...she won't. And if she kills him...he'll thank me from the other side."

I drew in a deep breath and let sleep take me. This was better. I'd been right to come to Gabe's place.

Of course, that was before Diana showed up and indeed, tried to kill me.

CHAPTER 24
Diana

I stared out over the dock, listening to the sound of the waves splashing up against the boat as the ocean bucked and stirred like a restless horse. How long would this lull in the weather last?

Not long if the tremor along the back of my neck meant anything. Something bad was coming, and at that point I was just praying that it was weather, and not something else.

Praying it wasn't Lilis winding up for another strike against us.

"Where the fuck is Hamish?" I hit my hand against the railing.

Maverick had gone below deck to rest. Despite his youthful appearance, the traumatic events for him over the last few days seemed to have taken a toll on him.

Or he's fooling you again, a tiny voice whispered.

I shook it off. I was not falling for Maverick, in any way shape or form. His presence was strangely comforting, yes, like an old friend from my past...even if I'd felt the way his eyes had lingered on me. Even if I'd felt a strange connection to him that pulled me toward him. Not unlike the blood bond with Raven. What was it with these men trying to trap me?

No, there was nothing for me with Maverick. But I couldn't help but wonder at the way fate had worked, bringing us back together. Literally caging him so that I could track him down. Whatever it was between us, it hadn't come full circle yet. As much as I wanted to deny it, our story was not done.

Nicholas approached me cautiously, his scent reaching me first. "Is there anything I can do to help? Do you want me to go and see if I can find Hamish and the others?"

I shook my head, another wave splashing up over the deck. "We can't leave without a crew, and the crew is still fucking around hunting. We will wait. They will come back." Probably for the best anyway. They could burn off all their excess energy. Who knew how long we'd be on the boat, or when they'd get their next chance to truly stretch their legs? The full moon was still a good two weeks off, and by then...by then where would we be?

Back in the Territories?

Somewhere else on the mainland?

"Diana?" Nicholas pulled me out of my thoughts, and I circled back to his question.

"Hamish and the others, they will come back before dawn. They know to be here for the turning of the tide. The rest of our supplies have already been loaded by Gabe's men; we are as ready as we can be." I tried not to grimace. Owing a demon anything was just...bad news. And I already owed his brother Malach a favor. What would the two demons ask of me? That, I didn't want to think about.

Don't go borrowing trouble, as Lycan used to say. I'd deal with them both when the time came.

"Aren't you worried about Raven?" Nicholas asked, all innocent like. "I mean...he was having a pretty hard time watching you with Maverick."

I startled at his words. "What? What do you mean?"

"Well, you might not have seen it, but he just about blew his top before he left. That bond you have with him, I know you don't like it. Pretty sure he doesn't either. But you're rubbing salt in a wound Raven didn't inflict on purpose. You and Maverick had your heads pressed together looking as thick as thieves..."

Kevin, who'd been laying at my feet gave a woof in his sleep. I wasn't sure if he was agreeing or not.

I lowered my voice, my words biting. "I was talking close with him because with Lilis watching our every move, we don't know who's listening. We can't just be shouting our plans out to the damned universe, can we now? Maybe I should give in to Raven to make his time with this bond easier? Fuck him and be done with it?"

"That's not what I'm saying!" Nicholas replied, and just a tiny piece of me was disappointed. "I'm saying be mindful. Every time you touch another male, every time you lock eyes with another male...the fact that Maverick is still alive is a testament to Raven's control. Did you not see Dominic with Sienna? Do you not remember how possessive he was? The least you could do is be considerate of Raven's feelings until the bond fades. That's all."

The anger fled from me in a sudden rush...along with my connection to Raven.

For a second, I stood there frozen, searching for the pulse of energy between us. The realization that it was gone was like being hit with a brick.

I whipped around, panic rolling through me in a rush. "Something's wrong. Something's happened to him."

"What? What do you mean?"

I swallowed hard. "The bond, it's just...gone. As if he's..." Hurt. Or worse...I didn't even think, I leapt off the boat, shouting over my shoulder. "Stay here! Don't leave the boat!"

Nicholas shouted something back but I was running as fast as I could while following Raven's scent, breathing it in deeply. The bond that had been there for the last two days was suddenly gone, like someone had cut it with a knife.

Or cut Raven?

Killed him? Gods, not that. Please, not that.

My entire body seized up at the thought, seeing it in my mind so clearly that I stumbled and had to catch myself against the nearest wall.

Raven, lifeless, his eyes empty of any light, his mouth no longer smiling, teasing. Blood pooling around him. His body cold.

I was not a believer of random moments like this of seeing the future, and yet the image stuck with me in a way that I could not shake.

What would I do if I found him...dead?

A shudder ran through me and my wolf and she fought me for control, to howl and mourn him.

“He’s not dead. He can’t be,” I whispered, trying to calm the fear that threatened to drag me under.

I got my feet moving again and picked up his scent once more. It had been only an hour since he’d left the boat, and it was easy enough to track him.

His path took him back to the Wild Queen Casino. The bouncer out front took one look at me.

“Nope. Not supposed to let you in. Sorry.”

“Step aside, or you’ll live to regret it,” I snapped the words and put all my alpha strength behind it. I might not be able to stun him with my powers, but there were perks to learning to rule. The demon blinked a few times.

"Can't, boss said no."

My jaw ticked and I let my wolf rise to the surface, let her strength seep through me. I stepped up to the bouncer, putting my nose to his so that he could not look away. "Move."

For just a moment, I thought he'd throw off my command, but he was no alpha. Not an alpha wolf, and not an alpha demon.

I heard him gulp as he stepped to the side. "Don't blame me."

I didn't think about what he was saying, just left him there as I entered the casino. Raven's scent went to a set of stairs and led down to where the ring was that he and Gabe had sparred.

Voices floated up to me.

Raven's first. Slurred. Drunk.

"Nice kitty."

A woman's giggle.

As I came off the bottom stair, I didn't think about the fact that my wolf was still very much on the surface, humming along every piece of my skin. That I'd not pushed her back to the recesses of my mind.

Raven sat with his head lolled back against the top of his chair, one hand around a half-full glass of beer, the other looped casually around the waist of a beautiful red-headed, scantily clad, well-endowed woman. There was no one else in the room. Just the two of them, alone. Together.

There was no thought in my head, only my wolf. And her intent was crystal fucking clear.

Kill the woman for touching what belonged to me. My wolf didn't give a single shit about the fact that the bond between us had been severed.

Mine. Mine.

I was across the room, the woman's throat in my hand as I yanked her off Raven's lap and threw her behind me. She screamed, and it was all I could to not turn around and leap at her. As it was, I focused on the vampire in front of me. Relief that he was not dead, fury that he was touching another woman close on its heels.

"What the actual fuck, Raven?" Was I yelling? Yup. Could I stop myself? Not a chance.

He opened one eye and blinked up at me, whatever alcohol he'd imbibed still making him fuzzy. "Frostbite. I'm dreaming, yes? You found me?"

"I sure as hell found you, cozying up to some f—"

His hands wrapped around me and yanked me onto his lap so I straddled him, feeling his body react to mine, hardening in a flash. He'd not been hard with the other woman?

But for me, his body reacted.

I'd like to say that he kissed me first. But that was not the case. He was alive, and my wolf rejoiced.

Mine. Mine!

My lips were on his, tasting him, drinking him down. Whatever had been in his cup was still on his tongue, and the magic of it zinged through me, making my blood hot, and my need hotter.

Unable to help myself, I ground myself against his hard cock as his fingers gripped my hips tight.

"Well, seems I was wrong. First time for everything, as they say."

I jerked away from Raven and stumbled to my feet, heat flushing through me, like a teenager caught by their parent when they'd been making out with a boy they said was just a friend.

Gabe stood at the bottom of the stairs, the girl I'd thrown off Raven behind him looking a lot shaken and a little pissed.

"Wrong about what?" I demanded, struggling to catch my breath.

Gabe grinned. "Well, that's for you to find out. Good luck on your quest, Your Majesty." He gave me a two fingered salute. "And take care of my dog, would you? Kevin always was my favorite."

Without another word, he left me there with a drunk as a skunk vampire...and more raging hormones than I cared to admit to.

I closed my eyes and tried to rein in not only my emotions, but the desire that raced through me. My clit throbbed and ached to be touched, ached for Raven to lower his mouth to my center again and work me until I climaxed. I grabbed the table closest to me.

"Fuck."

Raven let out a low moan and reached for me. "Gladly."

I wanted him so much, that I wanted to run *from* him —ridiculous, I know, because I'd just basically thrown myself into his arms, willingly. But I had to get us both back to the boat.

"Come, we have to go save the world." I shook my head, my own thoughts jumbled up with desire and jealousy. I'd been *jealous* of that girl on his lap. And damn him for having a girl on his lap in the first place. The anger came rushing back.

Better. Anger was far better.

"What right do you have to be a dick about Maverick when you just ran off and grabbed the first girl you could, huh?"

"Nice kitty," he mumbled as I helped him stand. I pulled one of his arms across my shoulders and helped him up the stairs. He didn't lean on me too much, and as we walked back to the boat, I kept my mouth shut.

Nice kitty, or nice pussy? Had he had sex with that girl? If I thought I was angry before, the thought of him fucking the redhead had me raging hotter than the volcano we'd barely escaped. As soon as we got to the boat, I let him drop on the deck. But even as I let him go, he shook his head.

"How the hell did I get here?" Raven looked around; his eyes suddenly clear. "Gods, Gabe wasn't shitting me. That stuff hit hard and then gone...poof." He ran a hand over his head as a wave rose up and splashed over him, soaking him through.

My eyes went past him to the figure clinging to the side of the boat, grateful for the distraction. "Xefia! What are you doing here?"

"Thank gods you're back!" Her quicksilver eyes blinked rapidly. "They took two of your friends."

A chill of cold settled over me, dousing what was left of my desire and anger with Raven. "What?"

Xefia looked over her shoulder. "They took them north, in a big boat, with a big motor. You have to go now, or you'll never catch them."

Raven crouched next to the young mermaid, asking the question that I feared to ask.

"Who, who was taken?"

"I...don't know their names. The old woman. And a cute younger man," Xefia whispered, her eyes darting from Raven to me. "I couldn't stop them. I'm sorry."

"It's not your job to stop them," I said, crouching on the other side of Raven. "You watched, and you are able to give us information. That's more than we would have known otherwise."

She smiled, her sharp teeth flashing. "The old lady was very angry."

Raven grunted. "I'll bet she was. Do you know what they looked like? Did they have any markings on them, like a patch that looks like a spiral with spikes on it?"

Xefia gave a sharp nod. "Yes, on the back of their jackets, that symbol was painted on!"

Raven looked at me. "The Vanators."

And where the Vanators went, Lilis was leading them. "But what about the third person aboard? Are you sure only two were taken?" I asked.

From behind us came footsteps and the answer to my question. I whipped around to see Maverick step out of the hold from below. "What's going on? I thought I heard yelling—holy shit, is that a mermaid?"

Xefia squeaked and flipped back into the water. I was about to ask Maverick what happened and how he'd managed to sleep through a double kidnapping.

But Raven...well, Raven beat me to it.

"You piece of shit coward...You let our friends get taken?"

CHAPTER 25

Raven

The roar came from my gut as I leapt on him, seeing red.

He'd been so far up my woman's ass the past couple of hours, I could still smell her shampoo on him as I pinned him against the side of the boat.

"You hid like a fucking child, and let them kidnap our comrades? Tell me why I should let you draw one more breath, human."

"Because you'll have to take on both of us if you don't," Diana muttered. She was directly behind me and had something hard and sharp pressed against my kidney.

Damn. E tu, Diana?

Some small part of me wanted to call her bluff. To see if she would actually take Maverick's side over mine and stab me if I moved to tear out his jugular. But the bigger part knew if I rolled the dice and lost that gamble, the wound would've been far worse than just the cut itself. The betrayal would've killed me.

"He's exhausted, Raven. Weakened, hungry, tired. He isn't as strong as you or I," she whispered into my ear. "Don't do this."

I stared down into the other man's pale face, and knew she was right. But that didn't make it any easier to release him. "We don't even need him anymore," I reasoned. "He has no additional information. He said it himself and Nicholas confirmed. Wouldn't it just be easier for everyone if he "fell" overboard and acted as the chum he was always meant to be?"

"Easier, but not right. Come on, Raven. We wouldn't even know this Jade person if she walked past right now, we have no idea how much she's changed since she was a young girl. We need him and you know it. Besides, every second we waste infighting is a second further the Vanators get with our friends. Release him."

Maverick let one eye close for just an instant in a mocking wink that was nearly the end of him. It was only the thought of Diana hating me for it that stayed my hand.

I gave the bastard one last shove, hard enough to make him grunt, and he stepped back, hands up in surrender.

"As always, I'm at your command, Your Majesty. But I'm going on record one last time. This man cannot be trusted. I'll be watching your back...and your front, but I can only do so much if you choose to let him in."

I turned to see her tucking the dagger back into her belt as she met my gaze with a chilly one of her own.

"I'm not the stupid girl I used to be, Raven. I can take care of myself. And apparently, I can take care of you sometimes, too. You're welcome for dragging your drunk ass back."

With that, she pushed past me and helped Maverick straighten.

He winced, and slipped his arm around her shoulder, leaning in.

"I think I twisted my ankle when he shoved me. Sorry, Di, it's just been a long few days, and I'm whipped."

"I'm going to put him back to bed to recover, and then you and I can get this ship on its way," she called over her shoulder as she helped him across the deck. “We don't have time to wait for Hamish and the others.”

So it was "Di" now?

Di and Mav. How fucking cute was that?

So cute, I wanted to tear down the mast with my bare hands.

We would have days on end stuck on this ship together. I had to get it together or I was going to kill this man.

Fuck the end of the world. Saving it was secondary. And yes, of course we had to rescue our friends.

But I had my own mission.

I would make this woman love me or die trying—Maverick chose that moment to murmur something to Diana, forcing her to lean closer—And kill whoever tried to get in my way.

The End

DON'T MISS HIDDEN BY FATE

Hidden By Fate is coming later this year.

I can't wait to see how Raven handles the challenges ahead as he stops fighting his own heart, and starts fighting for his Queen's.

Caged by Fate is my first release of 2024, but it isn't the only one I'll be bringing you this year. Here are a few more:

- Midlife Vampire Hunter (The Forty Proof Series #9)
- Gossamer (The Golden Wolf #3)
- Hidden By Fate (The Alpha Territories #5)

And there may be a few surprise releases in there as well. Stay tuned to my Newsletter for updates on those.

Did you miss a 2023 release? There were seven of them.

- Golden
- Glitter
- Midlife Soul Hunter
- Hunted By Fate
- Claimed By Fate
- Ivy Touched & Bronze Blade

Connect With Me

Email me at Shannon@shannonmayer.com or find me on social media.

Join my newsletter for updates on upcoming books, behind the scenes info, and exclusive content.

facebook.com/ShannonMayerAuthor
instagram.com/hijinksink
bookbub.com/profile/shannon-mayer
tiktok.com/@hijinksink

www.ingramcontent.com/pod-product-compliance
Lightning Source LLC
Chambersburg PA
CBHW020338310726
48979CB00015B/2418/J
9781987933956